KILLER FOR HIRE

KILLER TRILOGY BOOK 1

ALEXIS ABBOTT

PATHFORGERS PUBLISHING

© 2018 Pathforgers Publishing.

All Rights Reserved. This is a work of fiction. Names, characters, places and incidents are the product of the author's imaginations. Any resemblances to actual persons, living or dead, are entirely coincidental.

This book is intended for sale to Adult Audiences only. All sexually active characters in this work are over 18. All sexual activity is between non-blood related, consenting adults. This is a work of fiction, and as such, does not encourage illegal or immoral activities that happen within.

Cover Design by Wicked Good Covers. All cover art makes use of stock photography and all persons depicted are models.

More information is available at Pathforgers Publishing.

Content warnings: mafia violence, human trafficking, murder.

This is part 1 in a 3 part series.

Wordcount: 76,000 Words

Get an EXCLUSIVE book, **FREE** just as a thank you for signing up for my newsletter! Plus you'll never miss a new release, cover reveal, or promotion!

http://alexisabbott.com/newsletter

LUCA

'm not doing this for me.

Drops of rain patter on the crumpled piece of paper I'm holding in my hand as I squint at the running ink on it. It's the only piece of evidence for what I'm going to do tonight. Written on it is nothing but the address and room number Claudio gave me. Leaning on the back of my car, cigarette in my mouth, my lips curls into a frown at the thought of that smug bastard.

The scrape of my lighter is the only sound beside the rain in the alley where I've parked, and once I light my cigarette, I flick the tongue of flame on again to hold up to the scrap of paper, watching the red glow eat away at it and the words on it before there's nothing but a blank scrap left. I let the little cinder fall to the ground and watch it die out in the raindrops on the asphalt.

I put out the cigarette and stick it in my pocket. I'm not leaving any evidence, even this far from what's about to take place. It would be a rookie mistake. I'm young, but I'm not that stupid.

And with so much on the line, I will not take any chances.

I set off through the alleyways, staying off the main roads as much as I can as I wind through the streets of the Bronx. I've lived here long enough to know my way around, and I know that I need to keep a low profile tonight.

Not that it's going to matter after I do what I'm about to. The Bronx is big, but my community is small. We're tight-knit. Word will spread. It'll be on everyone's mind when they see me.

Mafioso.

I feel anger boiling up inside me as I walk, my footsteps nearly silent. That word cast a darkness over my childhood. I could sense it in every shadow. Now, that's the very same inky blackness I walk in.

But for her, I'd walk through the fires of hell.

I don't have far to go. I turn yet another corner, and a cat perched on a dumpster slinks off silently, a freshly-killed rat in its mouth. As I approach the corner, I glance out to make sure the way is clear.

I hold my place and keep still in the cover of the brick wall as a pair of drunk men stumble by, arm-in-arm. As they laugh their worries away, I go unnoticed. I wait for their voices to fade away around another corner before I slip around leaving the side-walk and stepping onto the filthy, grassy space below an overpass. I can see my goal ahead of me.

It's a hotel, and not the kind business travelers reserve for ritzy trips or vacations. I'm looking at it from the back under a worn-down overpass, and I know from experience it isn't much prettier in front. It's attached to a storage facility with a rusted sign.

I'm tall, standing at least a head over most men, and I have the broad shoulders to match. My clothes hide the muscular build under them, bulked up and toned from years of manual labor. You can see a hint of that life in my rough, powerful hands when I let them slip from my front pocket. I'm clean-shaven, so I have my hood up and a pair of sunglasses covering my eyes. Intimidating as I am, this hotel would let me walk through the front door up to the rooms if I wanted.

But if I'm going to sink into the shadows. I'll do it with finesse.

I make my way to one of the pillars that support the overpass, and there I wait. I know time is pass-ing, and I don't have much of it. I glance to the service door impatiently. My window of opportu-nity is only open so long.

My job tonight is straightforward. A man must die. But like many men who've earned the mafia's crosshairs, he's skittish. Afraid. Always looking over his shoulder. A man like that could run at a moment's notice. A man like that could fight viciously. So a man like that needs to be taken by surprise.

That takes bait.

Tonight, that bait is a woman. It's a pretty common tactic for the mafia. They'll set up a call girl to meet with the mark as if he's going out for a good time, usually at a hotel like this. Usually at nicer ones, but this guy is apparently a real lowlife, an old loan shark they found out was taking a little more than his weekly cut.

They're all monsters tearing each other apart.

Except the girls. I know what the mafia can be like with women. And all Claudio told me was that this girl is new, and that she's not to be harmed, just dropped off somewhere on her way to her next job. I've got a bad feeling in my gut. I'm not just worrying about whether this girl will botch the whole job tonight. I'm worried I'll be driving her to something worse, and that I'll just be another set of hands sending someone innocent further in over her head.

And if I'm going to be working for the mafia, I'd better get used to it. There's more at stake than my conscience, in my case.

But I don't have any more time to think about this woman I've never even met.

I hear the click of the door, and I hear footsteps

traveling out, along with the loud clinking of a garbage cart full of trash bags.

I waste no time. The second the janitor has his back to the door, I dart behind him and into the building. I've stepped inside a small utility room with a cleaner's cart sitting unattended. Without wasting a moment, I grab a pair of latex gloves from it and move on. A moment later, I step out into the hallway. My hood up, and my heart is racing.

Maybe I was meant to be a hunter after all.

I know I'm going to be caught on camera. Maybe the mob wants me to take the fall for this. But if I'm fast enough and have luck on my side, the only thing the camera will catch is a tall hooded man with unclear features.

Room 232, I recite in my head. I head up the nearest set of stairs I can find, seeing nobody in the hallways. It's late enough that most are asleep for the night. I glance at the room numbers on my way through the hall, and I feel a pulse race through my veins as I see the number I'm after.

I pass it by, heading to the bathrooms just a few doors down. One more stop, and the timing has to be perfect.

I enter the bathroom and head for the second stall down, entering and closing the door behind me. As soon as I'm in, I stoop down onto the cool tile floor and slip the latex gloves on. Carefully, I reach around the back of the toilet. My fingers brush against something small and plastic.

A janitor's master keycard. It was planted earlier by a friend of the mafia. At least, that's what they call the men and women that are either paid off or under threat.

As I take the card in hand, I check my watch, standing and turning around. Right on time. Now I have to wait for the mark to get in place.

But that thought's interrupted as the bathroom door swings open, and footsteps echo in the ugly little room.

I freeze. My mind races with possibilities in an instant. Did the staff see me come in? Have the police been tipped off? Is it some random joe coming to waste my time? None of the options are good, and every muscle in my body is tense. Nothing can go wrong here.

One wrong move, and everything could go to hell.

Then my eye catches a glimpse of the man in the bathroom mirror when he walks past my stall. Skinny, white, wispy mustache, ropey muscles, graying brown hair, and green eyes.

It's my mark.

He turns a faucet on and starts to run cold water, splashing some in his face and rubbing it as he lets out a groan followed by an ugly shiver. I hear the rattle of a pill bottle, and he pops something into his mouth. As if there were any shadow of a doubt this is my man, he's taking a pill to keep him stiff.

My jaw is set. My hand is burning to go to the gun tucked behind me. All it would take would be one swift motion, and I could be out there. He hasn't noticed me watching. If a man as tall as me were to step out, dressed like I am, he'd bolt. Could I take him down before then? It could be quick, clean, and there would be no risk to the girl in the room.

I see him staring in the mirror, and his eyes flit to the closed door of my stall. I'm bent enough that my head doesn't stick out the top, but just how skittish is this man?

He peers at the door silently for a moment. Does he suspect something? Will he run? In that instant, I know what it means for the wolf to stare at a deer from the shadows.

The man crooks his arm and lets out a hacking cough, spitting something vile into the sink before washing his mouth off and popping a mint. I feel my muscles start to relax as he turns and makes his way out the door, no more alert than a moment ago. He doesn't suspect a thing. I know the walk of someone who's hiding something.

As easy as it would have been to take him, I had to restrain myself. There would be a cleaner coming after me to cover my tracks. They're specialists who make sure the crime scene was scrubbed clean of any evidence. It's grizzly work, but necessary for the people who do this kind of business.

People like me, I remind myself.

I check my watch, each second ticking by as if it were a minute. I have to give the mark time to get into the room and feel safe. If I burst out of the bathroom and barrel after him, he'll run. If I kick down the door the moment he goes in, he might try something stupid. The deer is most exposed when its head is down to graze.

I shudder. It's a disgusting thought.

But I take deep, slow breaths and let my body focus itself as I count to fifty, visualizing the man's movements in my head. I imagine him walking down the stained carpet of the hallway to Room 232...his cardkey slipping in...the door swinging open...the terrified sight of the girl on the bed...and he steps forward, closing the door behind him as he slips his jacket off. I can see his yellowed, grinning teeth in my mind's eye when I can't keep focus any longer.

The mafia wants to treat girls like disposable things to throw away when they're used up. But when I think of a young girl being used to lure such human slime in, my gut turns, and even though I have no idea who the woman behind that door is, all I can picture is one girl.

The one girl in the world I'd kill for.

I can't take it any longer. I slide open the latch of

my door as quietly as I can, and I let my legs carry me out of the bathroom, cardkey in hand.

The walk to Room 232 is like pushing through a dream. There's no going back after this. It isn't like fighting behind the workshop with the other Italians I call my brothers, my friends. It isn't like hunting a deer, either. My uncle's teaching is in my head like a ringing in my ears.

To kill a man is to cross a line there's no coming back from.

I hold the cardkey up to the slot and listen. The doors are heavy. I can hardly hear a thing through there. That's good, but…

The sound of a woman's voice on the other side of the door reaches me, and my blood runs cold. I know that voice.

No. It can't be.

Without another moment's wait, I slide the cardkey and push through the door, vanishing from the hallway like a shadow.

"The fuck?!" is the shout that greets me.

Then a girl's cry of fear, and my eyes fall on the both of them.

His belt and pants are already undone, and there's the unmistakable look of lust written on his face. But my eyes are only on her.

She's half-sitting on the bed, one hand up at the beautiful dress that he's already started taking off her. Her face is turned away, and she's raising her other arm to shield herself from what she knows is coming. Everything about her body language says she's terrified.

Instinct takes over.

I forget about the gun I brought. I won't need it. I lunge forward as the man dives for his jacket, no doubt reaching for his own weapon. Before he can reach it, I'm on him.

I seize his wrist and thrust my palm into his outstretched arm at the elbow. With a sickening crack, it snaps, and he lets out a croaking gasp of pain.

Without thought, pure, raw adrenaline coursing through my body and awakening what I was built to do, I easily wrap my arm around his mouth, muffling his scream as he thrashes in my arms. But he's nothing compared to me. All the strength in his frail bones amounts to an ounce of mine.

He struggles in my grip, and his good hand grasps at my leg, pounding, doing anything he can, and finally, he finds his wits and reaches for something in his pant leg. I see the flash of a blade.

CRACK.

The man's knife falls from his hand as his grip slackens, and slowly, I feel his body go limp in my arms. His neck is broken, eyes going glassy as he stares up at the ceiling. All it took was one quick motion, and it was over.

Gently, I lower the body to the ground before standing up over it, looking down at my kill.

My first kill.

I'm still as I look at him. I expected my hands to be shaking, my body to be trembling, but my massive frame doesn't shudder. I'm poised. Ready for more. I'm not stupid, I know what my body is capable of. But it's something different to look down at a corpse and realize your body is ready to do it again.

"Oh...oh my God!" The shuddering cry snaps me out of my thoughts, and my heart comes alive again as I look at the woman on the bed. She isn't looking down at the body in horror. She's looking at me.

Our eyes meet. And even through the hood and the glasses, I know she recognizes me. How couldn't she? Her hazel eyes are staring up at me, as expressive and deep as the first time I'd seen them.

And they're full of fear. Fear of *me*.

How can it be her? How can she be the girl they got for this? Claudio never mentioned her. Of course he didn't. He knew it would be the one thing that would make me turn down this job. That putting her in danger would be the one thing that would keep me from acting.

I start to reach for her with the gloved hand that just took a life, and for the first time, I watch her recoil from me, clutching her clothes close to her as her lips part, quivering.

"...Luca?"

SERENA

SEVERAL YEARS LATER...

*I*t's early.

God, it's too early.

With a heavy sigh, I poke my arm out from underneath the comforter to swat the alarm clock, accidentally knocking it off the night stand in the process. The loud clatter of plastic on tile immediately sends my brain into full-on wake-up mode.

Well, that's one way to kickstart another grueling Monday grind.

I sit up in bed and push the hair out of my eyes, tucking it behind my ears as I blink blearily in the dim light of dawn. The sunlight streaking in through the cracks in the blinds tells me that I've probably snoozed the alarm at least four times before finally turning it off. I have never been a natural morning person, and if it were totally up to me, I wouldn't get out of bed until at least eleven. But I'm not one of those girls lucky enough to play to my own whims. I don't get to sleep in. I've got serious responsibilities, and if I don't get up now and get the day started, the delicate balance that keeps all the balls rolling in my life will be seriously disrupted. There is a lot to juggle, and it all starts right now. Every weekday at six in the morning.

So I launch myself out of bed, wiggling my feet into my worn-down slippers, and pad my way across the bedroom to the little en suite bathroom to start the shower. While I wait for the water to warm up, I yawn and lean over the sink to look at myself in the mirror. Sleepy hazel eyes with purplish bags below them blink back at me. I try to force myself to smile. It's something my dad used to always tell me: "Smile, even when it's the last thing you feel like doing, and you'll be amazed at how your outlook can brighten just a little bit."

But my smile in the mirror just looks lopsided and forced, and I quickly look away. I wish it were easier to follow my dad's advice, but these days, everything seems a lot harder than it was when he was still alive.

As the mirror begins to fog up, I shed my night-gown and slippers and slip under the hot stream of water. A pleasurable shiver runs down my spine while steam gathers around me. It's a bad habit, I know, taking such hot showers. "One of these days you're going to boil yourself alive in there," my mom has told me on numerous occasions. But I can't help it. I love the feeling of scrubbing all my worries away, feeling the hot water cleanse my skin and make me feel brand new again. Shower time is one of the few moments I get to purely be myself and give into my own needs throughout the day. There was a time, long ago before things got so hectic and crazy, when I used to sink into a hot bubble bath and stay there for hours reading or just daydreaming about the future. About pretty things and handsome boys and faraway places I would someday visit.

Nowadays, I've had to settle for a steamy shower in the morning.

Still, I can't help but wonder if my love for a good scrub is part of what fuels me to keep plugging away at the struggling family business. I manage a luxury bath goods shop called Bathing Beauty, and even though it's been a long, long time since I was last blessed with the opportunity to partake in any of my sweet-smelling bath bombs or shower gels, I still feel pretty passionate about going into work every day. Sure, it's a lot of effort for not a lot of pay-off, but it's close to my heart just the same. And it's lucky that I feel that way, because my passion almost makes up for the fact that I don't have much hands-on business experience. Nor do I have the kind of financial backing most people need to keep such a frivolous business afloat. But I can't give up. I refuse to.

As I shampoo my hair, I run through the list of

things to do today. First of all, I need to remind mom to drop off the power bill. Of course, it would make my life much easier to have all the bills set up to pay automatically online each month. But my mother is old-fashioned, and she likes the ritual of writing a check and handing it to a living, breathing associate. And she's held onto this almost vintage-level quirk for years, even though it's no longer her name on the check anymore. It's mine.

If it were up to her, she would still be signing off on everything. God knows how difficult it is for a woman of her bearing to give up control and lose face like that. I've tried a million times to convince her that it's no big deal, that I don't mind being the breadwinner. But even though these days she's finally given in and allowed me to take control of the finances— purely because the alternative was much worse— she's still quite bitter about the whole thing.

You see, my mother comes from serious money. She's a born-and-raised mafia princess, and she's had the best of everything since the day she was born. So, naturally, our fall from power and money in recent years has hit her pretty hard. Sometimes I find her just poring over old photographs, her finger tracing over the fancy fur-lined coats, Prada hand-bags, and Hermes scarves she used to wear all the time. She's had to sell a lot of her old wardrobe clas-sics, which to me doesn't seem like a huge loss, since I've never been quite as much of a clotheshorse as my mom, but to her I think it really does feel like she's lost a chunk of her identity.

Someday, though, I'm gonna put her back into the pearls and perfumes she's used to. I know good things are coming. I can feel it. After all, I've often heard that bad luck can only go on for so long until there's a bounce in the opposite direction. As far as I'm concerned, we hit rock bottom years ago, and everything has been on the up-and-up ever since.

But God, is it a long, slow ride back up to the top. And I've had to put aside my own pain to help my mom through hers. Losing my dad... well, it ruined her entire life. It just almost ruined mine.

I turn off the water and start towel-drying my hair, then move on to applying the kind of low-key makeup I tend to live in these days. When I was a teenager, I used to wear the raciest red lipstick and the most outlandishly vivid colors imaginable. Back then, I was never afraid of standing out from the crowd. It wasn't that I was starved for attention, either. Daddy spoiled the hell out of me, and like my mom, I walked around with the kind of self-assured cheekiness you get when you come from money. But I wanted to make a statement. I wanted everything. I wanted to wring every last drop of excitement out of life that I could manage.

Nowadays, I settle for some lightly tinted chap-stick, a splash of mascara, and a ponytail. Just enough to make me look professional, yet approachable. God, I wanted to be approachable. Anything to draw a customer into my shop. I was a hard worker, and I had passion out the wazoo, but none of that could matter if I didn't make a sale.

I dress in a simple pair of dark jeans and a summery pink floral blouse, paired with a navy blue blazer and some kitten heels, and then I'm on my way. As I pass my mother's bedroom, I knock gently on the door and say, "Hey, Mom, don't forget to take that power bill downtown, okay? It's in an envelope on the table."

There's the faint sound of the bed creaking and then I hear her footsteps trudging across the room. The door opens just a crack to reveal my mother's face, older and sadder but still beautiful. There is a regal air about her, still, no matter how drastically our circumstances have changed over time. She gives me a nod and runs her hand back over her raven-black hair.

"Of course, dear. I'll see to it this afternoon. Will you be home for dinner?" she asks, stifling a yawn.

I bite my lip.

"Um, maybe. Not sure yet. I have a lot of inventory to do today, and I would hate to keep you waiting on me," I reply, giving her an apologetic half-smile.

"Right, yes. Well, do let me know. I can always call for some pizza or something if you're going to be late. I can wait up for you," she says, and it's hard not to giggle at the way she says pizza, as though it's some bizarre exotic food. I suppose when you've spent most of your life eating caviar, a pepperoni pie delivery might feel a little pedestrian.

"Okay, Mom. Sounds good. I'll text you later," I tell her, blowing her a kiss as I hurry off down the stairs. I hear her door click closed as I rush out the front entry and into my car. I took a little too long in the shower this morning, and I don't want to be late for opening hours at the shop. After all, I am the only employee. If I'm not there to open the store, and a customer just so happens to wander up at 7:30 to find it closed, I'll probably lose that customer for life. One thing I have learned both in studying business and by running one myself, is that every single tiny human interaction counts. If I make one miniscule mistake, I might lose a potential patron. And every one I lose is another sale I lose. Or more.

I really hate math, but even I know that it all adds up quickly.

I make the long drive from our house in Riverdale down to Morris Park, thinking over the work I have to do today. Once I'm inside the shop, I turn on the little radio I keep behind the counter (I can't yet afford to install a real speaker system for background music) and get started. I turn on the coffee maker and start going through my inventory checklist, wiping down counters and making note of what labels need reprinting as I go. That's the cruel beauty of being the one and only employee: you learn how to multitask. Sometimes I think that I've gotten so used to being three people at once, I can hardly remember how to just be myself.

As I sip my coffee, I hear the telltale jingle of the front door being opened. My heart immediately skips a beat and I glance up eagerly, expecting to see a customer. And so early in the day, too! However, my excitement dims slightly when I notice that my customer is just a rough-looking guy, rather than the typical girly-girl the shop usually attracts. For a moment I wonder if maybe he might be lost, having wandered into the wrong business by accident.

Still, I have a role to play. With a big smile, I greet him, "Good morning! Welcome to Bathing Beauty, how can I help you?"

The man looks at me with two cold eyes that make my heart freeze momentarily.

Something about him feels... off. I can't quite put my finger on it, but something about him makes me incredibly uneasy. He's dressed in jeans and a beat-up leather jacket, and it's obvious that he hasn't shaved in several days, judging by the scruff along his jaw. He gives me a wry smirk and strolls up to the counter. Even as I feel myself bristling with nervousness, I don't let the smile fade from my face. *Maybe he's here to buy his sister a birthday gift*, I tell myself, trying to calm my nerves.

"Is there anything in particular you're looking for

today?" I ask, trying to keep my tone even and chipper as he stands in front of me, squinting as though he's sizing me up. He chuckles, then gives me an exaggerated once-over. I instantly feel stripped and exposed — a feeling that I despise. My mind immediately flashes back to another time when I felt degraded, and how I felt just like this before getting into that car.

But I force myself to stay strong. I can't think about the past right now. It's just paranoia, getting the better of me. My natural instincts trying to keep me safe, but they're being too over-protective. That's all. That's all.

"I think I found exactly what I'm lookin' for already," he replies, giving me a wink. His voice is gruff, like he's been smoking heavily for years. He does have an admittedly handsome face, and I might have found him attractive when I was a reckless teenager, but these days, guys like him just make me nervous.

"Oh," I answer awkwardly. He leans on the counter, peering toward me.

"This is a pretty nice setup you've got here, ma'am," he says, gesturing broadly.

"Th-thank you," I stutter, damning myself inwardly for being so weak.

"You know," he begins, rubbing his palms together, "I'm a discerning entrepreneur, and I really think you've got somethin' good goin' here. Is business good lately? How's your profit margin?"

"Uh, well, it's… um," I struggle, taken aback by this change in topic. Who the hell is this guy?

Without letting me answer, he continues.

"I've been watching this shop for a while now, and my people think it might be a good place to, uh, make our mark. It's a good thing you're doin' here, bringin' an upstanding business like this to Morris Park. I've got an interest in cleanin' up the neighborhood, so to speak, and it's nice to see a local girl like you set up shop."

"Oh. Well, thank you," I reply, surprised again. This is definitely not the way I thought this conversation was headed a moment ago, but I guess it could be worse.

"Yeah, yeah, so we're thinkin' you could benefit from our services. You know, as a part of the local community here and all," he adds, locking eyes with me.

"I'm sorry, I don't understand," I admit, frowning. If this guy is trying to sell me insurance or something, he's certainly got a weird way of making his pitch.

He takes a phone out of his jacket pocket and quickly sends a text before looking back up at me with a dangerous grin. Suddenly, my whole body is on high alert. Something is definitely wrong here. *Never ignore your instincts, Serena,* the back of my mind nags at me. *It's what'll keep you safe.* But what good is that? I can't exactly dart out of the store like a maniac. My hand reaches out for my phone, but it's too far away to do it discretely.

"Me and my guys, we're all about tackling risk management head-on. Just lookin' out for the neighborhood to maintain the integrity of our little community. I'm sure you understand, right? You're a business-minded girl, I can tell. So, listen up," he says, just as the front door jingles again.

Two hulking, musclebound men dressed in similar clothes have entered the shop. They each flank the first guy, walking around the store with menacing glares on their ugly faces.

Shit. I may be fresh, but I'm not totally naive. This is a shakedown.

As the two goons have a grand old time knocking expensive soaps and displays off the shelves, making me wince, the first guy introduces himself to me.

"I'm Lorenzo. Nice to make your acquaintance, Miss De Laurentis." As soon as he says my last name, I feel my knees buckle. This is bad. This is very bad.

"Now, I like a nice, fragrant bath from time to time, but let's be real here. I'm a lot less interested in the shit you sell here than I am in your profits. And your rent for this lovely space. I know exactly who the hell you are, and I know you're not stupid," he says, lowering his voice to a growl. He comes around to stand behind the counter, effectively boxing me in. My stomach churns and I feel sick.

"Now, look here, I'm a generous man, and I would hate for our little partnership to start out on the wrong foot, so I'm gonna grant you a little more time. I'm not even gonna penalize you for your late payment, see? I've got a heart, you know," Lorenzo says, grinning. The two goons laugh.

"Please don't hurt me," I manage to murmur, the small of my back pressed hard against the countertop while Lorenzo towers over me.

"Oh, I would never. Unless you make me. But I see no reason why we can't have a feel-good agreement. I think you'd rather keep this civil, right?" he answers, narrowing his eyes at me.

My breath is lodged in my throat, my words totally fallen silent. I give him a vigorous nod.

"Atta girl," Lorenzo sneers, patting me on the shoulder. I flinch slightly and he chuckles again before turning and gesturing for the two other guys to follow him out of the store. As he steps out the door, he glances back over his shoulder and says, "Nice doin' business with you, sweetheart. We'll be seein' each other again real soon."

As soon as the door closes and the men disappear from sight, I collapse to the floor behind the counter, pulling my knees in close to my chest. My heartbeat slowly starts to calm again, and I close my eyes, forcing myself to take deep breaths. I should have known this day would come. They just couldn't leave me well enough alone, could they?

I know better than to try and fight them. It's pointless. I'm just one girl against a whole bunch of guys. This isn't my first rodeo. I know how quickly shit goes south when gangbangers are involved.

Still, I find myself asking the question: if Bathing Beauty is barely breaking even right now, then how the hell am I gonna be able to pay protection fees to the mafia? And what's the cost when I can't pay up?

LUCA

*T*he orange afternoon sun is on my back when I bring my car to a stop about a block away from the well-to-do little store on the corner of the street. When I turn my ignition off, I lean back and just stare at it, letting out a deep breath.

How long has it been?

The light playing off the glass window panes make it impossible to see inside the shop, but the sign outside is clear as ever: Bathing Beauty. I feel a smile on my face. As many mixed memories as it stirs up in me, there's something comforting about knowing it's still there, unchanged as ever. Maybe even a little nicer.

All thanks to her.

I catch a glimpse of myself in the car mirror. I've changed so much over the years. It feels like a lifetime

27

ago that I was just a teenager, freshly landed in America. I kept my hair cut short back then, and my face was clean-shaven. I run a hand through the long locks that hang nearly to my shoulders now. It's grown out thick and wavy. Even I have to admit it's unkempt, and the short, coarse black beard on my face matches.

My voice sounds different, too. I think back to the thick accent I had in those years that I was still learning English, fresh from the old country. I'm so used to it now that English almost sounds as natural as my native Italian on my tongue. I might as well be a different person.

Better that way, I think. When I look into that mirror, I'm not sure I even see myself anymore. What I do see is the face of a man who's done terrible things. A "made man," they call us in this country. *Mafioso.*

What are you really doing here, Luca?

My mind flashes back to her face, that gorgeous face that's kept me going all this time. A bright candle in the darkness.

That face doesn't need to know fear ever again. It doesn't need to know me.

So why am I here, coming to risk dragging the past back? I don't dare turn the ignition and drive off. I've made my decision, and I'm a man of my word.

After all, I remind myself, I'm not here just to see

her, to remind myself that she's alive and living happily, that what I did for her was all worth it. I'm here to make sure she's safe.

The Cleaners.

Their name makes my lip curl. They are a gang that sprung up almost overnight, and they've gone from being a nuisance to a threat in just as little time.

A few years ago, they were nobodies in East Harlem. But times changed, East Harlem started to get cleaned up, and that meant the gangs had to move around. Soon, the Bronx found itself with new faces hitting warehouses on the south side. And goddamn, they're vicious.

The Cleaners fight like men who have nothing to lose. I learned that the first week they hit our streets, and hit it hard.

I hit back, harder.

Those days left me with scars and them with worse ones, but the Cleaners have dug their heels in. They've been shaking down business left and right, and one of my boss's associates gave us a tip that some of them might be skulking around here, Morris Park.

This is a nicer part of the Bronx. Places like Bathing Beauty can do pretty well for themselves, if they play their cards right. It would be a gamble to go after businesses this deep into our territory.

But if experience has taught me anything, it's that the Cleaners are gambling men.

I pop on a pair of aviators in case there could be any chance of her still recognizing me—well, that, and a good pair of aviators can do a man some favors—and I step out of the car and cross the street. It's a walk I've thought about taking a long time, but I never wanted to make her see this face again.

I've never wanted Serena to go through that pain again.

But I won't stand by and let a rival gang get to her, either. My associates know that this store in particular is off-limits.

If Serena knew the reason why, it would kill her. All the more reason I must stay a stranger to her.

And the fact that we can't touch Bathing Beauty makes it a prime target for the Cleaners. That's something I can't tolerate.

I reach the simple door and push it open.

There's a rush of fragrant air from inside as a little bell jingles. I nearly have to stoop to step inside. If I felt out of place just being in the nicer side of town, I feel *really* out of place in this quaint little shop. But even so, the place so clearly has her personal touch to it that I can't keep the faintest smile off my bearded face.

At least, until my eyes fall to the floor.

There's broken glass all over, freshly fallen from some of the shelves and ornate displays lined up all around the shop. Expensive liquid soaps pool on the floor in puddles, some of the sparkling colors swirling together and changing color as they mix. In one corner, one of those fancy chalky balls you throw into a bath has fallen over, and it fizzes and pops in the liquid soap spill.

There's something almost beautiful to the big mess, I have to admit.

I can see brightly-colored footprints leading back and forth from the door to the back of the shop. The space near the checkout counter seems to have been recently cleaned up.

And no sooner has the front door closed behind me than the back door swings open, and the afternoon light filtering in behind me falls on her.

Serena.

I have to keep my jaw from dropping.

Her dark blonde hair shines like gold in the sunlight, playing against her shoulders as if she were posing for a painting. It's grown out a little since we were younger, and it suits her beautifully. Her hazel eyes could be jewels, gazing at me, taking in my form in that first split-second. Her olive-toned skin gives away the Italian blood running strong in her. And as the years passed and the sun kissed her skin, time has been very, very good to her. The Serena I knew as a teenager was a beautiful work-in-progress, and what I'm looking at now is a masterpiece that takes my breath away.

But then I see fear flash through her eyes. An old, familiar fear I'd hoped never to see again. Does she recognize me?

I then realize the sun is behind me, half-blinding her. I must look like little more than a 6'2" silhouette, clad in jeans, a tight-fitting white shirt, and a worn leather jacket that's seen better days.

"Are you...closed?" I say slowly, trying to keep my Italian accent buried.

"Oh, oh no," she says, and I can see the worry melting away from her face. An anxious smile replaces it, and she brushes a strand of hair from her face. I notice she's carrying a large bucket of cleaning supplies in her other arm, and she sets it down on the counter. "Just, um, taking care of a little mess, nothing to close early for!"

"What happened?" my deep voice rumbles as I carefully step into the shop, trying not to step in the bright blue and violet rivers of moisturizer creeping along the tile.

"Well, you know," she laughs nervously, tearing off a few paper towels to gingerly step over to the colorful chalk-ball and pick up the remnants of it. "It's kind of a messy business!"

"I...see." I arch an eyebrow, watching her drop the fizzy thing into a garbage bag. "There are worse things to spill everywhere."

"Yes," she says, as much to herself as to me, visibly trying to keep calm as she looks around at the damage surrounding her. "Yes, there definitely is. Yeah. I've got this. No problem." As if remembering she has a customer, her eyes flutter back toward me, and she bites her lip apologetically. "I'm so sorry, just give me a minute or two and I'll have all this cleaned up!"

She starts to dig through her bucket, but I've already made my way across the shop to the mop leaning against the wall and picked it up. A look of horror crosses her face when she sees me start to drag the thing through the mess.

"Oh- no, you don't have to do that! Really, it won't be long."

I want to glance up at her and silence her with a wink, but I keep my head down as I get some of the fragrant slop pushed into a more manageable puddle. "I came in here to try some soap, didn't I? This can be a test run. What's this one called?" I ask as I dip the mop into a puddle of bright blue.

She's stunned to silence for a few moments, but she finally says absently, "...that's *Blue-bury the Hatchet.*"

"Good one," I say, suppressing a grin on my face, and I can feel hers from across the room.

"Thanks."

Not even a minute with her, and I already feel like we've never been apart. But I can't let her feel too comfortable around her. I'm a stranger, after all. I have to play the part.

"Don't you have any other help around here?" I ask, glancing at the back. "It can't be just you running this place alone."

"Just me," she says, emptying the bucket of supplies onto the counter and carrying the bucket to a sink to fill with water. "I've usually got a handle on everything—I promise I'm not *that* much of a mess," she laughs off, and as her back is turned, I can't help but look up at her.

Her ass looks even better than I remember. I feel myself thickening between my legs, and I look back down to the mess as she brings the bucket over to set next to me.

"Usually isn't this bad, I just...had a *really* bad spill this time," she says, raising her eyebrows as she hesitates. I know what she looks like when she's holding something back. She always was a proud girl, and now she's a proud woman.

The years haven't taken her spirit. Nothing could do that.

I dip the tip of my mop into the water and wring it out. I feel her watching me, and it makes me want to work all the harder. But I didn't come here just to clean up.

"Just think of it as free advertising," I say as my strong forearms work the handle. "People will be smelling this from a block away."

I hear her gentle laugh, so full of life and quick

wit, and it makes my heart just a little lighter to be able to draw that out of her so easily.

"It certainly helps draw in burly strangers to work for free," she quips, and I grin as she breaks out some paper towels and spray to start scrubbing the floors in detail where I've already passed by. But I still have my suspicions to chase down.

"From the looks of this place, I'd say burly strangers are the last thing this shop needs—let me guess, did a football team come through here and get a little rowdy?" I'm probing to see how much she's willing to tell me about what happened, because I have a feeling this isn't the kind of mess that happens on accident.

"No, no," she says with that slight flippant scoff that tells me she's lying. Even after all these years, I can read her like a book. Thankfully my new look, the bright light and the rough voice cigarettes gave me keep her from recognizing me. "Just...you know, someone bumps into one of the displays, things start falling, and it's one big chain reaction."

"This is a big chain reaction," I say, glancing at the various bits of broken glass across the shop.

"Tell me about it," she says under her breath.

I'm not convinced for a second, but I let it go as we work together. It goes fast, both of us working as a team—it happened almost wordlessly, but it feels so natural. She still works quickly, thinking I'm a new customer and not wanting to embarrass herself, but I take my time to make sure the job is done well.

"Oh my god," she says as she checks the clock when I stand up from detailing the floors, wiping my hands on a towel, "we've been at this for half an hour!"

"Making good time," I say, looking around the shop proudly. It's cleaned up pretty nicely.

"No, I mean, you spent all this time!" she says, letting out an incredulous laugh as she washes her hands off and dries them.

"Don't mention it," I say, setting the mop against the wall where I'd found it.

"I think I should," she says, hands on her hips as she smiles at me. "Seriously, though, I really appreciate it. After everything that's happened today, I never expected a stranger to take that kind of time."

"What's happened today?" I ask, quirking a brow, and I see her cheeks tinge with a bit of color.

"Wh- oh, nothing. The guy who caused the accident just kind of ran off, is all," she lies, averting her eyes to the setting sun outside.

"Dirty move," I say, crossing my arms. "Good thing you run a soap store."

She just stares at me in disbelief for a beat before she bursts into a laugh at my awful pun, covering her face for a moment. "Oh...wow," she says, starting to take a few steps toward me. "Who *are* you?"

"Someone who can tell you've had too much on

your plate for one day," I say. Every muscle in my body wants to take a step toward her as well, to play the game between us that she's slipping into already. I want to flirt with her, charm her all over again, even as a stranger, take her out for a good time. If I'm *really* honest, I want to bend her over that counter and take her right here and now.

But for her safety, I have to keep my distance. I'm just checking in to make sure she's okay, and then I can disappear from her life all over again. With any luck, she'll never even realize I was back into it.

"Oh, who am I kidding," she says, running a hand through her hair and looking out the door. "You're right. Today's been a nightmare." She looks back to me, eyes flitting up and down my form. "Thank you, though. Really. God, I feel so silly, you didn't come here to--"

"Get some rest," I say, her name on the tip of my tongue before I reel it back in. "I'll come back by tomorrow. Maybe I can take care of any other messes that come up," I say, a boyish smile on my face.

I see the color flush into her cheeks, and she loses her words for a moment before she says, "I'll be here!"

She was a spoiled brat when I knew her, but even then, it was the easiest thing in the world to get her off her guard and swooning. But I liked that about her. She didn't feel shame for her feelings. She felt everything intensely. It was good to see that hadn't changed.

There's so much more I want to say, but I step out into the cool air without another word to her as I hear her voice calling, "Wait, I didn't get your name!"

I pretend not to hear.

Seeing how happy she is now, I can't let our tangled past flood into her life and upset everything she has. She's running her own business, for God's sake.

How would she feel about me if she knew I was an enforcer for the mafia?

I don't even know how I feel about myself.

No, the boy she once knew is gone. And now, there's just me.

I shake that thought off me as I start to walk away from the building. I have to keep my mind clear and focused for business. In truth, I had no plans to leave her for the night. A wrecked shop and a nervous business owner are telltale signs of extortionists coming through. Have the Cleaners gotten to her already? Whatever the case, I was planning to post up in my car and stake the place out for a night until I could watch Serena leave the shop and get to her car without incident. I'd even tail her home to make sure she gets there safely. I'm good enough at this kind of thing that I don't worry about getting caught by her. Hell, I'm good enough at it that I make myself uneasy.

And my fears are validated as I approach my car in time to see a black sedan roll down the street.

I slow my pace, eyes watching it, and I can feel eyes inside it watching me. My hand itches to go to the gun under my jacket. But just after what feels like an eternity, the car picks up speed again and takes off. My lip curls into a grimace.

Serena's being watched.

"Have you been doing those morning affirmations I taught you?" chirps my best friend Rafaela through the speakerphone.

I roll my eyes, relieved that she can't see me do it. It's midday, and the store has been dead-empty for two hours. At this rate, I'm half-tempted to call it a day and just go home, but that ravenous, desperate hunger for a sale keeps me riveted to my usual haunt behind the counter. Besides, my mind is distracted. It's hard to think about work when all my thoughts seem to center around that handsome, rugged guy who came into the shop a few days ago. Last night, I even dreamed about him, only I couldn't quite see his face.

Something about him is so shockingly familiar, but he kept looking away from me, speaking in a low voice. He definitely fit the bill of tall, dark and mysterious. I can't imagine where I would know him from. At first, I thought maybe he was a guy from my classes or something, but I don't remember seeing anyone looking so rough and unkempt on campus. Everything about him seemed to exude mystery, from the way he dodged my gaze and wore his hood up to the way he seemed to appear and disappear without giving me a chance to even ask his name.

My brain has been working overtime to try and figure him out. Why did my body have such a strange, visceral reaction to his presence? It felt almost like deja vu, like we have met before some-time, maybe once upon a dream. It's like he's just on the tip of my tongue, and I can't help but feel like if maybe I had seen his face properly, I would know who he is.

It's enough to drive me mad, especially when work is so boring and there's nothing to distract me from my thoughts. Luckily, Rafaela is between classes right now, so it's the perfect time to chat.

I lean over the phone lying on the counter and reply, "Yeah, yeah. Breathe in, breathe out, I'm a powerful goddess woman who can handle whatever life throws my way, blah blah blah."

"Hey!" she laughs, failing to sound indignant. "You know, that kind of thing really does help a lot of people with their self-confidence. It's not *all* just psycho-babble, I swear."

"I know, I know," I answer, resting my chin on my hands as I watch the rain streak down the front window of the shop. "Maybe that's why it's so slow today," I murmur aloud.

"What?" Rafaela asks, confused.

"Oh, God, sorry. I just zoned out for a minute. It's raining cats and dogs over here. I think maybe that's why nobody is coming into the shop today. You know how New Yorkers are— they're all too comfy in their apartments to go outside unless it's nice out."

Rafaela chuckles. "Yeah, like you wouldn't be snuggled up under a blanket back in Riverdale right now if you had the option."

"True," I admit, sighing. "I wish I was home right now. Watching TV, painting my nails, sipping some tea… ugh, now you've just killed the last measly dregs of my willpower today. If I can manage to get through the afternoon without calling it quits, it'll be a miracle."

"I feel you there, girl. I literally almost fell asleep on the subway this morning."

I burst out laughing, picturing my friend with her long, curly black hair and signature scarlet lipstick nodding off on the train, falling over into the lap of some scruffy homeless guy. Then I can't help but picture the guy who came into the shop a few days ago. My mystery man. He'd looked pretty scruffy, himself. What is his story? Who is he?

I shake the thought away and reply, "Yeah, that would've been pretty bad."

"I swear, between classes and the bar and studying and trying to still be a good girlfriend to Nico, the grind is about to put me out of commission for good," she laments. "And yeah, I know it's all good for my future or whatever, but really, I'm just tired. You know?"

"Oh, trust me, I know," I agree. "You and me both. We haven't even had a proper girls' night in, like, months. I miss being roommates with you. Are you sure you don't want to move into my empty old house with me and my mom? I'm only half-joking here," I add with a laugh.

"Hmm, tempting offer, but I don't think Mama De Laurentis would be too pleased to have me and Nico move into that old manor. She's a little old for our antics, I think."

I try to visualize what our household would look like—and it is not a pretty picture. My mom is a very private person these days, having retreated into a quiet loneliness to lick her wounds after losing everything years ago when Dad died. Vivacious, quick-talking Rafaela would be the opposite of a calming presence for my mom, even though for me, she's been a lifesaver in the past couple of years. Rafaela and I met in college, when I was studying business and she was a psychology Master's student. Somehow, we ended up having lunch together in the courtyard almost every week, and our friendship blossomed from there. I'm done with school after earning my Bachelor's, but Rafaela is still chiseling away at a PhD. She's six years older than me, but every bit as determined and ambitious, and for a while we even lived together. It was never a permanent situation, as I was still paying for the mortgage on my family home in Riverdale, but during exam times it just made more sense to crash at Rafaela and Nico's apartment rather than wasting time going back and forth all the time.

Living with Rafaela gave me a taste of freedom and independence I still crave, but my duty to keep the family home running and afloat, as well as take care of my mom, keeps me where I am. Sure, it's frustrating sometimes, but my dad taught me that family is the most important thing in the world. And I know he would want me to look after mom and the old house, so I do it for him.

"I'm working at the bar tonight if you want to come by!" Rafaela says brightly. She runs a bar called *Room With A View* alongside her boyfriend Nico, and when I was a student I spent a lot of time there. In fact, I wrote most of my reports and term papers sitting at the corner table of the bar. It was a cozy, homey atmosphere, and I missed it.

"I'll see what I can do. So, is your next class the

one with the hot professor?" I ask, quickly changing the subject. But before I can hear Rafaela's response, my attention is distracted by the flash of a shiny black car pulling up to the street parking outside the shop. My heart sinks, my instincts going on high alert. Something feels off, and I realize it's because that car looks like a mobster's ride.

"Nah, unfortunately this is the class with that weird lady who looks like Danny Devito's cousin or something," Rafaela is saying through the speakerphone. With a shaking hand, I quickly snatch up the phone and turn off the speaker, pressing the receiver to my face.

"Rafaela, um, I gotta go, babe. I-I'll talk to you later, okay?" I manage to mumble, staring at the front door with my heart hammering away in my chest.

"Wait, what? What's wrong? You sound weird. Is everything okay, Serena?"

"Uh, y-yeah. It's fine. I'm fine. I just—I gotta go. Love you. Bye," I reply quickly, ending the call before she can even respond. I glance down at the phone and shakily type in 9-1-1 before tucking the phone into my pocket. I want to have that number ready to go just in case things go sour. Of course, I realize with a sinking feeling, involving the police would probably only make the situation worse when it comes to the mafia. They've got cops on the take. I know what it's like. I learned just enough from eavesdropping on my dad's conversations years ago to know that I have to tread carefully here. One misstep, and I could lose everything. Hell, I could lose my life.

Just as expected, three skulking figures come through the front door a moment later, led by the same asshole who threatened me before: Lorenzo. And this time, there's no attempt at disarming me with charm or subtlety. The three of them come marching toward me with glowering expressions. I look around quickly, wondering if there's any way I can get out of this, any escape route I can take. But I know it's pointless. These guys are smarter than they look, I'm sure, and they're faster and stronger by far. No. The only thing I can do is stand my ground and take my beating.

I gulp back my fear and try not to let my eyes fill with tears as I face the wrath of the mob.

"Miss De Laurentis, you've been warned," Lorenzo snarls, cornering me behind the counter just like he did the other day. This time, he doesn't mince words. "Maybe I didn't make myself clear enough the last time we spoke, but you better cough up the money. Now. This isn't a negotiation, sweetheart, this is a shakedown. Do you wanna fuckin' die?"

"I-I'm sorry," I murmur. "Business has been slow. I'm barely breaking even as it is."

Lorenzo's eyebrows perk upward and he glances

back over his shoulder at the two goons behind him. "You hear that, boys? Hmm, sounds like an excuse to me. And a shitty one, too. Don't you lie to me, you little bitch. We know what kinda money is sunk into this place. Your daddy bankrolled you good, didn't he? You think you can hide that shit from us?"

"No, I swear. That money—it's all run out. I'm not lying. If I-I had the money I would pay you, I promise. It's just… it's not there anymore," I blurt out, feeling my whole body shake. Lorenzo glares at me so hard I wonder if he might be able to bore a hole in my face.

"Nice try," he scoffs. "But the thing is, I don't give a shit what your sob story is. Hard times, whatever. Everybody's gotta pay the rent somehow, and if you're not makin' ends meet sellin' soap to rich bitches, then it looks like you're gonna have to make up the deficit some other way."

He looks me up and down, stepping closer. The smell of his cheap cologne is so overbearing it almost makes my eyes water. I know what he's implying, and that's all it takes to send my thoughts hurtling back in time.

I'm shivering. It's not even cold, but my body won't stop convulsing. I feel sick to my stomach, but I know if I throw up they'll just hurt me more. What am I going to do? How am I going to survive…?

"Listen, you spoiled little brat. I know Daddy's

not around to spank you anymore, but if you need someone else to step in and whip your sweet little ass into shape, I'm your man," Lorenzo growls, the faint hint of a lascivious smile playing on his filthy lips.

Just then, there's the jingle from the front door, and all four of us whip around at the sound to see another man in the doorway. My stomach does a somersault. It's the guy from a few days ago! My mystery man. But what the hell is he doing here? I feel guilty instantly, knowing that now this man is in danger, too, because he's unwittingly interrupted mafia business. He's a witness now. And it's all my fault. I want to call out to him, tell him to leave, but my voice is caught in my throat.

"Who's this?" Lorenzo growls under his breath. Then, he shouts, "Who the fuck are you? Get out of here. This is private. Shop's closed."

The mystery guy pushes back the hood of his jacket to reveal a scruffy, handsome face with a coarse black beard, framed by long, gently curling black hair. There's a wildness to his face that thrills me, even in the tense danger of the moment.

"Shit, that's one of the Costa boys," says one of Lorenzo's goons.

Costa? My heart skips a beat. Another mafia guy. I should have known.

"Leave. Now. Before anyone has to get hurt," commands the mystery guy. His voice is like crushed velvet, deep and rumbling. It thrums through my body down to my core, and I shiver.

Lorenzo lets out a cruel laugh. "Yeah, you'd like that, wouldn't you? Have us just walk outta here before we get a chance to break that pretty-boy face of yours. You think that beard can hide you? I know who the hell you are. And this is no business of yours. Get out."

The Costa guy approaches slowly, shaking his head. "You really don't wanna mess with me."

All three of the others guffaw at his threat. "Right, sure, there are three of us and one of you. I'm sure we should all be scared right now, huh? You don't fuckin' scare me, man. But if you wanna go, we'll go. No sweat off my back. In fact, my boys have been itchin' for some target practice, right, boys?"

The two goons nod, grinning as they saunter toward Mystery Guy, squaring up for a fight.

"No," I breathe, terrified. But within the next few seconds, a flash of violent movement breaks out right in front of me, as the two goons move to swing at my Mystery Guy.

To my surprise, he manages to dodge them both, and there's a series of sickening crunches as his fist collides with one face and the other hand strikes a neck. They both swivel around, lumbering clumsily like two enraged bulls, only to be manhandled to the ground as Mystery Guy uses their own weight against him. He takes out a pistol, and with a flash of fluorescent light on silver metal, bashes them both upside the head. I scream at the sight of the gun, instinctively ducking down behind the counter. Lorenzo abandons me to take on the Mystery Guy, and even though I can't see what's going on, I can hear them.

"You wanna take me on, too?" growls Mystery Guy.

"You little fuckin' bitch!" yelps Lorenzo. There is a brief tussle and then I hear the telltale slam of knuckles against jawbone, and there's a stomach-turning cracking noise as Lorenzo cries out in agony. *Fuck, fuck, fuck.* Shit is getting real!

I hear the scramble of heavy, faltering footsteps and the jingle of the front door. Lorenzo sneers, "I'll remember this, you Costa piece of shit! This is just the beginning, motherfucker. You're gonna regret interfering with the Cleaners!"

"Yeah, you'll remember me when I mail your teeth back to you, asshole!" shouts back Mystery Guy, and the door slams shut. I stay cowering behind the counter, my knees pulled to my chest, while my heart races along at a stammering rhythm.

I hear footsteps approaching and I steel myself for whatever harm is due to come my way. After all, three mafia guys may be gone, but there's still one more left: Mystery Guy. He might hail from a different gang, but he's still a dangerous man, and I have no reason to believe that he's really here to help me. For all I know, that could have just been a tussle over territory, over who gets to terrorize me next.

So when Mystery Guy comes around behind the counter and offers me a hand to help me up, I hesitate for a long moment before taking it. I slowly look up at him to meet his gaze. I take in his dark clothing, the sleeves pushed to his elbows to reveal blood smeared along his hands and forearms, remnants of the battle. I stare at his face, that strangely familiar expression hidden behind a tangle of scraggly hair and beard. As soon as my eyes lock with his, it's like I'm hypnotized. His eyes peer down into my very being, to stroke the depths of my wounded soul.

It's almost overwhelming, that stare. Too much to take in.

But why? And how?

"I won't hurt you," he says softly, and that familiar thrum shakes through me. Stiffly, as though in a trance, I hold out my hand and take his. He pulls me to my feet, then places both hands on my shoulders, his eyes peering into my face with genuine concern.

"Are you okay? Did they hurt you before I got here?" he asks. I manage to shake my head. I somehow tear my eyes away from his and notice that some of the blood on his hands and arms seems to be his own, and that he's injured.

"I-I'm okay," I murmur, "but you're hurt."

He takes his hands off of me and curls them into

fists hanging at his sides. "No, I'm alright. It's nothing at all. As long as you're okay… I'll go."

As he turns to leave, some kind of strange impulse takes hold of my body and I reach out to stop him, my hands falling at his chest. He stops and looks down at me, eyes flashing. For a moment, I'm almost frightened by the wildness of that expression, but then he softens.

"Let me clean you up before you go, at least," I offer, biting my lip. "I mean, you can't go out all bloody and injured like that. It's unsanitary. And if there's one thing I do have here in abundance, it's soap. Just let me clean your wounds. Please. It's the least I can do."

He hesitates, clearly fighting some kind of internal battle as he looks at me, considering my strange request. Finally, he gives in, and I gently lead him to a sink, pulling up a stool for him to sit on while I grab the least-feminine-scented soap I can find and start lathering up his fists and forearms. Even as he sits on the stool, he's nearly eye-to-eye with me, he's so tall. And I consider myself to be relatively tall for a woman, too, at five-foot-seven, so it's unusual for a man to tower over me in such a way.

He doesn't even wince at the sting of soap on his cut-up, bruised knuckles, and from the number of scars I feel underneath my fingers as I wash them, he seems to have seen his fair share of fights. I wonder what kind of life he leads, how many times he has done this. Is this his job? Really? To go around protecting women he doesn't even know?

But Lorenzo and his goons called him a Costa guy. If he's a mafia associate, then why did he help me? Sure, when I was young and Dad was still alive, things were good. My folks and the mafia were more than just simpatico, they were family. But things have changed drastically since then, and as far as I know, the Costa family certainly don't make my safety and wellbeing a priority these days. I'm nothing to them. In fact, they probably hate me after everything that happened.

So why in the world did this rough-and-tough Costa enforcer come to my rescue?

As I make my way up his arm, scrubbing gently at the bloody lacerations and dark bruises, I come across a familiar sight. A tattoo. One I have not seen with my own two eyes in many years. The sight of it instantly throws me back, and a tidal wave of confused emotions overtake me. I freeze up, staring at the intricate lines of the tattoo, suddenly remembering all the things I have tried so hard to forget, dark things that time has buried.

And with it, an overwhelming sense of urgency to ask, to know for certain that this man is who my heart wills him to be. By chance, by fate, by magic. By whatever means necessary for him to have walked back into my world again, albeit beaten down and roughened up and subdued.

I look up from the tattoo to meet his gaze, and the answer to my question is there in his pale green eyes long before the words even leave my lips. It's him. I know it is. But I still can't stop myself from asking, just to be sure.

"Luca? Is… is that you?"

For a few long, sweet moments, we stare into each other's eyes, frozen. Her hands are still holding my forearm, her soft fingers on my rough, hardened hands warm even as the water starts to get cold. Her touch is one of the things I've missed most from my old life. I never want it to end.

But as strong as my arm is, as powerful as the body sitting before her in the little shop may be, those eyes of hers hold me still. Her gaze searches mine. Those eyes are feasting themselves, staring right into my soul, making me want to let her know everything they want to know even as my own eyes hold her paralyzed.

Finally, I let myself give her the smile I've been waiting years to give her.

"Ciao, bella."

And just like that, we're teenagers again.

Tears swell up like springwater in those endless eyes, and her lip quivers for half a second as a tidal wave of emotion crashes through her system.

"*Luca!*" she squeals, and before I can open my mouth, she flings herself at me, little arms wrapping around my torso as she buries her face in my chest. My chest is rippling with muscle, but even I can feel how tight she's trying to squeeze me, and I couldn't keep the grin off my face if my life depended on it.

My thick arms wrap around her, practically covering her in me as I hold her warmth against my body, and I hear her start to sob before I can put my lips to the top of her golden head. My large hand strokes her back, and I feel my own heart swelling as I give her a gentle squeeze back.

"Serena," I say, and it feels so good, so free to feel her name roll of my tongue. I've held myself back from this moment for so long. I still don't know if it was the right choice. But right now, in this moment, I let myself just *be* with her as we hold each other tight.

I'm a hardened man, but I can still feel. And Serena is the sweetest feeling in the world.

After what feels like forever, she turns her head up to look at me. Those wet, reddened eyes don't dampen the smile on her face. "Oh my god, it really is you! I...I can't..."

"Shush, shush, you've been through a lot today," I

say, giving her a reassuring squeeze, my huge arms holding her protectively. I feel her take a breath and let it out slowly.

She bites her lip, trying desperately to bring her emotions back in line, but it's useless. And I can't believe the joy I feel in my own heart—the relief.

She isn't afraid of me? After everything. After how we parted ways last time?

Not only that, she's overjoyed to see me. To be with me.

"I just...I never thought I'd see you again," she confesses, half-laughing, half-sobbing. She sniffs, wiggling an arm free to wipe her eyes and laugh at herself all over again. "Oh my god, I'm such a mess, don't look at me!"

It's my turn to laugh as I hug her tight to me as she tries to get away, and she gives a little squeal of delight as I give her a bear hug that lifts her feet off the ground for a moment. It's like no time has passed between us at all.

I set her down and release her. She immediately grabs a paper towel from the counter and dabs her eyes, checking in the mirror to see what the damage is. She could have raccoon eyes streaming down her whole face, and she'd still be irresistible to me.

After another sniff, she takes a step back and looks at me with a gaze that really see *me* for the first time. "Oh my god, and you were in here yesterday! I... I can't believe I didn't recognize you!"

I give a cocky smile. "That was the plan. Besides the glasses, though, I've changed a lot, Serena."

"No you haven't," she says in a laughing sob, looking over my face as more and more recognition crashes through her. "If it weren't for that beard... but I'd know those eyes anywhere," she says, dreamily, and I can tell she only half-realizes the words are coming from her mouth. Catching herself, she blushes and runs her fingers through her hair, getting a stray lock out of her face. Another sniff.

"You're one to talk," I say, a warm smile on my face as I take her in, looking her up and down. Her face reddens at my gaze, but she doesn't turn away, either. She always was like that—she liked to play shy, but my gaze excited her. It always had, and it still does, I see. "Serena, you look... incredible."

A moment passes between us in silence as we just stare at each other, smiling stupidly. Teenagers all over again.

But her smile fades, and I see concern on her face. "Luca... my god, where have you been all these years? Have you been safe? Do... do you know those guys that were here earlier? How are you even still in town, I--"

"Serena," I cut her off gently, putting two hands on her shoulders. I feel her instinctively melt in my hands, shoulders relaxing immediately. I never believed her when she told me I have a calming presence, but it's true for her, at least. "Serena, you've had a terrible day thanks to some terrible men. You don't need more things to trouble yourself. Not today, at least." I return her smile as those doe-eyes look up at me. "But I do think you could stand to get out of here and get a drink. Why don't we go get something?"

A smile slowly creeps back over her pretty face. After a moment's hesitation, she says, "I think I'd like that. Yeah."

~

"Nice ride," she says as she climbs into the passenger's seat of my black company sedan. "Nicer than that beat-up old pickup I remember."

I smile as she shuts the door and I pull out onto the road.

A lot of baggage comes with this car, Serena.

Still, it feels good to make her happy. I shift up through the gears and start tearing down the roads we've both grown up around.

"So," she says after a moment, "got anywhere in mind?"

"Well," I half-laugh, "the places I usually go, I don't think you'd find the most relaxing."

She smiles. "Still running with the old crowd, huh?"

"Something like that," I say. The only place that

comes to mind is a dive that some of the rougher Italian crowd haunts. It's dingy, falling apart, and doesn't have anything you could call service, but it's been my place for a while. It's got a homey feel to it. But just because it's homey doesn't mean it's the place I'd take someone shaken-up to calm down.

"I've got somewhere you'd like, though," I say, remembering somewhere... cozy. It's a mob-run place, and while it's a little closer to work than I'd like to bring her, it's somewhere I know is safe.

I follow the roads to a place that I'm not sure I'd call a hotel, exactly, judging by the outside. It's an older building, but people have taken care of it over the years. Good people. As good as you find in this business.

"Room With A View?" I hear Serena say as we pull up on the side of the road and climb out of the car.

"I haven't been here in a long time, but I remember it being a good place. I'm sure it doesn't look like much from the outside, but-"

"Are you kidding?" she laughs, a bright smile on her face, crossing the street with me and looking at me as if I'm unreal. "I totally know this place, come on!"

I blink in surprise as she runs ahead of me to the door, but I follow. She's really been getting around, hasn't she?

The interior is all wood—and good wood, at that.

It's an old building. A few candles are burning on the tables, and the windows are just dark enough to make the whole place feel cozy. Past the tables and the bar, I see a set of stairs leading up to the next floor, to what I assume are a few rooms. It can't be many. The place is tiny, and it looks like most of the people here are here for the drinks.

There's a woman with light brown skin and dark, curly hair behind the bar, and her eyes light up at the sight of Serena.

"Hey girl, you didn't tell me you were coming over!" she says, coming around to cross the floor and hug Serena around the neck. Even as she does though, she gives me a suspicious look, eyeing me like a judge. "Who's your tall friend?"

I crack a smile at the protective edge in her voice.

"It was kind of a last minute thing," she says, breaking the hug and turning to me. "I'll explain later. Rafaela, this is Luca. He's... an old friend," she introduces me with an anxious smile, and I watch Rafaela's eyebrows go up in understanding as she glances at me. "Luca, this is Rafaela. She runs this place," she adds with a wink. Rafaela rolls her eyes.

"Co-owns. Nico's around here somewhere. I'll have him come get your orders. I'm... guessing you two want a table?" she asks, giving Serena a curious look. Serena rolls her eyes, holding back a grin.

"That'd be great," Serena says, "thanks." Rafaela watches us as we head to a quaint little table by the window, surprise written all over her face. Serena must not bring guys through here very much.

I have to be careful as I slide into the tiny seat. The table's a little low, so I put my legs out to the side as I awkwardly fit my way in. Serena giggles as she watches me, and I grin back.

"Rafaela and I go way back," she says once we're situated. "She's like, my best friend. I wouldn't have survived college without her."

"Sounds like she keeps an eye out for you," I say.

"Yeah, she can be like that. Kind of like a big sister, too. She likes putting that Psych degree to use."

A man with his sleeves rolled up approaches the table, looking at both of us with a warm smile. This one, I recognize, and we give each other a knowing nod.

His name is Nico Tosetti, and he's what we call an associate. One of us. He must be the boyfriend Rafaela mentioned. I've crossed paths with him once or twice, but he's small potatoes—which is a good thing to be, in this business. He's a tall, goofy-looking guy, and he's got a good heart. He doesn't need to be tangled up in this business too deep.

"Luca," he says with a smile, "didn't think I'd see you around here."

"You know each other?" Serena asks, looking surprised.

"Yeah, we've met," I say, clapping hands with the guy. "Didn't know this was your place."

"Me and Rafaela," he says with a nod back to the bartender. "They said running a bar would be a nightmare, but between the two of us, it's the dream," he says with a boyish smile.

Probably a hell of a lot better than enforcement on the south side of town, I think, and I give him a nod.

"So, what can I get you two?" he asks, putting his hands on his hips. I make eye contact with Serena before I speak.

"Got any Campari back there?"

"Of course."

"How about a couple Americanos, then? Hold the Vermouth."

"So...just Campari and soda water?"

"That's right."

Nico nods with a smile before darting off, and I catch Serena grinning at me across the table.

"Bastard Americanos, huh?" she asks, and I feel a grin spread across my face. An Americano in this case isn't the coffee—it's a cocktail with Campari, a little Vermouth, and soda water. Back in the day, when we were younger, I'd find ways to sneak a bottle of Campari every now and then, but I never bothered with the Vermouth. So, I called them 'bastard' Americanos.

That was also because I was a teenager still

learning English, and I'd just learned the word 'bastard.'

"I'm surprised you remembered," I say.

"'An Americano for my Americana?' How could I forget that?" she says, and I cover my face with a massive hand.

"Oh god, I forgot about that," I laugh, remembering that cheesy line, and soon I can hear her laughter too.

"It was cute!" she says, and as our laughter fades, her face gets a little more pensive. "Feels like a lifetime ago. Sitting on the back of that old pickup you and the other boys worked out of. Sneaking drinks from some Italian place I couldn't pronounce."

I look at her, sitting there, the picture of beauty. The dim lighting in here just makes her all the more alluring, and I want to just take her right now, as if years hadn't passed between us.

But we're moving fast. Too fast. We need to talk, and I know it. And yet... why spoil the moment while it lasts? As if on cue, Nico sets our drinks down in front of us and heads off.

"It's been too long, Serena," I say, watching her as she takes her drink and stirs it pensively.

"I know," she nearly whispers. "I still can't believe it's real. You, here, I mean." She looks up at me and hesitates a moment. "Those guys, back there at the shop..."

"The Cleaners," I say in a low tone, glancing

around the bar. I don't want to stir up commotion here, and talking about a rival crime syndicate is a good way to do that.

"How did you know they were gonna be there?" she asks.

"Things are getting rough, Serena," I say before taking a swig of my drink. "I was worried someone might come causing trouble around your place. I was right." She's watching me with wide eyes. "I have to be my own eyes and ears. It's how it always is, with these people."

"So it's true," she says softly, looking into my eyes. "You're working with…"

The words *the mafia* hang between us. I nod.

"It's been a long few years, Serena," I say. Even low, my voice is gruff, and the beard and long hair don't help the image. I reach over and cover one of her small hands in my large, warm one. "For now, just know that I'm not going to let anything happen to you. And you don't need to worry yourself about all that right now, okay?"

She looks at me with that glint in her eye I know so well. Serena doesn't like things being held back from her, and I know she'll come back to this soon enough. She's a precocious girl like that. So it's all the more surprising to me when I hear her say, "Alright, sure." She tilts her head to the side, narrowing her eyes at me. "Just tell me one thing, if you're gonna be all secretive... what's with the beard?"

I'm left speechless for a moment, then burst out laughing, putting a hand to my face. "I don't know, really. What, you don't like it?"

"Do you?"

I frown. "I've had it since…" *Since life tore us apart.* "For a while."

"I think I miss your face," she decides.

"I've been missing yours, *passerotta mia.*"

She blushes before hiding her face with her drink, which she finishes with a tinkling of ice cubes. "Woo, I forgot how strong that stuff is!"

"Careful now," I say after finishing my own. "I know how much of a lightweight you are."

"I'll have you know I've gotten *lots* better," she says playfully. Before I can reply, the sound of music floods the bar as someone turns on the speakers, and I flash a glance at the little open space between the tables—a wooden floor perfect for dancing.

Anyone who passes up the chance to dance with a pretty lady is no man at all.

"Alright, let's see it then," I say, standing up, and Serena flutters her eyes in confusion as I reach down to take her hands.

"Wait, what?"

"Rafaela, two more!" I call to the bartender, and she winks at Serena as I drag her out to the dance floor.

"Luca, what are you doing?" she laughs as some of the patrons give us amused looks.

"If you're so good at holding your liquor, let's see it! What good are a few drinks if they don't help you dance?"

She yelps as I swing her onto the clearing between tables that passes for a dance floor, and the next moment, I'm drawing her by the hand all around me. It's lively music, the kind you jump into to shake off your embarrassment and get into the heat of it. Serena is laughing already. After the first few awkward seconds of jerking around, we're dancing. I'm normally not a man who expresses himself much. Especially not the past few years. But the way Serena dances around me, the way I can lead her so easily, it kindles an old fire in me.

That, and well, dancing is in my blood.

A song goes by, and by the time the one after that is done, a few people around the bar have joined us. Our blood is racing, and after Serena and I grab another drink, we dive right back in. It's like there's nothing else in the world but the two of us.

We don't need words. All that gets shed by our body language. And as I'm watching her body move with mine, leading her on effortlessly, I realize how much I've missed her.

More dangerously, I realize how much I want her.

I need her.

Her soft hands brush against my muscular fore-arms, my strong hands on her hips, her ass against my crotch, the energy between us draws us closer and closer.

She turns, and our eyes meet for just a second, and it's like lightning flashes between us. Primal desire is bursting through, even though both of us have been trying to ignore it this whole time, but its message is plain as day.

We want each other. Now.

My heart is racing and I can feel every pulse of blood in my veins. Despite the three cocktails I've had, my brain doesn't feel fuzzy or out of focus. In fact, everything around me seems intensified, my senses all heightened, the colors in the bar seem brighter and more garish than ever before. It's like someone has turned up the contrast on the photo lens of the world around us. I feel exhilarated. I feel alive. I know exactly what I want.

And he's standing right in front of me. I look up at him with a dizzy smile on my face, drinking in the vivid green-peridot of his eyes, the fullness of his lips, the gentle slope of his nose. Even with that thick beard and scraggly hair, he's painfully attractive. He's grown up a lot since I last saw him, and I suppose that I have, too.

The scrappy young man I fell head over heels for as a teenager has transformed into a towering, musclebound, scarred, and stoic lumberjack type. If someone had told me years and years ago that we would meet again this way, I would never have believed it. After everything we went through, I assumed I would never see Luca again.

And even if we did, I thought he would turn away from me. I'm a reminder to him of dark times, just as he is to me. I can't pretend that running into him, resparking that old fire hasn't knocked me off my feet. Those memories, the ones I have worked so hard to put in the ground, float around me like the remains of some tragic shipwreck. Every now and then I wade too close to a piece of shrapnel, and the warning sirens go off in my head. As we talked and caught up with each other tonight, I had to remind myself that things are different now. That old danger is in the past.

Of course, there are new dangers now. Lorenzo and the Cleaners. The shop barely making a profit. Trying to keep my old, expensive, and empty family house up and running. And now there's a new, added fear to the mix: losing Luca again.

It's like a dream, a surreality, an impossible twist of fate that we should find each other again years after the horrors that broke us apart. Throughout the evening, I've been occasionally tempted to pinch myself, to shake myself awake. This has to be a dream.

But when I reach up to brush my hand along the wiry hair on Luca's jaw and feel him lean into my touch, closing those beautiful eyes as though he's losing himself in the ecstasy of the moment... I know for certain that this is real. This is actually happening. And I can't lose him again. Not now. Not yet. There are still so many things I need to ask him, need to find out. I want to know him again the way I used to. We just need time—the one thing there never seems to be enough of.

Luca turns his face slightly to kiss the soft skin of my palm, sending a curious thrill down through my body, burning down to my very core. I can feel that vibration way down in my toes. His warm, whiskey-tinged breath is like a jolt of electricity to my soul.

"Luca..." I murmur, my voice trailing off and getting lost in the raucous thrum of competing conversations all around us in the bar. The counter is packed with patrons, and every table is full. Luca and I have been standing against the far wall for... god only knows how long. Just talking. Reminiscing gently, both of us too afraid to really push too far and split open old wounds. I can tell, without even having to ask, that he's not ready to talk about what happened yet. Not fully. I don't blame him. I wish I could push those terrible thoughts of my mind, make room for better things hopefully to come.

Like right now.

I'm more than ready to make a new memory with Luca. A much better one.

And it appears that he feels the same, leaning toward me, talking close. All evening he's been pressed right up against me, that glorious, powerful body moving rhythmically with mine. It's delicious, it's intoxicating, and I can't believe I've managed to survive all this time without it. Sometimes, someone can enter your life and remind you just how much you've been missing out on. Luca was mine once, and nothing in the world has ever compared to the thrill of belonging to him.

I want him to claim me again. Tonight. As the two struggling grown-ups we are now.

"Passerotta mia," he whispers, brushing his lips along the shell of my ear. A tingling warmth spreads through my body and I shiver, feeling goosebumps rise across my skin. I turn to catch his face mere centimeters from mine, the tips of our noses barely touching. We lock eyes for a tense, clenching moment, and then he glances down ever so quickly at my lips and I know.

He wants to kiss me. He's feeling the same fire that I feel.

But he pulls back before giving in, lifting a calloused, powerful carpenter's hand to stroke the hair back out of my face. "Where can we go?" he asks softly.

It's a bigger question in my mind than he probably intends for it to be. Where can we go? In what world does our relationship belong? Where are we safe, the two of us? Right now, right here, I have an idea for a temporary safe haven.

"Stay here. I'll be right back," I tell him. Then, as I'm turning to walk away, I add, "Please... don't leave."

Luca gives me a brilliant, warming smile. "I'm not going anywhere without you, Serena."

It's hard to tear myself away from him, even for a moment, but I have to. I rush through the crowd, squeezing past various groups of bachelorette parties and post-grind investment bankers tossing back a few beers, finally reaching the bar counter. I wiggle in between two women giggling with umbrella drinks and locate Rafaela, who is engaged in a battle with one of her old nemeses: the daiquiri blender. At any other time, I might have burst out laughing at the sight— god knows we've talked about that evil blender a million times. She's even confessed to me on one occasion that she's pretty sure it's possessed by a demon. It's that bad.

But not as dire as my current situation.

I finally catch her eye, giving her an urgent expression. We know each other well enough to pick up on unspoken cues, and she immediately abandons the evil blender to hurry over to me.

"What's up, babe?" she asks, her voice miraculously cutting through the din of high-pitched laughter and yells coming from all directions here at the center of the activity.

"I need a room," I tell her plainly. I'm too determined to be coy about this. There's no time to waste. Every moment I'm here instead of standing in front of Luca is a moment I can hardly bear.

To her infinite credit and grace, she doesn't razz me at all. Rafaela simply nods, swivels around, bends down to unlock a little gray safe behind the counter, and take out a room key. She places it in my hand and gives me a wink.

"Room 6. King-sized bed, en suite bathroom, window overlooking the community garden next door. Go get 'im, tiger," she says, grinning.

"Do I need to—?"

She shakes her head. "Don't worry about paying. It's an empty room, you need it, and you're my best friend. Consider this an early wedding present," she adds, laughing. Blushing, I reach out and squeeze her hand gratefully.

"Thank you. Seriously."

I turn away and start maneuvering back through the crowd again, my eyes peeled for Luca. Finally, I arrive at the same spot where we were standing just minutes ago and he isn't there.

My heart sinks down into my stomach and the room starts to go dizzy.

Where is he? Did he leave? How could this have

happened? Maybe I spooked him somehow. Maybe he thought better of this and decided to make a break for it before things got too heavy. Maybe I only imagined the magic sparking between us. Maybe… it wasn't meant to be.

Just as I'm about to give up and go back to the bar to return the key to Rafaela, I feel an arm snake around my waist. I look down, then back up, and to my uncontrollable joy I see Luca beaming down at me, a fire in his eyes.

"I'm here, Serena. I told you I wasn't going anywhere."

Wordlessly, I hold up the key. His expression changes instantly, that affable smile melting into a white-hot smoulder. He nods and takes me by the hand, leading me to the staircase down the hall, tucked away just out of the hubbub of the bar crowd. Before we can even make it all the way up the stairs, Luca pushes me against the wall, leaning in close over me. His chest is heaving and I can tell that he's working as hard as he can to control himself, to stay level-headed. It's a thrill to think that he's as intoxicated by me as I am by him.

The noise at the bar fades into nothing as he takes my face gently in both of his rough, strong hands. Luca peers into my face as though he's searching for something, some answer hidden in the shape of my features that he's desperate to decode. And then, with only a split-second's hesitation, he closes the space between us and captures my lips in a passionate kiss.

Immediately, I feel my entire body going limp and pliable, the sensation of his full lips moving against mine like a shot of Everclear straight to my brain. He's like a drug, like the most addictive dream, and I need more. His tongue gently pushes into my mouth as his hands slide down to my shoulders, then down to grip my waist possessively. I am riveted to the spot, afraid to move for fear that this magical dream will fade away and leave me standing alone in the stairwell.

I feel his hands roving back over my hips to cup my ass, feeling his fingers digging into the soft flesh of my upper thighs. He wedges a leg between my thighs and presses the full length of his body against me. I'm warm between my legs and the sensation of his thigh rubbing against me is delicious. I moan into his mouth as he takes my wrists in his hands and pins them up above my head, making me feel both vulnerable and powerful at the same time.

He breaks our kiss for a moment, nudging me to turn my head to one side so he can kiss a line down my jaw to breathe softly in my ear. I tremble and arch toward him as his lips press into the ticklish skin of my neck, sucking and nipping gently in a way that makes my whole body shake. He remembers me so well, perfectly mapping out each of the places on my body that are sensitive. He knows me better than anyone else in the world, and after I lost him so many years ago, I never thought I would feel this good again.

How can this be real? Am I dreaming?

Suddenly, the echoing clack-clack of high-heeled shoes interrupts us and I glance around Luca's shoulder to see the shadows of some women approaching. Quickly, Luca hoists me up and I wrap my legs around his waist as he carries me up the rest of the stairs.

"Which room?" he asks, his voice rough and gravelly with desire.

"Six," I whisper. We find the door at the end of the hallway and he bends his knees so that I can fish out the key and fit it into the keyhole with a laugh. Once the door is open, he takes the key, shoves it in his pocket, and pushes through into the room.

Rafaela really, truly came through for me on this one. I've seen some of the rooms here, and while all of them are decent, standard-issue lodging, this particular room stands out. It's designed with a kind of 1960s vintage charm, and there is a king-sized canopy bed by the massive bay window.

"Wow, she really hooked us up," I murmur as Luca sets me down on my feet. But before I can say anything else, he pulls me close into another kiss, stealing the breath right from my lungs. I close my eyes and fold into his arms easily, letting him lean me backward onto the bed.

"I've thought about you so many times," Luca growls, bending to kiss me again. His hands reach down to peel my blouse up and over my arms, leaving me bare-chested except for my bra. He cups my breasts while his leg wedges between my thighs again, and I let out a groan of frustration. I need more, more, more. He's got me craving him like an addict.

"Please, don't take your time," I beg him. "I-I can't wait, Luca."

He groans and stands up to strip off his jacket, shirt, and then unzip his jeans. He pushes them down to stand in his boxers and I can't help but sit up and lean toward him, my fingers roving across the massive bulge in the fabric. He's much bigger than I even remember.

"Take off your clothes," he commands softly. Without a word, I obey, unclasping my bra, then pulling off my shoes, skirt, and panties to sit totally naked in front of him.

"Can I...?" I ask meekly, almost licking my lips at the sight of his cock straining to break free of his underwear. Luca nods and I hungrily tug his boxers down so he can step out of them. His cock springs free, bouncing in front of my face. I reach up to stroke him with both hands, feeling his enormous size and warmth. I can't resist. I need to taste him.

Adjusting to kneel on the bed, I lower my head down to take his cock into my mouth, stretching my lips to accommodate his size. As I slowly begin to work his shaft with my mouth and both hands, Luca groans appreciatively. His hand comes down to press lightly against the back of my head, pushing me down on his cock further until I'm almost choking on it. I wish desperately I could take his full length into my mouth, feel him swelling and pulsing against the back of my throat. I bob up and down, sucking him hard and fast until his hips are moving in rhythm with me. I can feel myself getting wetter by the second, just from the intoxicating taste of Luca's cock in my mouth.

But then he stops me suddenly, gently pushing me back away from him. I don't get a moment to feel sad, though, because he lifts and tosses me further back on the bed before climbing on top to straddle me. Once again, he takes hold of my wrists and pins my arms down, this time on either side of me. Then he leans to kiss his way down to my breasts, his lips nipping and suckling at my nipples until I'm crying out with need. Every kiss and bite sends a thrum of heady desire down to that secret place deep inside me, and before long I'm nearly teary-eyed with frustration.

"Please, Luca. I need you inside me. I'm so wet… I've waited so long for you," I murmur, hardly even aware of what I'm saying.

"Are you sure?" he asks gruffly, and I know it's taking every ounce of his self-control to resist.

"Yes! God, yes. Please! Fuck me, Luca," I plead desperately, yelping when he lets out an animalistic growl and bites harder. I'm arching my hips toward him, my body lifting up off the bed.

Finally, he pulls back and readies the head of his cock at my slick opening, and just this gentle touch is enough to make me tremble. For a few moments, he swirls the tip of his beautiful cock against my clit, making me groan and grip the sheets. My pussy is aching, swelling with desire.

"Fuck me," I mumble. "I want you so bad! Don't make me wait any longer."

And with that, Luca shoves the entire massive length of his cock inside of me in one smooth motion, until the tip brushes against that sweet spot deep within me and I wrap my legs around his waist, pulling him down to me. I need him close. I need to be flush with his body, to feel every part of him at once all around me.

"Oh my god," I whimper as he starts to thrust, pulling almost all the way out to slam back into me again and again and again. He groans and kisses my neck, his teeth grazing my skin. I can tell he wants to let go, to use my body like a fuck toy. But he's too gentle, too careful with me to do so.

But I want him to let go.

"You don't have to be gentle, Luca," I whisper, my breath tousling his hair softly. "You can fuck me however you want to."

And that's all it takes. Permission granted.

His teeth sink into my skin while his hands grope at my breasts, squeezing my nipples between his fingers while his cock slides in and out of me faster and faster. "Fuck, I've thought about this so many times, *mia passerotta*," he hisses through gritted teeth. "I've thought about how badly I wanted to touch you, fill you up with my cock."

"Harder," I breathe, scarcely able to form coherent thoughts as I lose myself in the swift rhythm of his thrusts. My pussy clenches with every movement, tightening around his cock. Luca reaches down between my legs to massage my clit with two fingers, making me scream in pleasure. His other hand comes up to cup over my mouth while he fucks me mercilessly, making my pussy ache with every powerful push. Finally, I feel my pleasure mounting to a climax and I cry out, orgasming against him. He moves faster and his fingers don't relent, even as I try to pull away from the overstimulation. He isn't going to give me a break. Not at all.

I come again and again, tears burning in my eyes as I toss my head back and twist the sheets in my fists. "Oh god, it feels so fucking good," I pant.

"I want to fill you up with my come, baby," Luca growls. "I want to pump you full."

"Do it," I reply, with a daring tone. "Please. I want your come inside me!"

With a few short, rapid thrusts, Luca comes.

"Fuck, Serena!" he shouts. His cock pulses with jet after jet of thick, hot come, filling me up while I orgasm again. He fucks into me a few more times and then collapses next to me, peppering my face with kisses.

We lie there breathing heavily for a few minutes, just soaking in the magical afterglow. He pulls me into his arms and holds me there, both of us totally silent and content. If this is a dream, then I never, ever want to wake up again. This is perfect. This is… paradise.

Finally, I make the suggestion that we should shower off. I slip out of his arms and prance across the room, feeling his hot seed slipping down my thighs mingled with my own juices. "Come on," I beckon flirtatiously. "Let's get wet again."

Luca sits up and smiles at me, lighting a fire inside my heart yet again. "I'll be there in a minute. I promise." But just then, there's the buzz of a cell phone going off. I wait in the doorway of the en suite bathroom while Luca gets up to check it. His face pales slightly, and his smile fades away.

"What… what is it?" I ask, a little worried.

Luca looks up at me, a pained expression on his handsome face. "I was summoned by the *Capo*." My heart drops into my stomach. Is Luca in trouble with the Mafia?

And if so… was it my fault?

The scent of her is still on me when I get into the car. It's something that's going to be on me all day, I know, and I'll remember it even longer. And when I see her next, what's to stop me from getting her on me all over again?

My eyes flick down to my phone before I stuff it into my pocket and check behind me to pull out into the road.

When I first saw the message, I wanted to crush the phone in my bare hand and throw the remains out the window. My instinct was to tear down anything that would dare step in and interrupt what I was having with Serena. And under any other circumstance, that's just what I would have done. But this message came from the very thing that forced us to be apart. It was one thing that I hated more than anything, but I knew it was also the only thing that would make sure she could be safe.

My bosses. The mafia.

This message came from Diego Milani, to be precise, a capo. The capos are the guys who manage enforcers and associates like me in our business. I've known Diego as long as I've been involved with these men. A message from someone like him means either something very good or very bad.

And considering what happened back at Serena's shop, I have a feeling I'm about to get chewed out. I don't care. I did what I had to for Serena's protection, and that's all my whole career has been about. That's all I acted for.

Is it, though?

I grip the steering wheel as I move through traffic, trying not to let my thoughts distract me. My mind flashes back to Serena on that bed, me tearing her clothes away, the feeling of her bare skin in my hands, the way my bare cock felt sinking into her to the hilt…

My manhood starts to swell between my legs. Just the thought of her stirs up a beast within me I can hardly control. And that's the problem. Everything I'm doing with these thugs is to give her a chance at life. I've done terrible things to make sure she'll be kept safe, out of all this ugly business.

I gave up my life to protect her, but I can't protect her from myself.

When I was a teenager, I let the fire in my soul rule me. I did what I felt was right, what I wanted. Serena makes me feel like that all over again, no matter how much the short years tried to snuff that fire out. It's dangerous. She makes me dangerous.

I feel a smile tug at my stony face as I pull up on the side of the road. I've beaten men down with my bare hands, fought off seasoned enforcers in knife-fights, and rained gunfire on rivals, but this woman who barely stands to my chest makes me more dangerous than any of them.

I climb out of the car and head around the side of the building to step into the room we "rent" at the back of this liquor store. It's been a place we use for last-minute meetings for a while, and the owner is an associate of ours. It's not a bad deal for him. He gets a break from protection money in exchange for letting a few musclebound Italians meet in the back of his store. I have my gun on me. I know it'll get taken, but it's a formality to show that I'm never unready.

In my business, you could come out of a meeting with your boss with a promotion or in a body bag.

When I get up to the door, there's a man outside it waiting for me. I've seen him before, but I don't know his name. He just nods to me and opens the door to usher me in. My eyes regard him carefully as I step inside, but he's relaxed. When a man's about to fight, he has tells, like a gambler about to lie. I've gotten good at recognizing them. A twitch of the finger, legs poised a certain way. You can even see it in the eyes.

But as I walk through the door, he just closes it behind me and gestures for me to hold my arms out. I smile.

"Diego's not that jumpy, is he?" I ask as he takes the gun from me and pats me down for any other weapons.

"Apparently I need to be," a voice calls from further in the room, past shelves of stacked liquor and beer, "if my men are gonna start jumping the gun like you. Get your ass in here, Luca."

That's Diego's voice, no doubt about it. I snort as the doorman finishes checking me over, and I stride down the aisles of stock to the cleared-out space where he takes care of business. I've been in here only once before, and it wasn't on the best terms.

When I step forward, I start to rethink whether I'm about to be killed.

Diego isn't a man who likes a lot of ceremony, but this looks like a miniature courtroom. Diego himself is looking over a stacked box of expensive Scotch, and in a semi-circle around him are men I recognize. Some, I know by name. Most are enforcers like me, but one man sitting on a crate next to Diego takes me by surprise.

It's a consigliere. In every business like ours,

there's usually only one man like him, maybe two. Consiglieri don't stick to our hierarchy.

He's the Don's own advisor, which makes him the most important man I've been in the same room as for a long time. It also means that this meeting is serious. I feel his hawkish gray eyes watching me carefully as he sits there. Diego turns to look me up and down before I can say anything.

"Luca," he says, crossing his arms, "I'm sure you're familiar with our consigliere, Antonio Tomasi."

I give the man a nod with a tight but respectful smile. He doesn't react.

"Mr. Tomasi thought it would be wise to sit in on this little business meeting," Diego goes on, his formality starting to relax into his usual self. "Because when our men make waves as big as you did out of line earlier today, he likes to hear the *very good reason* I'm sure you have firsthand."

"News travels fast," I say, keeping my eyes on Diego evenly.

"That it does," he says, pacing in a slow circle around me, "especially when a soldier like you takes it upon himself to pick a fight with the likes of Lorenzo Abruzzi."

That last name gets my attention. But I don't show the slightest hint of emotion. I'm being grilled, and Diego can smell a crack in someone's defenses from a mile away.

"Didn't get his name while I was knocking his teeth out," I say, and I watch Diego's jaw set. "He was in our territory, boss. Deep in our territory."

"Don't pretend that's what this is about, I know where the fight went down," Diego says, coming to a stop and resting his hands on his hips as he glares at me. "I know you got your reasons to go stalking that girl, and before today, I didn't give two shits."

My fists clench instinctively at what Diego is hinting, and Diego steps forward as I say, "It was still our territory, Diego. I caught some Cleaners starting to start shit deep in our territory, and I was taking care of business. I was doing my job."

"Your job is to do what the family needs," Diego says, restraining the anger in his voice as much as I'm holding back mine. "And the family did *not* need to spark a turf war with the goddamn Cleaners!"

There's a silence in the room for a few moments that everyone can *taste*.

The Cleaners have been like a bad word the past few months, a curse you don't say out loud. They've been trying to cut in on our territory like nothing our family has ever faced before. Our family—the Costa family—has its heels dug into the Bronx deep, but everyone's feeling the tension with the Cleaners.

That nickname, "Cleaners," that's stuck with them since day one. They're fast, they're good at what they do, and by the time they're gone, the cops have lost their trail before they've even started on it.

But as much as us Costas don't want to admit it, the Cleaners are a rival family of Italians—the Abruzzi family. The family Lorenzo belongs to.

"We've butted heads with Cleaners all over town," I say, not giving an inch on this, "don't pretend *I'm* the one out to start a turf war here."

"This is different, Luca," Diego nearly growls. "Lorenzo Abruzzi isn't some nobody cleaning up the streets-"

"Like me," I interrupt with a smile, and Diego gives a cruel smile back.

"Yeah, like you, a walking death-wish. No, Lorenzo is Abruzzi blood. You didn't wonder why he thought he could waltz into our territory like that and push that girl around? He's a spoiled little daddy's boy, Luca—Lorenzo Abruzzi is their boss's *son*."

Shit.

"That asshole calling himself 'Don Abruzzi'? He's letting his snot-nosed brat run loose?" I ask with a grimace.

"Yeah, *that* asshole," Diego says, striding back to the stacked bottles of beer, looking like he wants to pull one out, bad.

I let out a chuckle that makes Diego raise an eyebrow at me. "You think this shit's funny?" he says incredulously.

"Kind of," I admit. "I like seeing 'royalty' knocked down a peg."

Diego shakes his head with a smile of disbelief. "Been trying to send your ass on jobs to get you killed for years, and you keep comin' back with this shit. You're something else, you know that?"

He's only half-joking, and I know by the look in his eyes he'd like to try to beat that smile off my face if he weren't in front of the consigliere, whose face hasn't changed this whole time.

"Listen, you son of a bitch," Diego says, stepping toward me slowly, "I don't care if you're the best man I've got on the ground out here, you were out of line. You were out somewhere you weren't supposed to be, doing shit you weren't supposed to be doing, and you beat the shit outta some guy you weren't supposed to touch with a thirty-foot pole."

"So you dragged me out here to tighten my leash?" I say, raising my eyebrows. I hold my arms out, exposing my torso to him and the enforcers in the room. "Well then, take your shots. I can take a beating, I know how this goes."

Diego gives a cruel laugh, glaring daggers at me. I'm embarrassing him in front of his superior, and he knows it. The man could put a bullet in my head if he wanted to, though, so I know better than to push it. My temper is flaring, but in the back of my mind, Serena's safety is still my number one priority. If I get myself killed, she won't be safe. I lower my arms.

"Nah, if this was about that, you'd be feeling it

already, and we wouldn't be getting the floor of this fine establishment dirty," he says. He then moves back to stand beside the consigliere, and both of them look at me like judges.

"The Cleaners are going to take Lorenzo's smashed-up face as an act of war," Diego says, "and if there's one thing I know about the Abruzzis, it's that they take insults like that very personally." Diego pauses to take out a cigarette and light it, and the smell of tobacco fills the space between us. He stares me down. "You got us in some real hot fuckin' water, Luca, you know that? Things are tense with the Cleaners as it is—I've had people calling me to tell me I oughta have your ass killed to smooth things over with them."

"Don't give me that shit," I snarl, and even some of the enforcers in the room looks surprised at my talking to my boss like that. Diego just watches me, burning cigarette in hand.

"I gave my life to this family, you all know that," I say, looking around at the gathered people, even making eye contact with the consigliere. "I haven't forgotten that, and I'll take as many bullets as you have me dish out to those *stronzi*. But you know Serena's safety means more than anything to me, and it has from the very start," I say, looking back to Diego.

"Think about the past few months," I say, knowing it's time to show my bargaining chips if I want to get out of here unscathed. "The fight at the warehouse down by the river? I had that gunfight on lockdown. The Cleaners would have put all our men in the grave that night if I hadn't been there, ask any one of them. Just last week, when that fucking rat Gabe tried to catch a bus out of state to cozy up to the Russians, I'm the one who put a bullet in his head coming out of his hotel room. When you need a job done right, Diego, you've come to me," I say, "I'm the best you've got, and you know it."

I can tell by the look in Diego's eye he's ready to start a fight with me right then and there. Some of the enforcers look to be of the same mind. Diego opens his mouth to speak, but to everyone's surprise...the consigliere raises a hand.

It's a simple move, but it silences Diego.

"You're right, Luca," his calm voice says simply. He sounds older than he looks. "Diego, Luca's a big boy. He does good work for our family, and he's proven more than capable. Which is why he's going to take care of his own mess here."

Diego and I both look at the consigliere blankly.

"Luca, part of your 'agreement' with us means that we don't touch Serena De Laurentis or her business. We respect that. But you've crossed the line here and dragged her into our business, whether she likes it or not."

I feel heat wash over my body. Damn him, I know he's right. I should have been protecting

Serena, not getting involved with her like this. I've endangered us both just by coming near her. That's the one accusation I can't fight off.

"But you're a man who takes responsibility," he goes on, folding his hands in front of him as he watches me carefully. "So I have a solution that should make us both happy. I'm assigning you to her and her business. You'll be her personal guard, and I expect you to handle the situation with all the stubbornness I've seen tonight."

So that's how it is. That's why he's here. He saw a chance to get the family to protect Serena's business, and he took it. He's good. And he's right—because I'd take a bullet to the heart before I let anything happen to Serena.

"Lorenzo Abruzzi takes these kinds of things very personally," the consigliere says. "If it makes you feel better about watching over Miss De Laurentis's place, chances are good he'll see this as between the two of you above all."

"So what, should I expect a hit squad to come shoot up my place sometime soon?" I say.

"I wouldn't rule that out," Diego speaks up, "but Lorenzo has a reputation... with women."

I raise an eyebrow.

"He's not good to his girls, and the Abruzzis don't shy away from the sex trade. Kid's got an ego so fragile even someone like Serena can shake it. Hell, *especially* someone like her. He won't like the fact that you showed his ass up in front of her. That shop of hers is going to be on his mind, Luca—and so is she. The Cleaners know who she is. That and this new history the three of you have makes her a high-value target."

They're goading me into anger, but as much as the heat is boiling up inside me, I won't show it. "What are you saying?"

"I'm saying," the consigliere says, standing up and locking eyes with me, "that going after you isn't enough for a man like Lorenzo. We got a tip. Lorenzo has his eyes set on Serena. If he gets his hands on her, he's going to make her disappear into the sex trade. Or worse."

*L*ast night was a whirlwind.

I was still reeling from the rush of it all when I finally made it back home last night around two in the morning. Thankfully, Mom was already in her bedroom with the lights off by then, instead of waiting up for me to come home like she often did. I wonder what time she gave up waiting for me, and the thought is almost enough to deflate my high spirits. In the back of my mind there's a small voice telling me I should feel guilty for leaving her here all alone for so long when I know good and well that she's prone to worrying about me. But then again, I do spend all my time working and doing everything in my power to look after Mom and the house. Don't I deserve a break every now and then?

Besides, there's no way in hell I could have resisted a reunion with Luca, even if I wanted to.

He's the one who got away, the knight in shining armor who has finally returned from a long, arduous eternity at war. From the very second it clicked in my brain who he was, it's been totally clear to me that I have been waiting for him all this time, without even realizing it. Even though I thought I was over it, over all the awful stuff that went down several years ago between and around us, there's always been a little part of me who kept looking for him everywhere I went.

And now he's back. He's back! It's almost impossible to fathom, that we could find our way back to each other again after all this time. He's changed, that's for damn sure. No longer the scrappy, rebellious teenager who first captured my heart. No, he's a man now.

Standing in the shower after waking up late — I somehow managed to sleep through my alarm again — I think about how much he's changed. That face of his, always handsome, has gained a more serious, world-weary expression. Like he's seen and done things that the teenage version of him could never imagine. It hurts my heart to think of him in pain.

And then there are the more physical changes: his height, his rippling muscles, the scruffy beard obscuring his strong jawline and making him look like some rugged mountain man in the very best way imaginable. I shiver involuntarily, feeling myself getting wet between my thighs just at the thought of him. If I thought I was subconsciously longing for him before, there was no hiding the fact that I *very* consciously wanted him now. Especially after last night, when I found myself wrapped up in the most explosively fantastic sex of my life.

Until the evening was cut short by that phone call.

I still have no idea what that was really about, but right now is not the right time to think about it, since staying up late last night made me oversleep, and now I'm late for opening the shop! I've never allowed a man or my emotions to override my intense desire to maintain my responsibilities. I'm a hard worker, and I know that the future of my little, broken family is in my hands.

So I hurry through my shower and the rest of my morning routine, get dressed and dash out the door. It's not until I'm already driving to work that I realize I forgot to even say good morning to my mother. That familiar, heavy feeling of guilt settles down over me and when I pull into a gas station to fill up my tank, I take out my phone and send her a text message.

Good morning! Sorry I had to rush. Slept thru my alarm.

Barely ten seconds pass before I get a reply: **You were very late coming home last night.**

My heart sinks. So she was awake for that. I type out, **I'm sorry, did I wake you up? Time got away**

from me. As I put the gas cap back on and slide into the driver's seat to start my car, the phone buzzes again.

No, I was already awake. Just waiting for you to come home. I do worry when you're out so late, Serena. You're young and you should be enjoying life. I know how hard you work, dear. But things aren't the way they were when I was your age. Not anymore. It's dangerous out there.

I sigh, wondering how to respond. I decide that because I'm already late for work, I don't have time to write out a long reply. I simply answer, **I know, Mom. I'll be more careful. I love you.** Then I start the car and make my way downtown to work. Even my mother's worrying can't totally puncture my giddiness as I dreamily relive the events of last night, playing it over and over in my head.

However, when I walk up to the shop front, my good mood instantly melts away and my heart begins to race. Right there, on each of the two wide windows that I keep so spotlessly clean, is bright red graffiti. Both windows have a massive skull with three legs coming out of it. The symbol looks vaguely familiar, and then it hits me. In one of my introductory college history classes, I remember seeing a symbol similar to this one in a list of various national flags from around the world.

If I recall correctly, this particular one belongs to Sicily, only with a normal human face in the center instead of a gruesome skull. It dawns on me that this must be used as some kind of gang or mafia insignia around here. Probably the same guys who threatened me for protection money. I swallow hard, almost afraid to even go inside my own shop, the beloved store I call home for the majority of my waking hours. The one asset left of my father's former dynasty.

Tears burn in my eyes as passersby cross the street to avoid having to walk close to my shop. I can feel them all whispering, averting their eyes, making mental notes to never set foot in Bathing Beauty, because it's now tainted with mob activity. I can just hear them gossiping at the office water cooler with their stuffy, white-collar coworkers, talking about how my shop has been marked. Discussing the inevitable failure of my business. Hedging bets on how long it'll be before Bathing Beauty shuts down forever. The thought makes me feel dizzy and weak in the knees.

"What am I doing just standing here?" I murmur to myself angrily. I shake myself out of my stunned, tragic state and go inside to grab some rags and window cleaner, then set to work trying to scrub away the graffiti. I'll be damned if all my hard work gets undone by some arrogant hooligans. I may be just one young woman, but I'm also my Dad's daughter, and he would be disappointed to see me fall apart so easily. I'm better than that.

However, the window cleaner doesn't seem to be affecting the graffiti at all, and after about an hour of fruitless scrubbing, my arms are aching and I decide to just leave it for now. After all, there's inventory to do and shelves to clean and stock. So I go inside and get to work, turning on some upbeat radio station and trying my best to pretend everything is okay.

A couple hours pass before there's the jingle of the front door and I glance over eagerly, hoping that maybe some brave customer has decided to look past the graffiti and come in anyway. But it's actually even better than that: Luca is walking in!

Despite everything, my mouth immediately upturns into a smile as I take in his freshly-shaven face, the sexy button-up shirt he's wearing rolled to his elbows, and the giant bouquet of exotic-looking red flowers in his hands. He grins at me and it's almost like the beauty of his smile knocks me back a step. God, he's handsome.

"Good morning, *mia passerotta*," he says, his voice a delicious deep thrum.

"Luca, I wasn't expecting to see you," I say, feeling as bashful as a preteen girl with a schoolyard crush. I nervously tuck my hair behind my ears as he steps up to the counter and offers me the bouquet. "What are these? They're beautiful!" I ask.

"Nearly as beautiful as you," Luca adds. "In fact, you're the most beautiful thing I have ever seen since I last saw these flowers growing wild back home in

Italy. It just so happened this morning that I noticed the neighborhood florist had some in the window and I had to get them for you. It's fate."

His words immediately warm my soul and help me relax a little. Luca has always had a calming presence about him, and it's intoxicating to be around. But then his expression darkens a little.

"I can't help but notice the new artwork on your front windows there," he points out, those green eyes locked with mine. There's a deep sympathy there. I look away.

"Yeah, it was there when I got here this morning," I answer, fiddling with the bouquet. "I tried washing it off but I couldn't get it to even smudge."

"It's the special kind of paint they use. I'll have to get you some heavy-duty industrial-grade cleaner to get rid of it," Luca tells me. "In fact, I'll go get it now. I know just where to find it. I'll be back in twenty minutes."

He nods and turns to leave, clearing the space to the door with several long strides.

"Luca, you don't have to—"

He glances back and gives me a consoling smile. "I want to."

Then he walks out and gets into his car to drive off, leaving me standing here slack-jawed and stunned, still holding the beautiful flowers. I quickly find a vase in the back room, fill it with water, and by the time I'm finished trimming and arranging the flowers into the vase, the door jingles again and in walks Luca with a giant white bottle of cleaner in his hand. It can't have even been fifteen minutes, much less twenty!

At my shocked expression, Luca laughs and says, "I know a guy. Now, just give me a few minutes and I'll have this shit come right off."

I stand inside, watching through the window as Luca easily scrubs away the red graffiti until the glass sparkles and shines again. It's like magic. Luca is like magic. When he comes back in, he goes to wash his hands and I follow, thanking him profusely.

"It's no big deal," he assures me. "I can't have you trying to run a shop with that ugly shit on the windows. Problem solved. The nightmare's behind you now, sweetheart. However," he adds with a grin brightening his face, "you're all shaken up. Too shaken up to try and keep the shop running today. You need a break."

I blink a few times, confused. "No, no. I-I'm fine, really. I have a lot of work to do."

Luca glances around. "Looks spic-and-span in here, Serena. Not much to do."

I shifted uncomfortably, biting my lip. "Well, it's just…I can't leave. What if I have a customer? I need to meet my daily sales quota or the profit margin gets totally skewed, and I'm already barely breaking even, as it is, and—"

"Hey," Luca interrupts, his hands landing gently

on my shoulders as he peers into my face. I feel my body heating up just from this light touch. "If it's a quota you're after, just let me know how much it is and I'll make it happen."

I raise an eyebrow skeptically. "What, do you 'know a guy' who needs a few hundred dollars' worth of bath bombs and soaps?"

Luca chuckles. "Yeah. Me."

I stare at him blankly. "You. You want three-hundred-dollars of bath goods."

He shrugs and walks over to pick up a wicker shopping basket. "Sure. Load me up."

"Luca, that's ridiculous, you can't just—"

"Why not? You're really going to turn away a paying customer?" he asks earnestly, with a mischievous glint in his gorgeous eyes. Against my better judgement, I have to laugh.

"Okay. Fine. If you're totally sure."

"Oh, I definitely am. Now, do you have any manly-scented stuff or am I just gonna go full floral with this deal?" he asks, picking up and peering quizzically at a lavender-scented bubble bath gel.

I giggle and direct him toward the corner of the shop dedicated to slightly more masculine scents like sandalwood, cedar, and evergreen. I realize I'm not quite sure how to proceed. Usually I have to make some kind of eloquent sales pitch, going through the motions of giving free samples, gingerly soaping and rinsing a customer's hands while describing the various benefits and quirks of our homemade products.

"So, do you want to just kind of take some of everything or…?" I question.

"No, no. I want the full spiel. I want some testers and samples. Let's do this," Luca says brightly. I can't help but grin. He seems like such a serious guy, it's amazing to see how relaxed and whimsical he can actually be.

So we spend the next forty-five minutes testing out a ton of different scents and products in the sink while I explain how, every month, I spend a whole weekend in the back kitchen creating all these soaps, bath bombs, and everything else. It's a long, back-breaking process, but it's also really fun and relaxing in some ways. I get to zone out and listen to my favorite music while I play mad scientist, mixing essential oils and playing with new combinations. My mom taught me everything, which she learned from a summer of soap-making classes over a decade ago, back when life was easy and she was just a bored housewife looking for a new hobby. Long before this became the one business endeavor keeping us afloat. Barely.

And it's fun today, too, washing Luca's strong, scarred hands in the sink, the two of us leaning close together, so close I can feel the masculine heat coming from his powerful body. We flirt shamelessly throughout the whole process, and by the time we're done, we've moved from the men's section and outward, so that his basket is also filled with rose- and lavender-scented products, too.

"So, you're really gonna use this stuff? You're gonna squeeze your massive body into a little bathtub and take a sugar-cookie-scented bubble bath?" I ask him, giggling.

He gives me a wink. "Maybe I will. Or maybe I'll just save all that stuff so that you can use it when you stay over at my place. Gotta make my bathroom more lady-friendly, of course."

I can feel myself blushing, and I look away. But Luca takes me gently by the chin and turns me back to face him before leaning down and kissing me softly. A tingling warmth shoots all the way down my body and I melt into the kiss. Luca sets all three of his heaping-full shopping baskets down on the counter and pulls me in close, deepening the kiss. I lose myself in the moment, our tongues gently pushing against each other while his hands stroke the hair back from my face.

When we break apart, he says, "Well, I guess I'm ready to check out."

As I ring him up, the total reaches well over the daily sales quota and my stomach flip-flops.

"Luca, are you sure? This is...really expensive. You don't have to buy all this stuff."

He shakes his head. "Nope. You can't talk me out of it. Your sales pitch was just too convincing, and yes, I *do* need three baskets of bath products. It's final."

After he pays— in cash— I help him load all his purchases into the trunk of his car, and then he turns to me and says, "Well, now that that's over, I think it's time you take the rest of the day off. After all, you have officially met your daily quota. What else could there be for you to do?"

At first I open my mouth to protest, to tell him that it would be irresponsible for me to abandon my duties even now. What would my mother think? What would my *father* think? But instead, I realize that I have no way of resisting Luca's offer, and even if I did...well, I really do want to go with him and see whatever he has in store for me.

So I give in easily and decide to lock up the shop for the day. It's thrilling, like the feeling of ditching class for the first time as a teenager, that delicious, forbidden sense of freedom and danger. I have no idea what to expect from a day out with Luca. It's been so long since we last spent time together this way, and even though I know him, he's definitely changed since then. But I am so willing and excited to find out.

"So, where are we headed on this day of rebellious truancy?" I pipe up as I slide into the passenger seat of his sleek car. Luca revs the engine into gear and glances over at me with a smile.

"Have you ever been to the aquarium?" he asks.

"The aquarium?" I repeat incredulously. "Really? No, I-I haven't been there, actually."

"Well, today's the day then," Luca declares, reaching over to gently squeeze my thigh through the thin fabric of my dress. That telltale heatwave vibrates through me again.

But after a few minutes of driving, I realize we're not going in the direction of the New York Aquarium. In fact, I have no idea where we're actually headed.

I don't let myself glance at the rear-view mirror more than once every few minutes. I've learned to act natural in situations like this, to almost convince *myself* that nothing is out of the ordinary as I carefully weave through traffic. It's important to stay relaxed, not to show the slightest hint that you know anything is out of the ordinary.

Because we're being tailed.

I noticed it several blocks back, and it took a lot of strength not to swear. The black sedan that's been keeping up with us isn't one that I recognize. It's the Cleaners, I have no doubt in my mind about that.

And I want to unload every chamber in my gun at them.

Normally, I wouldn't feel so furious about getting tailed. Over the years, I've come to recognize it as part of business. An inconvenient part that meant things were soon to get very fast and very exciting, but still just another part.

But the thought that they would have the audacity to tail me right now fills me with fury that I have to force myself to hold back from my face. The reason is sitting right next to me. With Serena in the car, I feel a protective instinct rear its head inside me. It's not a new feeling. I knew it well when we were teenagers. I forgot how powerful it made me feel.

These men dare put Serena at risk, and if it comes to it, I won't hesitate to kill for that. But for now, I carefully plan out a path in my head that will take us through traffic where I know I can lose them. All it will take is a little patience.

I'm so caught up thinking of Serena's safety that I almost forget we're heading out on a date. That just makes me all the more furious at the bastards behind us for intruding on a moment with Serena.

"So," Serena's voice snaps me out of my concentration a moment, "I've gotta admit, you don't strike me as an aquarium kinda guy."

I raise my eyebrow at her. "No?"

"No, something about the rippling muscle and guns don't scream 'I love dolphins'."

"Dolphins are alright," I say simply. My face is still, but I can see her cracking a smile out of the corner of my eye as if she can't tell if I'm joking or not.

"But you've been here before, right?" she says, glancing at the road.

"Once." I take a turn, hand on the gear shift, and I'm at the other end of the road taking another turn by the time I see our pursuers come into sight. I'm gaining ground.

"Oh. Did some starfish owe you money or something?" she asks with a smile, and I can't help but feel a grin tug at my lips.

"Seal, actually," I say, and she giggles. It's nice to hear her joking, feeling at ease with me. But every time we share something lighthearted together, I can't help but feel that nagging voice at the back of my mind. It reminds me that I the closer I get to her, the more I could put her in danger.

I can't let that happen. But I can't abandon her, either. We've opened the Pandora's Box, and I'm not prepared to lose her again.

To let her go again, I correct myself.

"Really, though, who convinced you to go check out the fish?"

"My uncle," I say, my smile fading into a more wistful one as I think back to him. Along with Serena, my uncle is one of the few people I can think of in this country and feel happy.

"Carlo?"

"You remember him?" I say with a smile, glancing over at her before glancing back to the rear-view. Damn it, they're back on us again.

"You talked about him a lot," she says, "seems like a really nice guy."

I give a half-smile, thinking back to my teenage years. "Yeah, yeah he is."

"So what, you take your old uncle to the aquarium for his birthday or something?"

"Opposite," I say, leaning back in the seat. "When I first got here—to America, I mean—my uncle wanted to show me the sights, and for some reason he thought the aquarium was a good place to start. I think I was...thirteen? Fourteen?"

"Ohhh my god," she says, grinning broadly, and I know she's picturing my punk-ass getting dragged around New York by the old man.

"I was a little shit," I say with a laugh, thinking back to myself fresh off the 'boat.' "I think he didn't realize what age I was at, and he kept trying to get me interested in all the sharks and jellyfish and all the dangerous ones. All I did was grouch around the place. Every time he tried to show me something, I'd fuck off somewhere else or swear at him with some of the English words I learned."

"Wow, you were bad," she giggles, and I shake my head, chuckling.

"He got back at me, though. When he started teaching me his carpentry, he drilled me, constantly."

"Wait-"

"No, not literally," I say, "it was just intense. He wouldn't accept anything less than perfection. He's a poor man, but I've never seen carpentry better than what he'd make, and he expected me to be able to do the same. I was getting there, too."

That wasn't the only thing Uncle Carlo taught me, either. There were other skills I got from him, skills that made me so good at what I do now. Uncle Carlo has a lot of secrets Serena doesn't need to hear about. Not now, at least.

"Wow," she says, and I notice she's looking down at my hand on the stick-shift. "I always wondered what made your hands like that."

"Like what?"

A little color comes to her cheeks. "Hm? Oh. I dunno. Rough. It's...kinda nice."

I smile, feeling quiet pride swelling in my chest, and she twirls a lock of hair around her finger for a few moments of silence between us before speaking up again.

"Are you *sure* you've been to the aquarium before?" I hear her ask. Despite the situation, I smile. I was wondering when she'd notice. She's sharp. She always has been.

"I am."

"...are you sure this is the right way?"

"Yes."

She just stares at me blankly for a few moments, and I realize that I can't hide anything from her. It's better that she know, anyway—easier to keep her safe when she knows what I'm watching out for.

"Look up at the mirror and tell me if you see a black sedan three cars behind us. Be subtle."

Her body tenses up immediately, but she manages to look up at the mirror without jerking around. "Yeah."

"It's been following us since about five blocks from where we left."

"Shit, really?" she hisses, and before she can say anything else, I reach over and take one of her small, slender hands in my rough fingers. I give it a squeeze, glancing over at her to smile.

"Let me worry about him," I say calmly. "I might not have been born here, but I know the Bronx better than these *stronzi* from over the river."

She nods, and I shift gears and pull out of traffic through a side-road when I have the chance. It's a quick move, and I soon have us out onto another road that lets me weave through traffic a little more freely.

"I know a way Dad used to take us when things were...kinda heated," she says suddenly, and I'm so surprised I look over at her with a raised eyebrow. She looks a little unsure of herself, but she nods to the road up ahead. "About five blocks down, take a right. I think I remember it pretty well."

"Serena..."

"I'm sure about it," she says with a little more confidence, and I crack a smile.

Following Serena's direction, I take us on a winding path through the city, but I'm impressed by how Serena handles herself. I glance over at her now and then, and I can see she's scared, but she keeps herself calm on the surface. Her eyes go to the mirror periodically, but she knows better than to be obvious. She's strong. She's had to be strong for so long. She shouldn't have to be.

It takes us about half an hour out of the way, but around the third time I check the mirror and see nothing there, I hear Serena say cautiously, "I think you lost them."

"Yes," I say, turning onto a road to take us back toward where I still plan on taking her. "You shouldn't have to worry about all that."

"You seem pretty used to it," she says, and I watch her eyes move up and down me swiftly.

"Yes," I say, letting the matter rest there as I speed us toward the aquarium.

Sometime later, we come to a halt in the crowded parking lot.

Even as I get out of the car, my eyes are scanning the lot to see if we've been followed despite my efforts. The thought of work intruding on my time with Serena is infuriating, but not as infuriating as the thought of her getting hurt.

My glance around the lot is subtle, but as I walk around the car to Serena, I feel her meaningful squeeze on my arm, and I look down at her. She's smiling up and me, and I know she's telling me silently not to worry.

I give a smile back, but that won't make my demons go away so easily.

Inside the aquarium, oddly, the sights and sounds of a big and happy crowd puts me a little more at ease, and I can enjoy the feeling of the temperature-controlled rooms with slightly dimmed lighting.

It's a beautiful place. After stopping by the ticket booth, it's Serena who takes the lead, dragging me to the nearest exhibits that catch her eye, growing more excited with each minute that goes by. While soft, happy music plays all around us, we make our way around some of the big and small glass tanks.

"Luca Luca Luca oh my God!" she squeals, her arm half-submerged in one of the open touch pools. I step up beside her to see her gently touching a brightly-colored starfish that's lazing on the bottom.

"What's the matter?" I chuckle, raising an eyebrow at her.

"It feels weeeeird," she half-whispers, as if not wanting to offend the aquarium worker hovering around.

"You never felt a starfish before?" I say, a grin spreading across my face.

"You have?!" she shoots back.

I roll up my sleeve and sink my thick arm into the water, and I notice the worker glancing at me uneasily. I guess I look more likely to break something than Serena's small hand. I give the man a wink and turn my attention back to Serena.

"I grew up on the coast. We used to go swimming and find sea urchins and other things. You can let them crawl on your hand, if you're careful."

"Wow," she says, "I only ever went swimming in a public pool. You uh, really don't want to pick up anything you find at the bottom of those."

I chuckle, and we soon move on, drying our hands with cheap little paper towels.

As we walk, Serena slips her arm through mine, sighing gently as we stroll past the exhibits, and her eyes are wide as we walk through the glass tunnel that lets sea life float lazily all around us. I stand a head taller than most of the people around us, and I have a look about me that makes most people give us all the space we need.

I find myself watching her more than any of the fish, though. I didn't think an aquarium was all that special, but she seems really swept up in the atmosphere of the place. As her eyes travel around the half-cylinder of the tunnel, they fall on me, and she blushes as she realizes I'm looking at her. "Stop! Look at the fish," she playfully whines, and I give her hand a squeeze as we move on.

When I'm not looking at Serena, though, I'm glancing over my shoulder, at every corner, half-expecting to see someone following us. It would be beyond stupid for anyone to follow us in here, but I can't help but look.

Our walk soon takes us into a wide, very dark room, the only illumination coming from the soft blue glow of the tanks around us. The ceiling is low, and the only sound is the gentle droning of the machinery that keeps the place running. Only a handful of people wander around here—I suspect there's a show going on somewhere drawing most of the day-crowd.

As we walk, Serena's eyes are drawn to the beautiful displays of sea life floating around in view, but I catch her glancing at me from time to time. She's a perceptive girl. I know she can sense my tension, as much as I try to hide it. We walk across the soft carpet to one of the windows, peering out into the blue, fuzzy space beyond, and I feel her squeeze my arm.

"Hey," she says.

"Hey."

"Is something up? You seem kind of…"

I give her a tight smile. "I don't like being tailed, Serena."

"Not just that," she says, shaking her head, and I can see those round eyes looking straight through me. She can read me like an open book, as closed as I try to keep myself. "You've been tense all day. Did something happen at that meeting you had to run off to?"

"Serena, I don't want to worry you with business."

"Don't say that," she says softly, those beautiful eyes watching a shark glide around the bottom of its tank, "that's what Dad used to say all the time."

I'm silent for a few moments, but then she turns her head to look at me, a smile on her lips. "If you can trust me to lose someone tailing us, you can trust me with anything else that's going on, I think."

If you only knew the half of it.

I give her a sad smile, looking down at her, watching the wavy light reflecting off the water dance across her face, her hair, those eyes. "It isn't that I don't want to talk business because I don't trust you, Serena," I say, enveloping her hand in mine. I turn and take her small chin in my free hand, stroking her jaw with my thumb as she smiles up at me. "You thrive even though everything is stacked against you. You own a business. You're a survivor. And you're better than all this—that's why I don't want you getting wrapped up in anything dangerous."

She sets her hand on my hip, feeling the strong muscles under my tight-fitting shirt. "I've got you here, though," she says, her eyes playful, lidded, a smile creeping over those lips. "As long as you're with me, Luca, it's kinda hard to feel like anything could hurt me. I saw what you did in the shop. I feel...well, *safe* when you're around."

I feel warmth spreading through my chest, and I can't help but smile in pride. I wrap my arms around her waist, holding her protectively as the scent of her hair fills my nostrils. "You know how naive that sounds, *passerotta mia*," I say, only half-seriously, and she looks up at me with a challenging smile.

"Don't give me that," she says, her Italian blood showing, "you and I both know how well we work together."

I feel a chuckle escaping me, and I bring my face close to hers as I rumble, "All too well, Serena."

Our lips meet.

All the world seems to melt away as I hold her there. We're not standing in a public place, we're off in our own world, far away from all our troubles, all our danger. A place we've visited before when things got too heated. A place we went when we both *were* young and naive. Things haven't changed so much after all.

Just the world around us has.

But I eventually feel her soft lips leaving mine, and she looks up at me, her smiling eyes proud of the thickening shaft growing between my legs. But I can't let everything go unspoken between us. Looking at her evenly, our eyes locked, I level with her.

"You're in danger, Serena," I say softly yet firmly. "I won't lie to you." I watch the ghost of fear wash over her face briefly, but she swallows.

"You mean...those guys you fought with."

"The Cleaners."

She gives me a puzzled look, and I turn back to the aquarium tank with her in my arm, hugged to my side. "There have always been a lot of gangs fighting for dominance down in Spanish Harlem. There's always been a small Italian presence, but they've kept to themselves for a long time. Now, Spanish Harlem is changing, and they got pushed out with nowhere else to go. A group of them calling themselves the Abruzzi family showed up in the south side of the Bronx a while back. They earned a reputation, and the nickname stuck. They've been pushing into our territory.

"That's who was at my shop?" she says, her eyes widening. I squeeze her side. "Is that why they were there? Why would anyone bother with my shop if-"

"The Cleaners don't play by any rules, Serena," I say. My voice is low, both to keep our conversation quiet and keep her calm. "The man harassing you, Lorenzo—he's the so-called Don's son. He's a spoiled man in a family of upstarts," I say, not hiding the edge of disgust in my voice. I don't like mafia politics on a good day, and the Cleaners are the worst of the worst. I've been...tactful in how I describe the situation, though. The last thing I want is to scare her too much.

"Oh God," she breathes, leaning into me. "The

mark on the window today...this isn't going to go away, is it?"

"I've been assigned to protect you, Serena," I say, looking down at her, and I can practically feel her heart flutter as she looks up at me. "I don't want the rest of my associates getting involved unless I'm the one calling the shots. I'm going to keep you safe *and* out of all that business."

I know old memories are getting dredged up, and I see the shining hint of tears welling up in her eyes. I squeeze her, and she opens her mouth silently before saying, "Do you think that's going to be a problem? That the m- that your associates are going to start caring about my shop?"

"No," I say firmly, squeezing her hand. "I've made sure of that. And if that changes, Serena," I say, leaning in to whisper into her ear, "then the mafia can go fuck themselves. You and I are the only ones I care about, *carina*. I'll be right here, at your side, watching over you. As long as this heart of mine is beating, I swear, nothing will touch you unless you want it to."

Her lip is quivering, and I meet her embrace as she hugs me, sinking into my arms, and I feel a tear stain the shoulder of my shirt.

Growing up with families like ours, you don't escape the shadow of the mafia. But maybe together, we can keep just one light aflame to see us through the dark.

Sometime later, I walk her through the rest of the aquarium to ease her mind off of such heavy things. She's spacey at first, but soon, the play of the dolphins and the gentle, hypnotic floating of the jellyfish we pass help her smile, and by the time we get a bite to eat, she's chatting about some biology class she took in college as if she didn't have a care in the world.

It's the little things that give me some hope for the future. But even so, as the day winds down and we make our way out to the parking lot and look up at the dark sky, I know we can't escape our troubles that easily. I hold her tight to me as we make our way down the parking lot that's not lit up by nothing but street lights.

While Serena has a spring to her step, I'm already expecting what makes her freeze in her tracks when my car comes into view.

"Luca-"

"I know," I say, my eyes darting around the lot as my gun hand twitches.

Parked next to my car is the black sedan that was tailing us earlier today.

LUCA

"Be casual, follow my lead," I say as I guide her to the side, walking away from my parked car.

"Where are we going?"

"Just stay close to me," I say as softly as if I were teaching her how to drive a car. "Do what I say, and be ready to run if I tell you to."

"You know I won't," she says, tenacious even in a tense situation, and I can't help but smile. *That's my girl.*

"Then just be ready," I say, my hand on the small of her back as I guide her.

There's going to be trouble tonight. That much is unavoidable. I know we have eyes on us now, and it won't be long before they close in. But if we're going to have a fight, I will pick the battleground. We'll do things on my terms.

The boardwalk is next to the aquarium. It's still only as well-lit as the street lights will let it be, but there are less surprises in an open space than in a parking lot. I guide us onto the wooden planks, empty for a long way on either side by this time of the evening. Most people are either heading home or know better than to hang around the waterfront at night.

It's *mostly* empty, anyway. My eyes have been scanning the area as I guide Serena out, and by the time we step onto the boardwalk, I've spotted the men following us out there. There are three of them. I size them up. They're big, one of them almost as big as me.

"Luca?" Serena whispers.

"Remember what I said," I assure her as I guide her to the nearest light, watching the shadowy figures present themselves about ten paces away from us. The looks on their faces tell me they're about as ready to drop the pretense as I am. Riegelmann Boardwalk is basically a straight line—two of them are up ahead of us, and the big guy is behind us.

"You boys lost?" I say to them, looking between both of them. "This area can be a little dangerous at night."

"Shut the fuck up, Lomaglio," the big one addresses me by my last name, his deep voice rumbling from a mouth with a missing front tooth. "You know what this is about."

"Oh, Lorenzo wants his teeth back? Sorry, didn't bring 'em with me," I say, rolling my shoulders back as they take steps forward. "Tell him to meet me himself if he wants 'em. I'd say you could bring back some of your own and tell him they're his, but it looks like you tried that already."

As he makes a snarling face, I notice his hand twitch as if for a gun, but he stops himself. The NYPD station is just a block away. I have no doubt the cops have been paid off to turn a blind eye to the area for the next hour or so. That kind of thing happens all the time, even by my own associates. But even so, I'm guessing they didn't give a bribe big enough to ignore gunshots in the police's back yard.

Instead, I see the big guy's fist glimmer in the lamplight with a pair of brass knuckles.

"Fuck him up, boys, and take the girl," he orders, and he moves forward while the two in front charge.

I turn in time to see the two of them, the flash of a knife in the hand of each. Serena hunches down on instinct, and I step forward to put myself between her and them.

One lunges, but I turn with his strike and simply grab his wrist to pull him along, using his own momentum to throw him off-balance while I deal with the other guy.

The second knife swings from below, but I can see it coming from a mile away, and I simply catch him by the fist and squeeze. The muscles of my thick forearms ripple as he throws a wild punch with his other hand, but by the time it strikes my jaw, he's already screaming in agony as his wrist crunches with a sickening noise in my grip.

I hear Serena gasp from behind me. It makes me all the more furious that these fuckers are spoiling our date.

I answer his weak punch by seizing his other wrist, leaving him totally open, and my knee shoots up to the dead-center of his diaphragm, knocking the wind out of him. His knife falls to the ground as he doubles over and crumples to the ground. I kick the knife far away.

It might be useful, but it's not worth bending over to pick up.

Especially not as I hear a grunt from behind me, and the squirrelly man I threw off-balance a moment ago throws his arms around my neck. I catch his fist just in time to see the point of the blade aimed at my throat.

My jaw clenches as I hold the man's weapon away from me, both of us twisting as we struggle against each other. He's stronger than he looks, but not strong enough to overcome me.

"Turn him around!" the big guy commands, and I

hear Serena's yelp with the sound of flesh striking flesh.

My anger burns in me like a flame, and I see red.

Adrenaline surges through every corner of my body. I twist the man's knife away and crouch down to hurl him over my shoulder, hearing him *thump* solidly on the ground before my fist comes down on his face. There's the sound of cracking bone, and I know I've broken more than his nose when the force turns his head and puts him out cold.

An angry roar behind me makes me jump up to face the big guy, but what I see surprises me. He has Serena by the wrist, trying to hold her up and keep her off-guard—him grabbing her must have been the sound I heard. But in Serena's right hand is a little black cylinder.

She turns her head and shuts her eyes as the little can of pepper spray unleashes on him, and the man shouts out in pain and drops Serena, who scurries back while he wipes his eyes.

"Fucking brat! I'll kill you both!" he shouts, opening bloodshot eyes that fall squarely on me. His heavy footsteps carry him toward me, giving me enough time to square up and anticipate the jab he comes in with.

By his build and the way he carries himself, even with eyes full of pepper spray, I can tell this guy must be a boxer. A lot of them trickle down into the mob's ranks, and I know what to expect when this gorilla of a man comes swinging.

A jab and a cross first, brass knuckles humming through the air as if they were blades. A basic combo. With simple, quick movements, I dodge the blows, just like when I play-fought with the guys behind Uncle Carlo's shop. But instead of the hook I'm expecting, he surprises me with a left uppercut. I move fast, and it glances off the side of my face, leaving my ears ringing for a moment.

I see him getting ready for another onslaught—it's going to be hard to get this guy close enough to grapple. He lunges in for another jab, but I'm faster this time and catch him on the nose. He blinks in confusion, and then I see his face contort in pain after the sound of a thud from behind him. He reaches over his shoulder with his teeth gritted…

And I see Serena backing away from him in shock at what she's done, moments before the big guy turns enough for me to see the switchblade she just sunk into his back.

I take the opening. In half a second, I side-step him to get behind him, and in the instant that he rips Serena's blade out, I wrap my arms around him in a sleeper hold. He snarls—it's astounding he's even still standing—and he starts stabbing blindly behind him with the switchblade, trying to sink it into my leg. I hold my grip, an expert at controlling my foes this close up, and I feel the man's bulk start to get heavier as his strength leaves him.

Finally, the sound of the switchblade hitting the ground tells me it's over. I let the man collapse to the pavement awkwardly, and I step back, surveying our work. But I only do so long enough to make sure nobody's moving.

As soon as I have, I turn and embrace Serena, who's shaking in my arms as I hug her close to me, tears staining my shirt.

"O-o-oh my God, did I kill him?!" she stammers in a panic, and I can't help but smile as I rock her gently, stroking her hair to calm her down.

"No, no, Serena, everything's okay. You're okay. I've got you."

"Luca, I-I've never used that knife before, I just had it and thought-"

"You were wonderful," I say, holding her shoulders and pulling her back enough to look her in those shining eyes, beaming at her.

And with adrenaline still pumping through my body, she's never looked more attractive to me. Her slender frame feels so *right* in these hands of mine, fresh from protecting her without a weapon on hand. And as her panicked form stops shaking while she looks up at me, I see a glint of the same in her eyes.

As if we had the same thought, we dive at each

other in a deep kiss, and my hand goes to her ass when I feel my manhood growing between my legs.

But after a second that felt like an eternity, I break the kiss and whisper, "Come on, we need to get out of here."

~

"I'm staying the night," I say firmly once we're through the front door of her place and I lock it. I used one of the men's knives to slash their car tires before I drove us off. After that beating, those men would be lucky if they were awake by morning, much less able to track us down with their battered bodies.

Still, I'm not going anywhere. For more than one reason.

"Are you sure they didn't follow us?" Serena gasps, almost forgetting to take off her jacket when she steps inside, hand starting to shake again. She's gotten jittery in waves between then and the ride to her home.

"Yes."

"Oh my god, Luca, they were trying to kill you!"

"Yes."

"A-are you sure you're okay?" she says, rushing up to me and looking me over, "I-"

I silence her by putting a hand to her soft lips, looking at her steadily in the eyes. "Yes."

Without another word, I pull her into me and bring my lips to hers. I feel and hear a soft, surprised gasp from her before she starts to melt into me. We both have so much pent-up energy left over from the rush of the fight, and we desperately need somewhere to put it.

"You did well tonight," I say as she tugs my hand, beckoning me to be quiet as she leads me to her bedroom. It's on the far corner of the house, and she relaxes once the door clasps shut.

"I was so scared," she breathes as she tilts her head back, exposing her neck to me now that we're in private. I take the bait and attack her neck, kisses running up and down the sensitive skin, teeth grazing it and making her gasp. "Luca, if you hadn't been there-"

"You made me proud," I say, quieting her with a squeeze of her ass. "You've become a strong woman, *passerotta mia.*" We kick our shoes off in a hurry, and I haven't even gotten her top off before my hand gropes her chest, cupping a breast and savoring the feel of it through the thin fabric. She shivers at my touch. My other hand goes to her ass as I work her back toward the bed.

Finally, I sit her down on it, and I kneel over her, sliding my hand up to her back as we stare into each other's eyes, seeing the passion in each other's gaze. "*I've* gotten strong? What even was that?"

I run my fingers into her hair, letting the silky

feel of it run over my hand like water. "My work isn't something to be proud of, Serena."

"It does have its perks," she says, her eyes roving over the rippling muscle of my body, and I see her bite her lip as she runs her hands down my sides before reaching the hem of my shirt. She tugs at it, looking up at me with a pout to her lip.

It's a look I've seen before, and it still teases the same fire in me.

"You *are* a brat, you know that?" I tease, and a smile tugs her lips into a curl.

"Just for you."

I tear her top off up over her head, tossing it to the side. I glower down at her exposed form, nothing but a bra left on her chest, and with one hand, I unhook it and let it slide off her arms before easing her down onto the soft cushions.

Her breasts free, I descend on them. I let my hot breath wash over her nipple, panting over it like I'm about to devour it, and she arches her back, gasping as I play with the sensitive nub of her nipple relentlessly. My teeth toy with it, grazing against its sides ever so gently. Feeling the nipple harden under my tongue sends fire through me. My hand moves to her other nipple, and I run my thumb over it to excite it as well.

The taste of her is delicious. My tongue lashes back and forth over her nipple, darting out to play between my teeth before I toy with her stiff nipple and cover the area with my mouth.

My other hand gropes her breast, possessing her, letting her know she is *mine*. I push my thumb against the bottom of her nipple and flick it and rub it gently with my index finger. I can make my thick hands handle delicate things, when I want them to.

Her nipples stiffen, and her breathing is quick under me. I can feel her legs squirming, and I know just how much she's getting bothered between her thighs. It brings a smile to me, even as my mouth moves across her breast playfully, teasingly.

I shouldn't be doing this. This is dangerous for both of us. But if we're going to face danger anyway, I want to us to face it together.

I turn my eyes up as I nip her breasts, and I see a mess of blonde hair spilling around her neck and shoulders, mouth hanging open as she whimpers for me. I raise my head away from her breasts, replacing my teeth with my hand on her right breast. I have to look down on Serena.

On my woman.

Her limbs are sprawled out across the bed, long and willowy. She looks like some dancer exhausted from practice, but I'm just getting her started. She turns her eyes to me as she feels the change, and color rushes to her cheeks at the sight of me looming over her, thumbs roving possessively over her nipples.

She bites her lip, and I take my hands away to pull my shirt off over my head and toss it to the floor, displaying my body over her.

Even though she's seen it bare before, even recently, the light I see spark up in her eyes is like she's never seen anything like me before. I feel pride swell up in my chest as I roll my shoulders back, and her gaze meets mine.

To be able to get such a stir from a woman as beautiful as Serena is a thrill. And it should be—she deserves nothing but the very best.

I descend upon her again, this time cupping my hand under her neck and bringing my mouth to it. I kiss her, my other hand holding her by the wrist and splaying out her body as I start to rock my pelvis into her. Even through our pants, I know she can feel my hardness. I've been with women, sure, but nobody has ever made me as ready for love as Serena makes me. Every cell in my body cries out for her when I'm near her.

I run my hands down her body to her hips, and I bring my mouth to her lips. She lifts her head up with a whimper to meet me, and I smile into the kiss as I pull her hips up into me, rocking into her gently while her arms slip around my neck to hold on. Her lips are soft, and I let out a low groan into them before her tongue starts trying to tease mine out. I hold nothing back from her. My tongue dives into her mouth, and we play with each other while I feel a pulse go through my hard body.

I want her. I need her. We don't even need to speak to know how badly we desire each other. My rough hands run up and down her body, feeling every inch of smooth, olive skin. It's the easiest thing in the world to pick her up and turn her however I please, and when I slide her up the couch, she giggles at being held by me, squirming in the cushions, looking up at me with playful eyes.

"You're playing with fire, princess," I say with a low rumble to my voice, but I know Serena and the look in her eyes well enough to know that she likes playing with fire.

In a swift motion, I tear the buttons of her jeans apart, and she gasps when I tug her pants down over her thighs. She tries to kick them the rest of the way off, but I don't want to wait. I yank them the rest of the way off, panties and all, before I slide my hand under the small of her back and lift her legs up.

I run my mouth over her inner thigh, fingers squeezing her soft flesh as I let my breath wash over her, face tickling her as I rove over it.

"God, Luca," she whines, trying in vain, "God, I need you in me, don't keep me waiting!"

I deliver a quick slap to her bare ass, feeling the taut skin quiver under my touch, and she gives a yelp of delight as I squeeze her. "I'm going to take my time devouring you," I growl, "you're too sweet not to savor."

She opens her mouth to respond, but I silence her by lowering my head and dragging my tongue across her slit.

A long, hissing gasp escapes her, and I listen to it hang in the air like a musical note as I look at her lower lips. They're swollen with need like my cock is, and the darker, endlessly sensitive skin folds in on itself, just begging for attention. Her whole body is crying out for me. Just the thought that I have the power to bother her figure so much makes me swell so hard I think my shaft is going to burst from my pants.

I bring my face closer again, breathing heavily on the smooth surface of her pussy. I breathe in, and the heady scent of her makes me want to turn her over and thrust inside of her until neither of us can move anymore.

And I will. But not yet.

I let my tongue forth again, letting it slide through her lips and taste just how ready she is, savoring the flavor of the hot entry the tip of my tongue dances across. I slide my tongue deep into her, as deep as I can, probing and exploring like I own this sanctuary of hers. As the taste of her drives me wild, I reach up and grab her breast with one hand while the other cradles her ass.

Her honey is like wine to me. My tongue dives in,

again and again, and I feel her pushing her hips up at me with each stroke. Her breathing is shallow, and each time I reach some new part of her that I haven't touched yet, I hear a gasp to reward me. She's coaxing me further.

She's my brat, and she knows how to get me to dig into her. She likes getting more than she bargained for.

My tongue delves deep into her, drawing up more honey with each sweep. The inside of her vagina is hot, tense, endlessly needy. The more I enter her, the more she wants. I lose track of where my tongue has gone as it slides across the landscape within her.

All I know is that my face is soaked, and so are her lips. A few moments ago, they were puffy with need, and now, a gorgeous sheen glistens on them.

Her legs wrap around my sides as best they can— her legs are long, but my chest is thick with muscle. I can't help but smile at her efforts. I decide to reward her by driving her home.

I draw my tongue up to her clit, and the tip of my tongue darts onto her swollen nub to the sound of a sharp gasp. Fuck, she's close already.

I start to torment her, swirling just beyond her clit, edging nearer with each stroke as she claws at my back and the couch desperately. I think about all the years her poor clit has gone without my touch. I have a lot of time to make up for.

I drive my tongue in and lavish her nub with attention, pushing and flicking around it freely. It's a matter of seconds before her steady gasping becomes a high-pitched squeal, and she tries to close her legs as her honey flows onto my tongue, but I use my hands to keep her thighs apart. "You're not getting free so easy," I growl, and I attack her again.

My lips close around the area of her cunt as I savor her taste. My tongue dives deep into her, and I bring it up slowly, painfully slowly, to her clit, where I torment her until she's squirming relentlessly in my hands.

I raise my eyes enough to look at her, and there's a smile of absolute bliss on her face as I take her with my mouth. Her first orgasm left her glowing, and I know she's tingling head to toe, but even so, she wants more.

She's panting by the time I decide I've had my fill of her heady wine. Slowly, I push myself to my knees, looming over her like a statue. She bats her eyelashes at me, worrying her lip as her eyes stare up at me in a haze.

"Fuck, look at you" I say, running my hands up and down her thighs gently, wetting my lips at the sight of her. I dive back down to her nipples, my hands grasping her wrists as she gasps, but I feel them tug away.

"Wait," she breathes, and I stop, lifting my head to meet her gaze. As her eyes lock with mine, she loses her words for a moment, but I follow her gaze down to the bulge outlined in my pants. "I...I want to taste you," she says, the thirst in her voice so thick I can hear it in every syllable.

I give her a challenging smile. "You think you can do to me what I did to you?" I say, moving further up to her to hold her chin in my fingers. I lower my come-soaked lips to her mouth, and we kiss, a moan between us as I feel her hips push up into me. "Don't you know you already ruin me?" I growl when our lips part. "Or are you just a greedy little girl?"

"All of the above?" she says with a shy edge to her voice, and I sit back, taking my belt off and setting it on the floor. I see the hunger in her eyes as she pulls her legs back and folds them under her, and I take my time. My thick hands move to the button of my pants, undoing them one by one. The tight muscles of my stomach make a V leading down below the waist of my pants, promising what's below.

She waits, as if waiting for a word from me, but she fidgets impatiently as she watches my hands start to slide my pants down. She starts to move forward when she can see the thick base of the shaft. I want to tease her a little longer, but the sight of her so hungry for me, her lips so needy—I'm not so cruel as to keep her waiting any longer.

I pull my pants down and let my mast free, standing stiff and swollen. She reaches out for it carefully, as if touching something valuable, and when her soft fingers finally stroke up its length, I feel a shiver of pleasure run up me.

She's going to make me eat my words now that I've eaten her out.

She wraps her hand around the girth of my shaft, feeling its weight, and her other hand strokes it up to the bulging crown. It stands even stiffer at her touch. It wants to be inside her as much as she wants it. As much as *I* want it.

I lean back with her gently before she parts her lips and puts them to my crown, and warmth washes over me when I feel her tongue on the tip of my cock. She lets out a gentle moan into it as her thumbs slide down the sides of it, feeling every detail, every vein, and I see her hips squirm. She's imagining it inside her, and that only spurs her on as she opens her mouth a little more to take more of me in.

My neck leans my head back to the arm of the couch as my whole crown gets bathed in her tongue, and one of her hands takes my balls in her hand. She's soft and warm, innocently playing with the weight of my heavy, needy balls, not realizing how much tension she's playing with.

Or maybe she does. My woman likes playing with fire.

As her tongue starts to rove further down the soft underside of my shaft, I look down at her to see her eyes glittering at me. She slides more of my shaft into her mouth, and I can feel her whole tongue moving under me, sending wave after wave of pleasure up me. I let out a deep groan as she runs the tip of her tongue from the bottom to the tip of my cock, then again and again.

"Fuck, Serena," I groan, reaching out and taking a fistful of her hair—I don't hold her back, I just hold her, letting her know I can tug her around and steer her however I like. "You're the same brat I was sneaking around with when we were teenagers," I say, my voice gravelly.

She arches her back instinctively at my words, the warmth of her mouth utterly engulfing my cock. I'm impressed by how much of it she can take in, and her soft moans of pleasure spur me on, growing stiffer, more swollen, more ready for her than ever.

Her fingers play with my balls while her other hand feels the base of my shaft that her lips can't quite reach. My cock is so far in her that I worry she'll choke, but I'm keeping a close watch on her, ready to pull her back if she gets too greedy.

She lavishes my cock with attention like I tortured her pussy with my mouth, her face telling me how much she loves the feel of my cock sitting on her tongue, the taste of me, the feel of my shaft pulsing when she finds a way to stroke it that makes it twitch just right for her.

Dangerously so. She finds a way to move her tongue along the base of my crown to the head of my cock that makes my whole crotch tighten, and she can feel it in my balls. Excited by what she's discovered, she starts to stroke it more, her tongue lashing over it as her playful eyes flutter up at me.

My jaw hangs open, and I feel the tension building up in my whole body. It's so great that my balls ache with need, and I can tell just how badly she wants to release the pearly reward for her efforts.

It's tempting to give her what she wants—knowing that she takes so much pleasure from knowing how to unlock the best secrets of this massive, musclebound body of mine gives me so much pleasure. But as she starts unconsciously moving her hips when my body nears the point of no return, I know there are other parts of her that need attention.

Before that mouth of her makes me spill over the edge, I tighten my grip on her hair just enough to tug her back. She fights me a moment, but my hand is strong, and she reluctantly lets go of my cock.

When her mouth comes off it, it's more swollen than ever, now glistening with her. She sticks a lip out at me as I sit up and take her chin in my hand, brushing my thumb over that pouty lip.

"Do you think I'd let you drive me there when that pussy of yours is still so needy?"

She wets her lips at that, and her hands rove up my hips to feel my sides.

"You know I'm yours," she breathes, a blush in her cheeks as she says the words. "I just get greedy sometimes."

"I know," I say, reaching down to the floor. She follows my hand as it grasps the belt on the floor, and her eyes widen. "That's why I'm going to make sure you behave for me."

I stand up, nodding for her to turn around. She looks at me curiously, wonder in her face, but I reassure her, running my fingers through her hair. "Don't worry," I husk lowly, "I've got you. Tell me if you want me to stop. The safeword is Crimson."

"Crimson," she nods, licking her lips, and she doesn't resist when I gently take her hands and cross her wrists behind her back. I use the belt to tie them together, and she shivers as she realizes what I've done, testing her restraints. "What are you going to do to me?" she asks, her voice heavy with desire.

I take my shirt and rip it, making her gasp, and I do it again until I've got a black strip of cloth in my hands that I bring to her. "Show you that you're mine," I growl before I put the black cloth over her eyes and tie it behind her hair.

My Serena starts to squirm around on the bed, but I chuckle at her softly before I scoop her up in my arms. She yelps, and I carry her over to the wall. The way she feels in my arms never gets old.

"I could hold you forever," I whisper into her ear, and I feel her shiver, a smile playing across her lips.

"Where are you taking me?" she asks.

"No farther," I say.

Before she can speak again, I shift her in my hands so I'm holding her by the ass, and I let her back fall gently against the wall. My girl, my prisoner, sits there in my hands, wrapping her legs around my waist as best she can as she realizes what's about to happen. It looks rough, with her hands tied behind her back and her eyes blindfolded, but I'm careful with her. I wouldn't do this if I didn't know what I was doing.

When I look down at her exposed, vulnerable, tormented pussy, my cock stiffens as much as it had when it was a prisoner of Serena's lips.

"Remember," I say in a husky voice as I lower her just enough to perch her lower lips on the tip of my cock. The moment it touches, my cock swells to attention, and her mouth falls open. Every time I prepare to enter her, it seems she forgets just how big I am for her. "The moment you need me to stop, say Crimson. Until then...you're mine."

With those words, I let her sink onto my shaft, and she lets out a cry of pleasure as we lock into each other like my cock and her pussy were made for each other. Immediately, I start bucking into her, and she's utterly paralyzed by me, mouth wide open as her toes curl and her hips thrust forward.

"Oh, oh God, fuck!" she cries. We're both so slick that we grind into each other effortlessly, moving so fast, so wonderfully that I can already feel her tightening. "Luca, I'm gonna-"

She loses her voice to a silent scream, biting down on her lower lip to muffle it. I feel her whole body pulse around me, heels digging into my hips as I thrust myself up into her to the hilt. Her honey floods me, and I can hear it with each new thrust. I don't let up. I ride her pleasure like a wave that's about to break. Holding her effortlessly in my hands, I pull back and angle her back just so that I can hit the top of her inner depths better.

When the tip of my cock grinds against her g-spot, her silent scream becomes a real one. Just for a beautiful moment, she loses control of herself as I buck into her like a machine. My hips are a piston, moving with such precision and regular force, taming the wildfire that her body has become. Her mouth hangs open and her cheeks are blushing furiously. Every now and then, I see her trying to tilt her head back to look at my body past the blindfold, but another orgasm seizes her.

I can feel every inch of her, from the depths that my cock is thrusting into to the outermost lips kissing my base with every thrust. I feel her quick heartbeat through my cock, and I know she can feel my own powerful pulse.

That isn't the only pulse she's getting, either.

She's like a doll in my hands as I fuck her, but this is Serena. She tightens her pussy around me, thrusting as much as her spasming body will let her. Her golden hair spills over her shoulder as her head leans this way and that. She's totally in my power. And seeing that excite her so much fills me with pride.

I lean back to impale her on my cock, and now I'm doing most of the work, fucking her rough and hard while I move her. My pace never lets up. I'm hard as a rock, and I don't think I could get any harder or more needy. My balls are in such urgent need of emptying into her that they're sore.

The more I explore within her, the hotter my love for her burns. "You're my girl, Serena," I whisper huskily as I pump into her, "just as much now as you were before."

"Fuck, Luca," she whimpers, "fuck, I need you so bad!"

I let her sink onto my cock, letting more of her weight onto it, but my cock still holds her up as strong as ever. When I buck up into her, it's like I'm bouncing her on it alone, and a sharp cry from her lets me know she's come yet again.

I've lost count by now. She's trying to make me come, I can feel it, but I've won this time—I've got the control over her.

She clenches her pussy as tight as she can as she thrusts, struggling against her restraints like a little prisoner, and I wrap a hand around the back of her neck. "I'll fuck you until I'm good and done with you, Serena," I growl, and she lets out a desperate sigh, a pouting gasp as I buck up into her fiercely.

Her back is grinding against the wall, but she hasn't shown a single sign of letting up, no hint of saying that simple word that will make me stop. Crimson. She's a brave girl, that's for sure. My girl.

I feel another orgasm pulse through her body, but she's on the verge of going limp. "Luca," she gasps, "Luca, I-I don't know how much more I can-- oh God!" She whimpers the last words, and I groan into her as she writhes on my cock.

I slide my hand down from her neck to hold her back, and now, I'm holding her as much as she's leaning on the wall. She's utterly wrapped around me, calves tight against my rock-hard sides. She thrusts up against me with her chest out, and I feel my body revolt against me—it wants to *have* her, and it wants her *now*.

I let out a sharp groan as I feel myself crashing into those first few seconds before the orgasm, and I start pounding into her g-spot so that she lets out a cry of absolute bliss.

Just as I feel her honey wash over my red-hot cock, my balls tighten, and a stronger pulse of release than I've felt in a very, very long time shocks my whole frame. My jaw falls open, and my whole body goes paralyzed as a shot of hot come releases itself into her.

The first pulse hasn't even ended before the

second one follows, and it's even stronger than the last. My knees feel weak, and a lesser man might have buckled. The second shot spills into her hot and fast, and Serena sighs in ecstasy, letting her head fall back to the wall as she pushes her hips up, drinking me in with each pulse.

It lasts for what feels like an eternity, my body tightening and relaxing in a flurry of feeling that makes me want to stay buried in her forever. Finally, when the pulsing starts to let up, I stay rock-hard inside her, gently thrusting up and teasing a surprised little gasp from her.

My heart pounds in my chest as I feel such incredible relief. The look in Serena's blushing face tells me she's feeling what I'm feeling even more.

"*Cazzo*," I breathe, my whole body feeling like it could sleep for a hundred years. She's basically pudding in my hands, utterly limp as my thrusting slows to a stop.

"Luca, that was...I don't think I've ever felt like that," she says, genuine wonder in her voice. I give her a loving squeeze on the ass as I slowly step back. She gasps as I start to slide my cock out. It's a strange feeling, the cool air on my cock again as it glistens in the light. Some of my seed spills out of her with the cock, and I feel a strange pride at the sight of her.

I've marked her.

With my cock out, I gently take her in my arms

and walk her to the bed, where I lay her on her side before slipping my pants off the rest of the way and getting into bed after her. She's a melted mess, chest rising and falling. I move my hands to her wrists gently, and I take care in undoing the restraints I made for her.

The moment her hands are free, she brings them to her front again as I slip into the big spoon position behind her. My cock is still stiff, and she draws in a sharp, shivering breath as it slides against her. She lets the breath out with a pleased moan.

I take her tiny wrists in my hands and rub them with my thumbs. I bring one to my lips and breathe on it, kissing the light pink marks. "Are you hurt?"

"No," she says, smiling, "it's a little rough, but I like it. I just hope my mom didn't hear."

I smile and gently take off her blindfold. Her warm brown eyes flutter open, and she looks back at me. The heart I've worked so hard to harden over the years melts at the sight of those eyes. I wrap my arms around her and hug her to me, and she snuggles in with a contented sigh.

"God, I could fall asleep right now," she says, and I can practically feel the relaxation in her voice, the utter satisfaction that drips from every word.

"That's the adrenaline coming down," I say, rubbing her arm. I walk on my knees over to her and gently turn her onto her stomach. I straddle her, and before she can speak, I start running my hands up and down her back slowly, firmly enough for her to really feel it. Instantly, I hear a soft sigh of pleasure from her.

"Oh my God," she whispers, eyes half-shutting as I feel her relaxed muscles melt to my touch. "Are you like, a real person?"

I give her a light slap on the asscheek, and she squeals then giggles, wiggling her ass up into me as I rub her back.

"You did so well today, Serena," I say, "I mean that. Both the fight and... everything else," I say, my voice taking a husky undertone. "And you went through a lot more excitement than you're used to. You need to come down slow from that."

"I've never done anything with like, bondage and stuff," she muses into the blanket. "Is this uh, aftercare?"

"Something like that, if that's how you wish to think about it," I say, finding myself grinning at her innocence as my hands rub the spot on her back where she was against the wall. "Aftercare usually doesn't come after a knife-fight with a bunch of thugs, though."

"Doesn't it?" she laughs, but it soon relaxes into a sleepy sigh. "I think...I think I like it, though," she says. "I wish we could get some more alone-time that doesn't come with life-threatening danger every now and then."

I flip her onto her back and put my fists on either

side of her, looming over her and smiling warmly down at her form, then up to her face. Her golden hair spills all around her like the sun. I bend down and press my lips to hers.

When we part, I move my mouth to her ear and whisper, "If that's what you want, maybe you're with the wrong guy, *dolcezza*." Her face turns serious, contemplating my words so direly.

God, he looks good.

It's just shy of noon, and all morning Luca has been subtly keeping guard right outside Bathing Beauty while I tend to regular business inside. Well, he's about as subtle as someone who looks like him could ever possibly be. At first, I worried that his imposing figure might scare off potential customers. Especially considering his leather jacket and crossed-arm stance. But it turns out, it's not just me who feels a calming aura from him. All morning, he's been smiling and giving courteous nods to passersby, occasionally even striking up conversation. Many of those who stop to talk to him also come into the shop to browse, and by this time of day, I don't normally have this many sales in the bag. Luca has been less like an intimidating bouncer and more like an engaging shop attendant.

Only, you know, unbelievably rugged and sexy.

"Excuse me, do you happen to have anything that smells like lemon or lime? My grandmother's eightieth birthday is coming up, and she loves citrus-y scents," asks a young woman to my right. I manage to tear my eyes away from Luca and give her a helpful nod.

"Of course!" I tell her, taking in her appearance. She looks to be no older than fifteen, with her hair in a flouncy ponytail. She has a sweet, round face, and she reminds me of how I looked and acted at her age. Fifteen. Back when everything was so simple. Before my entire world shattered into tiny, razor-sharp pieces all around me.

I guide the young customer over to a shelf of lemon- and grapefruit-scented products, explaining to her how our soaps and lotions are made. I'm so used to doing the sales spiel that I can almost zone out entirely while my body goes on autopilot. As I'm talking, my mind can't help but drift idly back in time, to when I first met Luca so long ago.

He was so handsome, even back then, even when we were both in our awkward teenage years. He was never gawky or skinny. Never a jerk like so many guys that age are. God knows he had all the reason in the world to be an arrogant ass, with those good looks and smooth-talking style. But he wasn't. Sure, there was a hint of snarkiness in his tone sometimes, and he certainly was confident, but never cocky. He was just...perfect. From day one that he stepped into my life.

Bringing myself back to the present moment, I successfully persuade the young girl to buy a whole line of lemon soap, bubble bath, and a candle. I tell her I hope her grandmother has a fantastic birthday, and she leaves.

I look around the shop with a warm, fuzzy feeling washing over me. There are more customers here than usual, and so far it seems like almost everyone has bought something. I can't help but smile. Things might finally be turning up for me, despite all the mess with the mafia activity lately. If not for Luca, I would probably still be falling to pieces, losing my mind stressing over what to do and whether I should go to the cops. But with Luca around, it's hard to even let those negative thoughts into my head for a second. I just feel so safe with him, and no matter how many years have passed us by, I still feel like I can trust him with my life. In fact, I *know* I can.

After all, he's saved me once, and I have a pretty strong feeling he would do it again in a heartbeat. I don't quite see why he cares about me as much as he does, but I know I must be the luckiest girl in the world. Danger will always follow him, but so will I. Besides, I doubt there's much of anything he can't handle.

I ring up the rest of the customers and, just in

time for lunch, the door jingles and in walks Rafaela. She gives me a little wave and holds up a paper bag which I dearly hope contains some kind of burrito or burger. I've been so busy all morning here that I've definitely worked up an appetite.

Once everyone else has cleared out, Rafaela walks up to the counter, sets down the paper bags, and gives me a quick hug. "Class was canceled today so I figured I would surprise you!" she says, grinning her bright white smile.

"Oh, it's so good to see you. I'm glad class was canceled because I've missed your face," I reply happily, glancing down at the paper bag hungrily. "Please tell me one of those bags is for me. I'm starving, Raf."

"Yup! I went to that food truck around the corner from campus. Chicken burrito, no sour cream, extra pico. That's your order, right?" she asks, pushing the bag toward me.

I nod ravenously. "Oh yes. That's my order exactly. You have a damn good memory, wow."

She shrugs, smiling. "Well, yeah. Years of bartending will do that."

We both dig into our food, and I make sure to save half my burrito and chips for Luca, just in case he's hungry, too. It's the least I can do to thank him for hanging around all day keeping the shop safe and in business. Rafaela and I chat about her classes, how the bar is doing, how my shop is doing, and soon the conversation turns to more serious topics.

"So, like, what is your life plan?" she asks suddenly, shielding her mouth full of food. I lift an eyebrow and give her a quizzical look.

"Uh, what do you mean? And where did that come from?" I laugh.

She swallows and sighs. "It's just that I've been thinking a lot about how busy we both are and wondering if maybe we're, like, missing out on stuff. Life. Our youth."

"Okay, Miss *Eat-Pray-Love*, I guess I just try not to think about stuff like that," I answer, wrapping up the half of my burrito left over. "This is so not the way I thought my life would ever pan out. If you told teenage-me how my life would turn out, I don't think she would believe you. But you know, that's how it goes. I'm a planner, and I like to know what's coming, but if there's anything I've learned over the years, it's that some things just happen whether you plan for them or not."

Rafaela nods, a thoughtful expression on her pretty face. She crunches into a chip dipped in extra-spicy salsa. "You're right. I know you're right. It's just frustrating sometimes. Like, I'm so used to just being stuck in that daily grind of class, work, sleep, rinse, repeat that when I get a rare break like today, it really hits me how nice it would be to just slow down a little bit."

"You know what they say: youth is wasted on the young," I tell her, sighing. "And you and I are hard workers. I know what keeps me going is thinking about what my dad would say to me. He'd be so proud of me for taking on the family business and doing everything I can to take care of the house and Mom. I know he would want me to be happy, though, too."

"Yeah, whenever I get a chance to send some money home to my great-grandmother in Venezuela, I do feel pretty damn good about myself. You should see the letters she writes me, Serena. You'd think I was President of the United States from the way she talks. It's nice to know that she's proud of me. I'll try to focus on that," Rafaela decides, a dreamy look in her eyes. I know she's had a hard life, growing up very poor in Spanish Harlem. Her grandparents immigrated here to give her family a better life, and while Rafaela was born and raised in America, she still has close ties to Venezuela.

I, on the other hand, grew up in the lap of luxury, only to have it all taken away in one fell swoop years ago with my father's death. Rafaela and I couldn't have come from more different backgrounds, but we've always been able to find plenty of common ground. Suddenly, I feel the burning need to confide in my best friend.

"So, lately I've been having some trouble here at

the shop," I begin, launching into an explanation of the mafia activity threatening my barely-afloat business. I describe the 'rough types' who have been hanging around causing trouble, telling her all about the bright red graffiti.

"Holy cow," she says, shaking her head. "That's crazy, *chica*. How are you getting by? Have you gone to the cops? And, uh, is that guy standing outside the shop one of those 'rough types' you mentioned? Because he definitely looks a little intimidating."

I snort. "Oh, Luca? No, he's actually...been helping me, believe it or not. He's an old friend."

"Wait," she says, squinting as she stares at him through the window. "Oh my God, is that the same guy you came to the bar with the other night?"

I start to blush, my cheeks burning. "Yep. That's the guy."

"Nice catch," she says, giving me a cheesy wink. "He's a stud."

"Oh my God, stop," I laugh, rolling my eyes.

And almost as though he knew were talking about him, Luca walks into the shop, shrugging off his jacket and folding it over his arm as he walks by, giving us both a nod. Rafaela wiggles her fingers in a faux-flirtatious wave.

"Luca," I say, "this is Rafaela. We met in college. She's my best friend."

Luca shakes her hand and smiles. "Nice to meet you."

"*Encantada*," she responds, grinning.

"Oh! And she came bearing the very best of gifts: food. I saved half my burrito for you if you want it," I offer, handing the bag to Luca.

"Thanks," he says, taking a massive bite before heading into the back room to give Rafaela and I more privacy to keep chatting. He's still within earshot, but I know he doesn't want to hover.

He's so cute, Rafaela mouths silently at me. I nod emphatically.

"I know, right?" I whisper back.

Rafaela clears her throat. "So, anyway, wanna hear something weird?"

"Of course. You know I do," I laugh.

"Well, I mean, I guess it's not really funny. It's sad, actually. But it is definitely super weird, too. So, you know how my cousin Alejandro is a vet tech? Well, yesterday he told me that his office has been getting, like, an abnormal amount of injured dogs. Like, way more than they usually get. Everyone in his office thinks there might be some kind of dog-fighting ring going down somewhere in the city. Isn't that horrible?" she says, shaking her head as she eats another chip.

"Oh, wow. That *is* awful. Is there anyone looking into it? Cops? ASPCA?" I ask, concerned. I'm a huge animal lover despite the fact that my mom has never allowed pets in our household, and the idea of all these hurt dogs breaks my heart.

Rafaela shrugs. "I have no idea. I don't know if they would even know how to help, honestly. The cops probably don't care, and the ASPCA is so over-worked already. They might not have the resources to do much of anything about it."

"Well, Alejandro's office probably has all the dogs' information on file, right? That's got to be a good start," I suggest.

Before long, the topic moves away from this tragedy and we spend the next hour just catching up and talking about when we should meet up for a girls' night out. We're both so busy that we rarely get the chance to just relax and hang out like we did in college. I hope that when Rafaela graduates we'll have more opportunities.

"Oh shit, I gotta head to the bar," she says suddenly, looking at the digital time on her cell phone screen. "That shady dude Nico hired to help out on weekday afternoons has been really flaky about showing up for shifts lately. Nico's too forgiving to fire him just yet, so take a wild guess who's been picking up the slack?" She gestures toward herself with a sigh.

I giggle and give her a hug. "Tell Nico I said hi. It was really, really good to see you, Raf. I'll come by the bar sometime this week to hang out. Text me."

"I will, I will. Have a good day, *chica. Hasta luego.*"

"*Hasta luego,*" I call as she walks out the door.

Moments later, Luca comes out of the back room

with a stormy expression on his handsome face, and I know he's heard our conversation. Something is bothering him, and I have a feeling I know what it is.

"The dog fights," I murmur, biting my lip. He nods.

"Yes. It's pretty damn low, even for the Cleaners. Must be those East Harlem boys."

"I wonder what to do. I wish I could help somehow. I hate to think of those innocent dogs being abused for sport like that. Just horrible."

"It's inexcusable," Luca agrees, his voice low and gruff. There's a flash of terrifying anger in his gorgeous green eyes. He puts his leather jacket back on and adds, "I'm going out. Can you hold down the fort today? You've made enough sales already, I'm sure, that you could close up shop and head home if you need to."

I shake my head and reach out to take his hand. "I'll be fine. But...will *you* be okay?"

He lifts my hand and kisses the back of it softly, sending a pleasurable shiver down my spine.

"Don't worry about me. I've just got some business to take care of. I'll come back to you when the smoke has cleared," Luca assures me.

"Be careful," I tell him, a pleading note in my voice.

He gives me a devilish smirk. "I can't promise that, but I promise I will come back to you."

Tony's driving. I'm in the passenger seat. Mike and Paul are in the back. I'm loading the last of the 9mm pistols I have on my person. I can hear the two in the back doing the same, but there's an uneasy feeling in the car.

"Not much farther now," says Tony, keeping his eyes on the road, windshield wipers pushing aside the gentle rain that's been falling. It's not nearly enough to flush out an outside event like the one we're going to, but it's enough to give us the cover of darkness.

We couldn't ask for better conditions.

I put out feelers when I heard about the dogfighting rumors, calling a few friends of friends who owed me favors. And in this business, a good tip is as good as money.

My hunch was right. There's a junkyard on the

southeast side of town, right on the border of the territory the Cleaners are trying to make their own. If the word from my contact is good—and this guy doesn't disappoint—there's something going down there tonight.

We won't tolerate it. Not on our turf.

At least, that's what the bosses said. When I told them what I'd found out, I expected to be going in hot with a half-dozen men and a lot more firepower.

The bosses decided I could handle it with these two. Tony stays in the car, we'll need a quick getaway. I'd almost rather go in on my own.

"So, remind me what we know about these guys besides that we're gonna go fuck up anything they got goin' on," Mike says as he straps the gun to his side. They're are packed like sardines back there, but we're all used to getting ready in tight conditions.

"Not as much as I'd like," Paul grumbles.

"Shit, you're tellin' me," Mike says, his hand reaching for a cigarette he doesn't have. "Ever get the impression your boss is tryin' to kill you?"

Tony doesn't say anything. He never does.

"It's a low-stakes job," says Paul. "All the bosses need is to make a statement with a few good mooks and a lotta bullets—that's us. Not like we got bright futures ahead of us or nothin.'"

Mike gives a rueful laugh. "What, Paulie, you don't think I'm a model citizen? Look at me, I take a few more bullets for the family and I'll have a pension, just you watch."

"You take a few more bullets and the lead will be worth more than your pension," Paul chuckles.

The boys rib each other, laughing. Even I crack a smile. Joking about it helps, because the reality of everyday life for us is pretty goddamn grim.

"Nah, if the capo cared that much, we'd have a lot more people out here to take on Cleaners," says Mike.

"Luca's fought with 'em before, and he's here," Paul says. "Besides, Luca, you've got all that special-whatever training your crazy uncle gave you. You call the shots tonight, how 'bout that?"

"Think I'd leave you high and dry?" I say, raising an eyebrow into the mirror. "Don't bother thinking about the big men in the cushy chairs back home, we rely on each other while we're out here. But don't go saying stupid shit like that, either," I add with a warning glance. "We're soldiers. We're all on equal ground."

"One more block and I'm stopping," Tony says, giving us a heads-up. I nod before I look back to the two men. I feel like I'm obligated to give some kind of pep talk. These are good men, but they know as well as I do when we've been given a shit hand.

"Should be a small crowd tonight betting on a few dogs. We're coming in about ten minutes early, so I want us to be in there before the fuckers take the dogs out of their cages. Paul, you've got a pit bull, I don't have to tell you to watch your shot."

Paul nods with a hardened face. He's got a special hatred for fights like these. There's nothing about them that isn't monstrous.

"Cleaners don't have numbers on their side, but they're vicious," I say. "They don't pull punches, and neither should you. We've all been to this junkyard before, so no surprises. Hit them hard and fast, don't give them a second to organize. The gamblers are going to scatter, but unless one of them pulls a gun, let 'em go—the more people hear about tonight, the better." I glance between the two of them. "If I didn't trust the two of you, I wouldn't be bothering with this shit, alright? Let's show these assholes who runs the Bronx."

The men give me resolute nods just as we come to a stop on the outside of a fence with barbed wire running along the top. Tony turned the headlights off a while ago. All four of us climb out of the sedan, and Tony moves around to the trunk to take out a big, thick carpet.

As we make our way to the fence, Tony hands me the rug. I open my mouth to tell him we'd see him later, but he says, "Let me come with. Got a bad feeling about tonight."

I'm surprised, but after a quick glance to Mike and Paul, I give Tony a curt nod. "Lock the car. You carrying?"

Tony pulls his jacket to the side to show off a pair of glocks strapped to his chest. I smile. Tony's from the old country, like me. We don't fuck around with business like this.

I take the lead, climbing the fence up to the wire. With a quick motion, I toss the thick rug over it and use that as padding to climb over. This isn't exactly a high-security lot. They might as well have left out a welcome mat for anyone wanting to do what the Cleaners are doing tonight.

Once inside, the four of us start making our way through the shadows of the junkyard. Rain patters on crumpled, rusted metal all around us. The half-smashed, ruined cars and machines piled up all around us are like ridges of a mountain. I hear a rat scuttle away every thirty paces or so.

It doesn't take long for us to start hearing voices. I glance back at my men to make sure everyone's still good. I draw my weapon, and they do the same, triple-checking that they're loaded and ready to go.

As we get closer to the sounds, it's clear where the group is set up. There's an encircled dirt clearing not far from the center of the junkyard that's protected by a ring of stacked cars and warped metal. Perfect for things like this. Only a few ways out, but plenty of cover. You can't hear anything going on in there from outside the junkyard.

I know, because I killed a man here a year ago.

He was a loan shark who'd crossed the wrong people —I don't regret it.

I look back to nod to Paul and Tony, gesturing for them to circle around to another entryway. There's one almost directly across from the one I'm taking Mike toward. We should be able to see each other with no problem.

"What's the signal?" Paul asks in a low whisper.

"You'll know," I say simply. Paul gives me a look, but he knows better than to question me. He nods, and the two of them disappear, hugging the shadow of a semi-truck as they slide around to their position.

Me and Mike make it to a small outcropping made of what looks like the remains of a Volvo and a stack of tires, where we crouch down. Through the smashed-out window, we have a clear sight of the scene.

There's a makeshift ring set up in the middle of the clearing, set up from rebar, heavy metal barrels, and a few other odds and ends the ringleaders must have thrown together. A few people are leaning on the edges, beers in hand, while others crowd around a man standing on top of a small platform, taking bets. Next to him is a big burly guy with a scar across his face, bulging arms crossed.

That's one guard. I spot a second one walk by the opening between two stacks of metal, a third and a fourth by the ring. I always assume there's at least one more that I can't see.

"Something look off to you, Mike?" I murmur, narrowing my eyes at the scene.

"Yeah," he replies. "Where's the dogs?"

I notice the man taking bets checking his watch periodically. His brow is knit, and he's looking red-faced. He shouts at the guard every now and then, who looks unmoved.

"Must be running late," I say. "All the better. No risk of hurting anyone who doesn't have it coming." I reach into my coat pocket and pull out the little glass bottle I stashed in there on the ride over.

It's filled with alcohol and a little rag. The Americans call it a Molotov cocktail.

"That's your signal, huh?" Mike says through a smirk.

"Told you I was going in hot," I say with a wink before I see the patrol disappear behind the cars again and dart to the edge of the entrance. Crouching low, Mike follows behind me. I glance around the corner long enough to see Paul's face in the shadows on the other side.

I take out a lighter and set the tip of my Molotov ablaze. I give myself a half-second to take aim at the edge of the ring where two of the guards are standing, and I hurl it.

Chaos erupts.

The firebomb goes off with a crash, and the two

men scream as they stagger back, flames on their clothes keeping them from fumbling for their weapons. Like clockwork, I see Paul pop out of cover and fire at the big guy with the scar, who takes two to the chest and goes down. Immediately, the crowd scatters. Cursing fills the air as the gambling men run for the exitways, and a few people who spot us just start crawling out over the piles of cars.

The man taking bets pulls out a pistol and fires back at Paul, but I come out of cover with mine raised and put a bullet in his head before he can get off more than a couple shots that ricochet off the metal.

The two guards by the ring are burned badly, but they're getting to their feet and getting their weapons out, so Mike and I move in.

Mike fires at them, but I haven't forgotten the other guard just beyond the entryway. I blind-fire around the corner and hear a curse, and the first guard lunges at me from behind cover, closing the distance before I can aim a shot at him. But I'm ready.

I crouch down and brace for his impact, throwing him over my shoulder when he rushes in. Almost as soon as he's on the ground, I'm on top of him. I drop my knee down onto his throat with all my weight, crushing his neck instantly.

"Shit!" I hear Mike curse, and I look back to see him taking cover, holding his arm. He's been hit.

"Get down!" I shout, and I provide covering fire for him, hitting one of the two burned guards in the stomach. He crumples, and I see Paul and Tony moving in from behind the other side, guns out.

That's when I hear the sound of an engine.

I watch Paul and Tony's attention turn to their right from across the ring, and Tony cries out, pushing Paul out of the way as a truck comes barreling out of nowhere. It pulls a hard right as it flies toward the two, and I shout as Tony gets slammed by the side of the truck going God-knows-how fast.

His body goes rolling to the side as Paul scrambles to cover, and bullets are already flying from the truck. The truck flips its brights on, blinding me and Mike, and we're forced to cover, firing at it from behind the ruins of a car.

My adrenaline is racing, because I caught a glimpse of what's in the bed of that truck: about four more men, and the sound of those bullets told me they've got automatic weapons. Uzis, if I were a betting man.

"*It's a fucking trap!*" I shout, "Paul, get out of there!"

But there are already gunshots ringing out, and I can't see Paul. I grab Mike and pull him close to me. "I'll draw their fire, get Paul and get the fuck out of here!"

"What?!" he hisses, "I'm not leaving you, Luca!"

We both duck on reflex as bullets pelt the car, and I know I have to move fast. Then I hear his voice.

"Luca, you still alive?" calls Lorenzo from the truck, a mocking edge to his voice. "Think we have some unsettled business! My boys here have been dying to meet you, why don't you come say hi?"

"Fuck," I mutter. "Mike, I'm not fucking around, when I move, you move opposite me." I don't give him a moment to respond. Blind-firing to cover myself, I dart out from behind the car, crossing through plain sight. Bullets start peppering the ground around me, but adrenaline is pumping through my body now. I don't look back to see whether Mike listened to me, but in what feels like a second, I'm back into the labyrinth of shadows and cars, away from the ring.

If I want to survive tonight, I need to draw them into my territory.

I get low and reload my gun, making a wide circle to their position. I know they'll either be tailing me, trying to head me off, or both, depending on their numbers. I need to be ready for that.

"Your pal here left a dent in my truck, Luca," Lorenzo calls. "Don't worry, I'll try to keep your death nice and clean. Cleaner than this shmuck, anyway." His words come with the sound of a single shot as he puts Tony down for good.

I grit my teeth.

They'll pay for tonight.

I hear footsteps up ahead of me. They're moving quietly, but my ears are sharper. Without having to think, I move to the wall of cars and climb into the nearest gap I can find, pressing myself flat against it. I can hear my heart pounding. I never liked skulking through the shadows, but they'll be my ally tonight. Pistol still in one hand, I draw my knife.

In the blink of an eye, I watch two figures pass by me. I seize my chance. Like a specter, I lunge out from the darkness. My gun-hand wraps around the mouth of one while I drive the knife into the base of his skull with all the force I need.

His body hasn't hit the ground twitching before his comrade turns, wide-eyed, and fires blindly at me as I dive for him too. I feel the sting of at least two bullets in my shoulder, but that doesn't stop me from driving the knife into his throat.

Shit. I used the knife because I wanted to keep from making too much sound, but the man has given me away. As he crumples to the ground, I stow my knife and pistol to collect the Uzis from the men. Their blood is sticky on the handles.

The others must have been close, because no sooner have I picked up the guns than I hear the rush of running footsteps behind me. I whirl around in time to see another two of the thugs running my way, but they stagger to a halt as they see me and my guns.

On reflex, they fire off at me, and I dive for cover as I shoot back. There's a sting in my thigh, and I know I'm hit, but I see one of them hit the ground, dead, and the other groans. I think I hit him in the gut.

I can hear Uncle Carlo in the back of my mind, chiding me for being so imprecise. *You're the one who taught me how to defend myself in the first place, you crazy bastard.*

To my right, I see light filtering through the cars. I realize the light is coming from the headlights—there's a crack in the rusted machines just big enough to slip through and get back into the clearing where the ring is. And I wouldn't care to do so, except that I see a familiar figure walking nearby in that light.

Lorenzo.

There's a guard with him, though. I have to make this count. I draw my pistol again. I need to be precise. I move up carefully, as silently as I can be. My heart sinks as I see Paul on the ground, across from them, not moving. I get up just close enough to where I can make the shot, and Lorenzo's back is to me.

Broken glass crunches under my boot. The guard's gaze darts to me. I have to act *now*.

As he raises his gun to fill me with lead, I lunge forward and seize Lorenzo from behind, arm around his neck and pistol to his head. The guard has his gun trained on me, his face twisted into a grimace, but he freezes, and Lorenzo tenses up.

"You're a ballsy cock-sucker, you know that?" Lorenzo growls, struggling a moment against my grip. Our faces are so close I can hear his breathing. It's closer than I'd like to be to this piece of shit, but if my head isn't close enough to Lorenzo's to be a risk, I know that guard will take the shot.

"You're one to talk," I hiss back, "you've got guts, coming out here to die in a junkyard."

"I wouldn't be so sure," Lorenzo says as I keep my eyes locked with his guard, standing off with me uneasily. "I can feel the blood spilling out your wounds. My boys got you good."

"If you think this is bad, you're more spoiled than I thought," I chuckle.

"Tough talk. Serena's made you soft, Luca," he says in a taunting, almost singsong voice, "but she can get me hard, if you know what I mean."

I'm about ready to throw caution to the wind and pull the trigger when a hint of movement catches my eye.

Paul.

His firing-arm lifts up and aims at the guard from behind. I see it at the same time as Lorenzo. But just as Paul fires, Lorenzo throws his elbow into my side and twists away. He tries to get a hold of my wrist and take that with him. I wrench myself free, but I have to let my weapon fall out of my hands to do so. It falls to the dust as Lorenzo pulls himself away and turns to flee.

I hear the guard cry out in pain and fall to his knees, but I'm already chasing after Lorenzo, who's racing for the truck. My body is a better-tuned machine, though, and I catch up to him, diving into a tackle that brings him to the ground with a hard thud. The next moment, we're locked in each other's arms.

My legs twist to try to get a hold of him, but he's more careful than to let me have that. He throws a punch that catches me in the eye, but I push through the ringing in my ears to return the blow, then work my way around him to try to get him in a sleeper hold.

But before I can do that, he rolls away and pushes himself up onto his feet. I do the same, and he draws a knife, a trickle of blood running down his nose and out his mouth. His eyes are wide.

I smile. That's fear in his eyes. "Let's settle this like men, *codardo!*"

Lorenzo's eyes dart to his guard...but the man is dead, breathing his last on the ground. My jaw tightens as I realize Paul is gone, too. He used the last of his strength to give me a chance. My grip on my knife tightens as I ready to lunge at Lorenzo.

But as I move my leg, I feel a sharp pain shoot through my body, and I suppress a grunt of pain. I look down at my leg and realize that the entire side of my pants are soaked in red. My dizziness is catching up to my adrenaline.

For a moment, Lorenzo looks as if he's going to take me on, but he proves himself even more of a coward than I thought. He takes his chance and runs, hopping into his truck.

I run for my gun on the ground and pick it up to shoot at the vehicle, but he's already turned the ignition on and started roaring away. I fire my weapon and watch the sparks as it hits the back, but it just blazes on, tearing out of the junkyard.

I swear under my breath in my mother tongue. I have to go after him. I look around, and my gaze falls on Tony's broken body. Cursing, I stoop down beside him, fighting off the fuzziness of my vision. I say a quick prayer I remember from my youth as I reach into my dead friend's jacket to get the keys.

I start running toward where we parked the car. I have to go after Lorenzo. I have to end this tonight, dammit. I have to make sure he'll never lay another hand on Serena. As I move through the junkyard, I pass the bodies of the men I've slain tonight. It looks like a wild animal has been turned loose on them.

That's what this life has made me, I think in my delirious state. A wild animal. *Un diavolo.*

When I reach the fence, I realize that I don't remember running through the rest of the junkyard. My leg feels cold. I look behind me and see spots of blood I've left as tracks. Shit.

Tony and Paul, gone. Did Mike make it out? Did the stupid fucking idiot listen to me and save his hide? They set a trap for us. They cost me two damn fine men. I'll kill him with my own two hands. I'll…

I shout out in pain that jolts me awake, and I realize I'm sitting in the car already. "Luca, you son of a bitch," I talk to myself in Italian, using the sound of my voice and the pain to keep me awake, "you're not done yet. You're not done yet."

I fight off the blurriness one more time as my bloodied hand turns the key in the ignition.

"Seriously, you need to chill out, *chica*. This is supposed to be our one night to relax, right? You've checked your phone, like, thirty times in the past five minutes," Rafaela says, interrupting the dark train of thought I've been riding along in silence. I blink a few times and hastily put my phone in my back pocket, then look across the kitchen and give her an apologetic smile. I can feel just how unconvincing a smile it is, though. That nagging ball of worry in my gut just won't leave me alone.

"Yeah. Yeah, sorry," I murmur, swiping a hand back through my hair and sighing. Rafaela walks to the fridge and takes out a pre-cut lime section, then starts squeezing it over the green bowl of guacamole. She glances over at me as she mixes the contents of the bowl.

"You're really into him, huh?" she asks gently.

The genuine understanding in her voice almost makes me lose my cool—I've been fighting to keep myself composed the past day or so since Luca stormed out of Bathing Beauty with some vague, probably dangerous mission on his horizon. So I nod.

"I am. I know it's probably so stupid of me. I don't have time in my life right now for some torrid romance or whatever, but ugh, Raf. I just like him a lot. He and I go way back and it's just...I guess I was prepared to just never see him again. In fact, I'm starting to think that's partly why I've been so willing to just throw myself into work and give up on dating and all that. Whether I knew it or not, I think I've subconsciously been kind of, you know, saving myself for him," I finish, shrugging.

Raf raises an eyebrow and narrows her eyes suspiciously. "You don't mean, like...sexually. Right? I mean, I did go to college with you. I remember that one party where you made out with that frat guy on a couch at the club for, like, an hour."

Suddenly, the tension in my body breaks and I burst out laughing. "No, oh my god. I don't mean that I'm, like, a born-again virgin or anything like that. It's just that I haven't let myself fall in love since — well, since Luca stepped out of my life the first time."

"Ah, okay. So it's more like your heart is a born-again virgin. Saving your heart for him. Got it,"

Rafaela says jokingly, but there's a twinge of kindness to her sarcasm. I know she understands. After all, she and Nico have been together for as long as I've known Rafaela. It used to make my heart ache the way Nico and Rafaela look at each other, like each of them thinks the other put the stars in the night sky. I used to think I would never have that again. That I would just have to settle for finding the little pieces of happiness in my career, my broken family, my friendships.

And all of those things are well and good on their own. But now that Luca has come back into my world and tinted everything a rosy pink, well, I don't know if I could stand to lose that kind of endless, all-encompassing sunshine again. Even if it means that I'll be living on the edge of serious danger for the rest of my life. He's worth it. That much I know for sure.

"*Bueno.* Guacamole is done, we got the tortilla chips and the salsa, and Ryan Gosling is waiting for us in the DVD player. Let's get this girly night started!" Rafaela says brightly, gesturing with one hand for me to follow her into the living room while she grasps the bowl of guacamole in the other. I grab the bag of chips and the bowl of salsa and follow her to the big comfy couch.

As soon as we both settle into the couch and turn on the movie, Rafaela jumps back up. "Oh! I almost forgot the most important thing: tequila! Okay, I'll be right back. Just gonna make two very strong tequila sunrises."

"Should I pause it?" I call after her as she jogs back to the kitchen.

"Nah, I've seen this movie, like, seven billion times. Nico's starting to think Ryan Gosling is my second boyfriend at this point," she answers, amid the clinking of glasses. "He's my celebrity freebie, just in case."

I grin and turn back to the movie, trying to force myself to focus on the TV screen instead of letting my mind wander to the phone in my pocket. I distract myself with a few chips laden with guac. I try my best to focus on how cute Ryan Gosling is, how comfy the couch is, how happy I'll be to have a cocktail in my hand with my best friend beside me. God knows I need this.

Girls' night. We only managed to make it work tonight at the last minute, when Nico's new employee took Raf's shift at the bar in apology for all his missed shifts. Still, when Rafaela called to let me know she was free, my immediate reflex was to turn her down, to stay cooped up at home in my bedroom waiting for my phone to go off. I planned to sip tea and stare at my cell phone screen for as many hours as it took for Luca to finally get back in touch with me and let me know he was okay.

My stomach churns at the thought. What if he *isn't* okay? What if he's hurt and bleeding somewhere out there in the night, silently suffering while I sit here all warm and cozy at Raf's apartment. I bite my lip nervously and give into temptation, pulling my phone out of my pocket and lighting up the screen for the hundredth time. Still nothing. No text messages, no missed calls.

"I see you," says Rafaela, causing me to jump a little. I look up at her with what must be a panic-stricken expression, because she instantly hands me a tequila sunrise and adds, "Geez, are you okay? You look like you've seen a ghost or something."

I shake my head. "God, I'm sorry I'm such a mess tonight. I just can't stop worrying."

"Why? Just worried he's not gonna call you or worried because he's doing something dangerous and you don't know if he's okay?" she asks sagely. I take a sip of my drink, feeling the warmth spread down my body.

"Wow, how did you…?"

Rafaela rolls her eyes good-naturedly. "*Chica*, I could tell from the second I saw that boy that he's living some kind of crazy life. Those muscles and scars? Trust me, where I grew up, that's a neon sign for rough stuff."

"Okay," I begin, staring down into the gold-and-peachy colors swirling in my glass. "So, you know how you were telling me about the dogs coming into your cousin's vet office lately?"

"Yeah," she says warily. "What about?"

"Well, I think Luca is, um, looking into that."

Raf's eyes go big and round. "What, in like a cop kind of way?"

I shrug, giving a wishy-washy gesture. "Uh, not so much a cop. More like, well, I'm not really sure what he would consider himself, to be honest. But he's a good guy. That much I'm sure of."

"I could tell that, too. *Immediatamente*. He's a good one," Rafaela agreed, nodding.

"And so I haven't heard from him since he went off to look into the dog-fighting thing, and now I'm really worried that he got himself into big trouble and he's hurt somewhere and— I just don't know what to do," I blurt out, heaving out a breath I've been subconsciously holding in my chest all evening.

Rafaela reaches out to put a hand on my shoulder, looking into my eyes meaningfully. "*Chica*. Finish that drink. We're gonna go find him, okay?"

She turns off the movie, downs her tequila sunrise in a few short gulps, then snaps her fingers as she gets to her feet. "*Vámonos*," she adds emphatically. So I toss back the cocktail, letting the alcohol numb my nerves just a little bit, then I hop to my feet. Rafaela tucks the guacamole away in the fridge — always keeping her priorities straight— and then the two of us head out into the night.

"Where should we check first?" she asks. I think about it for a minute.

"Well, let's go to his apartment first. And if he's

not there— then I guess I'll just have to go track down a dog-fighting ring myself," I tell her honestly. Rafaela links her arm with mine.

"You're *loca*, you know that? But I get it. That's your man. You gotta do what you gotta do. But you're an idiot if you think I'm gonna let you do any of that by yourself," she adds with a conspiratorial smile.

So we set off for Luca's apartment, the address of which I have entered into my phone. He lives across town from Rafaela's place, so we take a taxi. The whole ride over, my stomach is twisting in knots, my heart hammering away like a tribal drum.

When we finally arrive, I'm surprised to see that it's a relatively modest, well-kept apartment building. It looks far too humble and innocent to house a guy like Luca, but I'm already learning once again that he is a man of many surprises. Rafaela and I exchange looks of nervous anticipation, and then we walk into the lobby. It's dimly lit inside, and there's no one around. We muddle our way through to an elevator, then take it up to the fourth floor. All the while, my mind is racing in a million directions, terrified that he'll either not be home or, possibly even worse, he *will* be home but in bad shape. The thought of seeing him hurt is enough to send my thoughts into a frenzy.

We get to his door and I hesitate a moment before knocking. There's a long silence, and then I knock again, leaning forward to try and peer through the peephole. I look at Rafaela, who shrugs.

"Maybe he isn't home," I whisper, feeling crushed. But I look through the peephole once more and nearly fall over with shock to see an eye looking back at me. A green eye.

Luca's eye.

There's the sound of several locks clinking open and then the door opens just a fraction. Luca's face peers through the crack, looking confused and almost angry. My heart skips a beat.

"Serena?" he asks, his voice low and broken.

"It's me. And— and Rafaela. She's here, too."

"Hi," she squeaks from behind my shoulder.

Luca sighs and opens the door wider to reveal his white t-shirt and loose flannel pants— and a few patches of deep red blood staining through the fabric. One on his left thigh, one near his shoulder, and the third— most worryingly— slightly below his ribs.

"*Mierda*," Rafaela breathes, letting out a low whistle.

"Oh my god, Luca, what the hell happened?" I ask, my voice higher-pitched than usual, as it often does when I'm panicked. Luca leans out the doorway, looking up and down the hall with a slightly suspicious air, then nods for us to come in.

"Come inside before someone sees," he growls. "You, too, Rafaela."

We both rush into the apartment, which is exactly as spartan and neat as I would expect from a guy of Luca's self-discipline. But I'm a little too distracted by the massive bloodstains peppering his body to pay too much attention to the details of his residence.

He walks gingerly to a stool pulled to the center of his little kitchen area, with an open box of bandage wraps, a bottle of rubbing alcohol, and a needle and thread sitting on the otherwise pristine granite countertop. My stomach turns when I catch sight of the drops of blood on the white tile floor.

"I was hoping you wouldn't see me like this," Luca says, sounding genuinely downtrodden. "I remember you being squeamish about this kind of thing."

I can't even protest. It's true. I've never been good with blood and guts. Hell, I have trouble watching some TV shows involving hospitals because they all make me queasy. Rafaela, however, immediately jumps into medic mode.

"Okay. I know I'm just a head doctor, but I took enough med courses to help," she says, a look of determination on her face. While I'm feeling woozy, Raf is already scrubbing her hands in the kitchen sink, preparing to do God knows what.

"Neither of you should be getting involved with this," Luca protests softly, staring at me with those hard, green eyes. Rafaela is going through the cupboards, looking for something.

"Well, tough luck. Because she's involved with you, and she's my best friend, so I'm automatically involved. Plus, it's like a Hippocratic Oath kind of thing. I may not be a real doctor yet, but I'm still not gonna turn away a guy bleeding out in his kitchen from what looks to be three separate gunshot wounds. Now, where the hell do you keep your rubber gloves? This apartment is spic and span, so I know you've got some hidden away somewhere," Rafaela says matter-of-factly.

A smile twitches momentarily at the corner of Luca's mouth. "Hallway closet. Second shelf."

"Thanks," she replies, and walks off to find them. When she returns, she tells Luca to take off his shirt, which he does obediently. Against my better judgement, I take a few steps closer, the breath hitching in my throat as I take in the gore of the situation. Dried blood. Bruising. Nicks and scratches.

The world spins for a moment and I carefully sit down on the tile floor while Rafaela tends to Luca's wounds. She gently dabs them clean, then begins the painstaking work of stitching him up. Thankfully, she's as professional and focused as a true doctor, even under these strange circumstances, and before long she has him as patched up as well as could be expected for this kind of serious injury.

"You're lucky," Rafaela says, tossing the rubber

gloves into a garbage can. Turning to me, she continues, "It looks really bad, I know. The rib shot and the thigh shot were just really bad grazes. The shoulder wound is the worst, but your guy here managed to wiggle the bullet out on his own before I got here. It'll all heal. As long as he takes care of himself."

"Thank you," I murmur, feeling overwhelmed.

"I could have done this myself," Luca says, "but probably not as neatly. So, thank you."

Rafaela waves off his gratitude. "Just doin' my job. Now, you really, really do need to take it easy. I'm serious. No crazy acrobatics or bad boy moves or whatever it is you do. Just chill out for awhile. Spend some quality time with your lady. She's been worried out of her mind all night about you, ya know?"

A flicker of pain crosses Luca's face and he locks eyes with me. "I'm sorry, Serena," he says softly. "I didn't want to worry you. This—all of this—you shouldn't have to deal with it. This is my bloody, filthy world. Not yours."

I stand up and walk over to him, taking his hands in mine. "And you are *my* world. So, like it or not, I'm here to stay. Don't push me out again. Please. I'd rather know what's going on."

Luca lifts his good arm to stroke my face. I close my eyes, leaning into his touch.

"I promise. And I will do everything in my power to keep you safe, *mia passerotta*. But you have to trust me," he replies. I nod, turning his hand to kiss his open palm.

"Okay! And that's my cue to leave, I think," Rafaela says suddenly, reminding us both that she's still here. My cheeks burn with embarrassment, having gotten caught up in the moment with Luca.

"Thank you so much again," I tell her earnestly, walking over to give her a tight hug. I whisper in her ear, "You have no idea how much this means to me."

"It's all good, *amiga*. Now, I assume you wanna stay and look after your boy. I'm gonna head home and go to town on that guacamole until Nico gets off work. Just me and Ryan Gosling for a few hours," she says, winking.

"Sorry our girls' night got ruined," I tell her.

"Eh, it's okay. More guac for me. But you do owe me. Just buy me a drink next time we're out, and we're square," she says good-heartedly. I give her a big grin.

"You got it. Text me when you get home."

Luca carefully gets to his feet, fishes a wad of money out of a wallet on the countertop, and hands it to Rafaela. At first, she shakes her head, refusing it.

"Take it. You've done me a huge service here. Not to mention taxi fare. It's the very least I can do," Luca insists, and she gives in.

"Okay," she says. "I'm leaving now. Take it easy. Seriously. I'm pretty good at stitches but you still don't want to risk them reopening or something."

I flinch at the thought. Once Rafaela is gone, I rush into Luca's arms, laying my head against his powerful chest, careful not to touch his wounds. I look up at him, overwhelmed with feeling.

"How did this happen? What did you do? Who did this to you? Did you go to the cops? Where did this all go down? Are you safe now? Is someone looking for you?" I ask, the words stumbling over themselves in a rush to get out.

Luca gently strokes my hair, calming me down. "It's okay. It's over for now. There's no need to rehash all this mess—it's *my* mess. And besides, you heard Rafaela: we have to relax, right?"

I want to protest, but I think better of it. "Fine. You've got to be exhausted."

Luca yawns. "I actually am. Nothing like a firefight to knock you right out."

"I'm staying here tonight," I insist.

He doesn't fight me on it, and the two of us carefully make our way to his bedroom, both of us curling up under the sheets and falling asleep pressed up against each other. We both sleep like the dead, probably because of all the stress of recent events, and when I wake up in the morning, it's to the glorious smell of coffee. *Good* coffee.

I roll out of bed, the events of last night returning to my foggy brain as I stretch and make my way into the kitchen. There, I find Luca shirtless, using his one uninjured side to pour coffee and arrange fresh fruit and pastries on two plates.

"What's all this?" I ask, sidling up next to him.

"Proper Italian breakfast. It's light, but it's something."

"You're supposed to be taking it easy, aren't you?" I chide him gently. He chuckles.

"It's not like I'm an invalid, Serena. I can handle putting fruit and *sfoglie* on plates."

"Still," I interject, running my hands up his chest. I stand on tiptoe to kiss him. Even though he's wounded, I can feel that powerful strength rippling through his body, and it thrills me to my core.

"Careful, *mia passerotta*," he growls, pressing against me so that I'm pinned into the counter. "Touch me like that and I might change my mind about what I want for breakfast."

A shiver runs down my legs. Suddenly, I can't resist egging him on. "Oh? What are you hungry for this morning, Luca?"

He leans down to kiss me, gently at first, and then more passionately. I can feel myself growing wet between the thighs. I become acutely aware of his cock pressing hard against my leg as his arms come down around me, pulling me tight to him. "We have to take it easy," I murmur between kisses.

"I'll do my best," he says, and immediately hoists me up with his one uninjured arm, setting me on the counter. Within thirty seconds, he whips off my panties, pulling me forward so that my ass rests on the edge of the counter. He bends down and wrenches my thighs open, parting me to get easy access to my flower. Glancing up at me with a devilish glint in his gorgeous eyes, he begins to swirl his tongue around my clit, making me cry out.

"Oh my god," I mumble, my head falling back as I close my eyes.

Luca gently nips and sucks at my clit, his tongue exploring my wet folds as my body shudders around him. It's like he knows me instinctively, knows exactly how to unlock and unravel me with the flick of his tongue and the softness of his lips. Before long, I'm writhing on the counter, trying not to move too much and risk knocking our breakfast to the floor.

"Luca," I gasp, feeling my pleasure mounting ever higher. "Feels so...fucking...good."

Without warning, he slides a finger inside of me, hooking it to stroke my g-spot just right. Combined with the expert lashing of his tongue, I fall apart instantly, my orgasm exploding in his mouth.

"Fuck!" I whimper, bucking my hips. Luca holds me still, never letting up even though it almost hurts —but it hurts so fucking good. A moment later, a second climax shakes my body and my hands wander down to tangle my fingers in Luca's dark hair, gently pushing his face into my pussy.

He fingers me harder and faster while his tongue

rhythmically laps at my clit, sending me into ecstasy again and again. Finally, when I'm totally spent, he kisses his way up my body to gently kiss my breasts, my neck, my lips. He strokes the hair out of my face while I slowly return to my senses.

And when I do, I immediately slide off the counter, dropping to my knees without a word, to return the favor. I'm aching to feel his cock in my hands, in my mouth. I need to make him feel as good as I do. And he doesn't stop me.

I pull down his flannel pants and boxers, letting his massive length spring free. I'm careful not to touch the wound on his thigh, kissing my way to his cock. His hand strokes the back of my head, gently guiding me to his shaft, and I have to smile. I love the way he can't resist, the way he wants so badly for me to touch him, to suck him. The fact that I can have such an effect on a guy like Luca is intoxicating.

But I want to take my time. I gently begin to stroke his cock with one hand at first, my thumb slowly sliding up and down along the underside of his shaft, making soft circles around the sensitive head. I adore the feeling of him in my hands—hard, hot, and smooth. My mouth is nearly watering for it. I add my other hand, applying a little more pressure as I work his shaft, letting his enormous length slide through my fingers as I lean forward and give the head a tantalizing kiss. Luca groans, his hand pushing a little harder against the back of my head. I peer up at him, smiling sweetly. I know what he wants, and I want it, too.

I want it so bad.

I open my mouth and take the tip of his cock between my lips, letting my tongue gently swirl around the end while my hands continue to pump his shaft— faster now, a little tighter.

"Yes, sweetheart, that's it," Luca growls, and I feel myself getting even wetter at the sound of his voice, the neediness in his tone. I can't stand it anymore. I need him.

I open my mouth and take him in as deeply as I can in one movement, feeling Luca tighten up as I envelop him. He begins to move his hips, and I can tell it's taking all his willpower not to just let go and fuck my mouth mercilessly. He needs this as badly as I do, and that knowledge makes me all the more determined to make him feel amazing. I start to bob my head up and down along his shaft, my hands working his cock in tandem with my mouth. I suck him harder, moaning a little to send vibrations through his body.

"Fuck, baby, that's so fucking good," he groans, pushing me down on his cock so that I can feel the tip gently grazing the back of my throat. Before I start to choke, he relents. I can tell he's trying so hard to maintain control, to be gentle. But I want him to fuck my mouth. I want him to use me. I want him to let go completely.

I move faster, reveling in the sensation of his hard, smooth cock in my mouth as I gently work his balls before wrapping my arms around his thighs, deep throating him again and again. He pushes me down on his cock, bucking his hips as I move faster and faster.

"Gonna make me come, baby," he murmurs roughly. "Swallow for me, sweetheart."

With a few rapid, deep thrusts, I feel him seize up and then shoot his sweet, hot honey down my throat. I swallow it back hungrily, not wanting to waste a single drop. "Fuck, Serena!" Luca snarls through gritted teeth. I work his cock until he's totally spent, pushing me off.

He pulls me to my feet and kisses me deeply, not giving a damn about the taste of his own come in my mouth. "I think I'm awake now," he says, holding me close.

"Good," I reply, wiping my mouth. "Because I'm starving."

"Still?" he asks wryly.

I laugh. "Yes. For real food. Breakfast."

We both clean up and sit down to finally eat, both of us glowing and happy. It's as if the events of the past twenty-four hours have all been power-washed away. But no sooner has the peace arrived than it gets broken.

Luca's phone buzzes. I pick it up to hand to him,

catching a glimpse of the text message on the screen. It says simply, **Don't go home.**

We both look at each other, sharing a dark expression.

We're already home. And only God knows why we shouldn't be.

"You made one hell of a splash last night, Luca" says Antonio. I'm not sitting in the back of any liquor store today. I'm in a proper office, standing in the middle of a room that's packed with shelves of thick books. The consigliere lives pretty well. I've heard he was a lawyer a while back, or maybe he still is.

We got the hell out of the house after I got that message, and I took Serena to Rafaela's bar to lay low for the day. The guy who sent the message was one of ours. He must have assumed I'd go straight to one of our medics, because word of what happened at the junkyard spread fast.

It wasn't long after I'd gotten Serena to safety that I'd been summoned here, to the consigliere's own house.

This isn't a grilling, though, not like last time. I'm

not surrounded by other soldiers this time. There are only three people in this room, and all of them are way over my pay grade. Two of them are familiar faces: the consigliere and Diego, my capo. The third is a man even I've never met and only seen once.

Giacomo "Jackie" Pisano, the underboss. Where he goes, business is serious.

The consigliere is sitting in a leather armchair, but not behind the big desk in the room. Jackie is leaning on that, while Diego sulks by the window.

Jackie scrolls through his phone, his face hard to read. He's a massive, meaty guy with thick, heavy features, and he always looks vaguely pissed-off. "Haven't seen a body count like this in a while."

"Neither have the Cleaners," I say, and Jackie's small eyes look me up and down, appraising me. I don't let it faze me. "Have we heard from Mike?"

"Mike's fine," Jackie says, putting his phone down. "Got himself patched up with one of our guys. We've already had a word with him."

"So you know how things went down," I say.

"We know," says Jackie, crossing his arms and pacing around the room, "that things were going fine until Lorenzo Abruzzi pulled up with a truck full of fuckers packin' military-grade weapons. We know our intel was bad, and the guy who gave you that tip is being dealt with right now. We know that you told Mike to get the fuck out of there, and we know he assumed you'd be hauling ass too, like any reasonable goddamn person would." Jackie stops to turn and look at the bandages visible on me. "But judging by the way you look and the fact that the Cleaners are out for blood, I'm guessing that didn't happen."

I clench my teeth for a moment before I force myself to relax and speak. "Lorenzo knew I was going to be there. He was after me. It was business between the two of us. He killed Paul and Tony, I wasn't about to let him get away with that. So I hunted his men down, and I almost killed him, too. But he fled. He's a coward."

"Mike told me what he saw," Jackie says. "He saw the guns those maniacs got a hold of. How the fuck are you alive?"

There's a pause between us as we hold each other's gaze. "My uncle," I say after a moment, "he taught me, when I was young. Taught me how to defend myself. He was in the army." That's a lie. Uncle Carlo was part of a Special Forces unit. I don't want to tell them too much detail, though, or they'll have me doing hits for them with Diego. I gesture to my body with a nonchalant expression. "The rest? Good genes, I guess. Luck?"

Jackie's ugly mug twists into a smile, and he chuckles. "You're a stupid son of a bitch, you know that?"

"I'm alive, aren't I?"

Jackie stops chuckling, but he holds his smile for

a moment before it fades. "You weren't the only target last night."

My brow knits. "What?"

Jackie scrolls through his phone to pull up a few messages. "That dive bar we run, Pete's? They got hit hard right before last call."

"Fuck," I breathe, running my hand over my face and clenching my fist. Bad enough that I couldn't keep a hold on the situation with Lorenzo, but another place too? "What happened?"

"Driveby," Jackie explains, and he holds out his phone to me. It's a picture of the bar in question, an old place I've gone to before. The front is riddled with bullets, all the windows are shot out, and I recognize bloodstains on the walls. "Pete made it out with a bullet in his side, but he'll pull through. The bar's done for, though."

"So, two places in one night and more bodies than the city's seen in a long time. Do we know who they've got on the take?" I ask. We have our own cops on our payroll, but if they're turning a blind eye to this much…

"Our boys in blue suddenly don't know a thing," Diego speaks up ruefully. "I don't know who they've got to, but it's someone who can pull some major strings."

"This has become a war," the consigliere says calmly. "They're making moves fast and hard, and if we don't act now, they'll have their heels dug into our territory even deeper. That's why I'm promoting you, Luca."

That hits me like a bolt of lightning. I stare at him, and I realize both Jackie and Diego are eyeing me expectantly. So this is why I got dragged out here.

"A promotion?"

"That's right," says Jackie, making no show of pomp or circumstance. "What happened last night would have gotten all four of you killed under most circumstances. Nobody could have been ready for that. But you and Mike got out of there because you can think on your feet, and god knows how many bullets it takes to put your ass down."

"That's the kind of initiative we need calling shots on the frontlines," the consigliere says, finally turning to look up at me. "Luca, I'm putting you in charge of the block the de Laurentis girl's shop is on."

Serena's block.

"So what, you're using her as a front line now?" I say, and the look Diego shoots me tells me I'm out of line, but I don't care. I'm sick of her getting endangered, dragged back into this life.

And I admit that the guilt in my gut is wearing me down. If I'd just avoided her…

I shake the thought away. No, I didn't bring this heat down on her. Lorenzo was shaking down her shop before I ever got there, and there's no way

Bathing Beauty could've paid the protection fees. Besides, her father was the one that put the target on her back. I was just the one that made Lorenzo take it more personally.

But Serena would've been in danger, with or without me. At least now, I'll have the power and authority to keep her safe. And once I kill Lorenzo…

"No," the consigliere says, putting out a hand, shaking me from my thoughts. He must have anticipated my reaction. "This is a sign of trust, Luca. I'm giving you more control over something that's very close to the heart all this violence."

"In other words, it's you that Lorenzo's got a beef with," says Jackie. "And you're one of us. If he wants a war, it's you he'll come after first. We're giving you the means to defend yourself."

"So we let them come to me," I say, and the men nod in agreement.

"I'll send you a list of the men who'll be under your command," says Jackie. "They'll be headed your way ASAP, because the Cleaners aren't gonna wait around long before they try to strike again."

"Good," I say. Not because I'm proud of the responsibility—I don't forget for a second that these mobsters are only interested in covering their own asses through me. "There are two alleys that run through that block that'll be to our advantage, and there's an office building on the opposite corner that will be useful for keeping an eye on the area. I'll give the men the rundown personally."

"You've got promise, Luca," says Jackie, nodding at me. "That's good. Show your men you're in control, and don't let 'em see weakness."

I crack a smile. "How could they see something that isn't there?'

~

Hours later, I'm back out to the only place I care to be—with Serena.

We're in Belmont, another little Italian corner of the Bronx. It's a nice little place, perfect for a peaceful moment away from everything else that's been going on.

"Are you sure you're okay?" Serena says as we walk down the sidewalk, glancing up and down at my body. I've got a slight limp, but with each step I get better at hiding it.

"Don't worry about me," I say, "you'll know when I'm feeling it. This is nothing."

"I can't *not* worry about you," she says with a smile, and I squeeze her hand.

She's wearing a sundress and a wide-brimmed hat today, and compared to me in my rough leather jacket and t-shirt, I feel like the bodyguard to some celebrity. I might as well be. Every time I glance over at Serena, it's like looking at someone out of a movie or a fairy tale.

Colorful streamers are strung up between buildings over the street, and the red brick buildings look warm in the afternoon sun as we stroll down the sidewalk. Serena keeps smiling, and I have a hard time tearing my eyes off her. She catches me once or twice and blushes, and the third time, she bumps her hip into mine and says "Quit it!" as we laugh.

After a moment, she looks over at me with those warm eyes glittering in the sun. "It feels weird to have a breather with everything that's going on."

"Weird?"

"Nice-weird," she says, and I take a hold of her hand as we turn into a fresh produce store.

It's a quiet little place with a few fans lazily running overhead, and there's that familiar scent all produce stores seem to have. A few flies are buzzing around the place, and the floors are just plain brown concrete. It's nothing fancy, but we're not looking for anything fancy today. Just a little time together.

"This is probably the most Italian place in the neighborhood," I say, looking around the place with raised eyebrows.

"Oh yeah?"

"All it's missing is a few people smoking outside," I say with a smile, and she giggles as we start to look around at some of the assorted stuff.

"You know, you don't talk about it very much, come to think of it."

"Italy?"

She nods her head as we pick out a couple of apples to eat on the way out. I pay for the food and look pensively up at the little Italian flag hanging from the window of one of the shops. "No, I guess I don't. It's a complicated place, where I'm from."

"Where is it?"

"Taranto," I say, a faint smile crossing my face. Taranto brings up a lot of mixed feelings. It's a far cry from the picture of Italy most Americans think about.

"That sounds familiar," she says thoughtfully.

"Probably because it sounds like Toronto," I say playfully, and she slaps me on the shoulder. "Don't laugh, that's where most people thought I was from when I first got here."

"Seriously, though."

"Seriously, okay," I say, looking up at the sky, trying to think of the best way to describe my hometown as I can. We're soon strolling through a park in the Bronx, but my memories take me back nearly ten years.

"It's in the far south. If you think of Italy like a boot, it's on the heel, facing the gulf. The land is very sunny. It's like the whole place is bathed in gold sometimes, and we don't get winters as harsh as the rest of the country up north. Taranto itself is very old. It was a Greek settlement, a long time ago."

"Woah," Serena says, raising her eyebrows. "The house I grew up in was built in the forties, and I thought *that* was old."

"All the buildings are sun-baked, for the most part. Imagine if you turned gold into stone, they'd look kind of like that. Only not as pristine. There's a lot of black soot on everything because of the factory nearby."

"Sounds romantic," she says with playful sarcasm.

"It's an acquired taste," I say with a chuckle. "The old town looks a something like the Little Italy up in Manhattan. Lots of clustered apartments, clothes lines strung up over narrow alleyways that *motorini*—er, scooters—zip down, big churches here and there...and the old military fort looms over everything on the water. Something about the palm trees and shining sea puts you at peace, though. It's hard to describe if you haven't seen it."

Serena is quiet for a moment before saying, "And you're from the old town?"

"No," I say, tossing the cores of our now-eaten apples into a trash can as our shoes click on the paved walkways. "My family lives a little ways out of the city. In the country. It looks like..." I frown, trying to draw a comparison. "Have you ever seen those old Western movies?"

Serena blinks, then bursts out laughing. "Wait, what?"

"No, seriously," I say. "They filmed some of those down in southern Italy. It's like a desert, but...more trees," I say, realizing I've never been to an American desert to compare to. I shake my head, laughing at myself. "My dad used to take me on drives around some of the villages in the area. They're really beautiful. They use a lot of smooth white stone that never goes dark like the ones in Taranto do. And some of them are up on mountains where you can see for miles in any direction."

"Wow," she says softly.

"When I was...very small," I say, holding my hand down to my knee to show how tall I was, "my dad would carry me on his shoulders and point out some of the other villages from this park up on a mountain ridge. Then we'd go get gelato from the little shops close by, and he'd tell me about the places he went when he was growing up."

I feel Serena's steady gaze on me, and the look on her face reminds me that I'm starting to get a little misty-eyed. I blink it away, and shake my head. "That was a long time ago, though."

There's silence between us as we walk slowly, and finally she says, "Your dad sounds like a good guy."

I nod.

"The place reminds me a little of what my dad

used to describe," she says, and she wraps her arms around my bicep to lean her head on me as we walk. "He was just a teenager when they left Sicily, but it sounds like they're a lot alike."

"Sicily and the mainland? They have everything and nothing in common," I say. "But they're both beautiful places. We ought to go sometime."

"Just up and go to Italy?" she says, a slight laugh to her voice, but I smile at her perfectly sincere.

"Why not? I'll make sure you get time off from work to close the shop for a few days."

"Oh god, I could never!"

"When customers come in, I'll 'encourage' them to make a few purchases," I say, playing up my best menacing accent and cracking my knuckles. Serena giggles and slaps my chest in protest, but I surprise her by scooping her up off the ground and spinning in a circle with her, then planting a kiss on her lips as she throws her arms around my neck. It was painful in my condition, but worth it.

We look at each other for a long moment, smiling, and I know we're both losing ourselves in the fantasy for a little bit.

"It's starting to get dark," I finally say, gently setting her down. "I ought to get you back."

We make our way back toward the car and climb in, but once we're driving, I can't help but feel like something's lacking from our little date. After a moment, I look over to Serena.

"Feel like going for a drive?"

"A drive?"

"I know someplace nice," I say. "It's too nice a night to waste inside.

A few minutes later, I turn off to head toward Orchard Beach, an idea forming in my mind. When Serena realizes where we're headed, a confused smile plays across her lips. "Luca, it's like, eight at night!"

"I want to show you something," I say simply, parking the car. "It's on the far end of the beach, this way."

As we approach the sand, Serena gasps at the sight, and immediately, I start looking around for danger, but then I hear her voice.

"Oh my god, Luca, look at the water!"

My concern melts away as I look up at it. The full moon is low on the water, casting a carpet-like stream of white reflective light on the gentle waves. There's not a cloud in the sky, and it couldn't be more beautiful.

I feel Serena looking at me, and I turn to see the most pleading eyes I've ever seen. "Do you want to go for a walk on the beach?" I ask with an arched eyebrow and a wide smile.

"How'd you guess?" she says, laughing before she darts over to the sand, kicking off her shoes and picking them up. I shake my head as I catch up to her and do the same.

We make our way out onto the beach proper. We're not the only ones out here tonight—I can see a few people further down here and there—but we're the only ones in this area. No other sounds but our feet crunching in the sand and the gentle sounds of the waves kissing the shore.

Serena goes almost to where the icy waters touch, and I start leading her to where I have in mind. The beach is pretty flat and open, and we're technically not supposed to be out here this late, but nothing's going to bother us while I'm around.

Before long, we come up to a little outcropping of rocks, and I lead Serena around it. "What's this?" she asks, and I crouch down to squint at the rock, looking it up and down. After a moment, I smile and point to something.

The words *VOGLIO TORNARE* are carved in a crude hand, a little weathered but still there. Serena blinks at it blankly.

"When I first got here, to America," I say, "well, I told you about how I was kind of a shit. I ran away from home once, the first few weeks. I *really* didn't want to be here. So I ran all the way out here to this beach and hid out for...I don't know, a few hours." I grin. "I was a rebel, but I got bored easy."

Serena reaches out and brushes her hand over the words. "Did you write this?"

"It means 'I want to go back,'" I explain, nodding. Serena is quiet for a few moments.

"It must have been hard, getting used to somewhere this new," she says. I'm thoughtful for a moment, but then I reach up and pull her down with me, rolling onto the sand, and she yelps as I hug her close to me.

"I might have settled down if I'd had you to distract me sooner," I whisper into her ear, and she wiggles in protest, giggling. Soon, though we find ourselves sitting up, Serena between my legs as we watch the bright, moonlit water.

"Think it's dangerous out here?" Serena asks, leaning her head back against my shoulder. Wisps of her hair flutter as I breathe in and out.

"Could be," I say, reaching to my pocket, "I've never had to worry about that kind of thing." I pull out a switchblade, opening it and letting it gleam in the moonlight as Serena looks down at it.

"Are you kidding? Giant, musclebound Italian guy with a knife?" she teases, but I squeeze her to me, chuckling as I plant a kiss on her neck. She squirms away from it with a smile, and I pepper her neck with kisses until she starts turning her neck up and scooting her butt into my crotch, her playful giggling melting away to short breaths.

"Why, are you afraid of something?" I ask, lowering my voice, and I bring my knife up to her collarbone. She hold still as I let the blade glide across her skin, and it gives her goosebumps.

"...Maybe I like a little danger," she says, and I feel

her shiver wonderfully against my hardening manhood. I smile, and my throat rumbles as I bring the blade up to her chin and whisper into her ear.

"Little lady like you should be careful, coming out so far with a dangerous man."

Even in the moonlight, I can see her cheeks start to flush with color. Her eyes flash to the rest of the beach. "We're pretty exposed out here," she breathes.

"I don't care," I growl, my hand reaching up to her breast and squeezing it. She suppresses a yelp, and she bites her lip. "I don't care if someone sees, I want to take you, Serena."

"God, I want you, Luca," she whimpers. She gives the shore one last worried look, but the same energy within her I've always known she has overtakes her. "Are you sure it's safe?"

"Trust me," I say, and I slip my jacket off to lay on the sand before I pull her onto it carefully. Her chest is rising and falling, hair spilling over her shoulders as she looks up at me and the knife, terrified yet full of need.

I take my shirt off and toss it aside, letting my whole torso gleam in the moonlight, and her eyes devour me. She reaches up to run her hands over my muscled body, and I put the knife in my teeth to rip her shirt up over her arms. Her bra comes the next moment, and I feast my eyes on her exposed body.

I take her wrists in my hand and hold them up

over her head, planting a knee on either side of her as I draw the blade slowly across my tongue.

"Be still," I caution her, slowly bringing the cool metal down to her torso. Her breathing is quick, but she nods softly and relaxes a bit at my deep, reassuring voice. "No sudden movements. I need all your trust, Serena."

"I want this," she says, red cheeks beautiful under stray locks of hair. "I want you, Luca."

I bring the knife down to her left breast and trace a circle around her nipple. She draws in breath at its cool touch, but I'm careful not to make more than the faintest contact. I've practiced this on myself before trying it with anyone, much less my Serena.

The blade slides around her breast, and I bring it to the other, playing dangerously close to her areola. My hand brings the knife to the nape of her neck, where I draw it across slowly, so slowly, wetting my lips as I watch its progress.

I pause to look up into her eyes, and they're wide with excitement, and she's breathing through her mouth. I smile and look back to the knife to bring it up to her chin, then to her lip, where I let it linger for a moment before gently using it to nudge her mouth open.

When that's done, I close the blade and toss it aside. The next moment, I attack her mouth. Our lips lock, and my bulge is growing rock-hard.

Our tongues explore each other's mouths, and

my hands slide down to her hips, squeezing them greedily, possessively.

We don't even talk. The heady drive of our lust is too strong for that tonight. I bring my mouth down to her nipple where I'd had the knife just a few moments ago, and my teeth do what the knife was too shy to do. I hear her gasp as my tongue washes over it, and meanwhile, I use my hands to start working her pants down. I have no patience tonight. I'm going to claim her, hard and fast.

As soon as her pants are down, I put my fingers to my mouth to wet them, but when I put those fingers to her lower lips, I find her already soaking-wet.

"That's my girl," I groan between kisses. I let my teeth graze her nipples one last time before I undo my own pants and let my shaft out, eager to meet her needy pussy.

His cock spears deeply inside of me as I cry out and arch my back, my hands grasping at either side of me, only to grab fistfuls of sifting sand. I close my eyes and feel my whole body tense up. The coarseness of the sand brushing against my back is just ever so slightly painful, adding a sharp edge to the pleasurable sensations between my legs.

Luca pauses for a moment, letting his massive length and girth fill me, the head of his shaft pressed squarely against that lovely, forbidden spot. I open my eyes again, slowly, to blink up at Luca with anticipation. He's looking down at me with an almost peaceful smile, but there's that fiery spark in his green eyes that tells me I'm in for the ride of my life.

I can't believe that the seed that was planted

between us so long ago still blooms so strongly. The trust, the love, the lust I have for him… He makes me feel like a love-struck teenager all over again. He's awakened things in me that I didn't even know were there.

And somehow, his presence in my life… it's soothed those old pains instead of inflaming them. When he first came back in my life, the memories I'd repressed came rushing back, and I had to face the demons in my past. The darkness that was lurking in the corner of my psyche.

But when I'm with him… I feel such love. Such trust. I knew he'd never hurt me, not even by acci-dent, as that cool blade had run up and down my body. So instead of frightening me, it simply thrilled me, and made me feel so… alive.

He runs his hands down my body, from my neck all the way down to squeeze my thighs, prying them open wider as he gradually slides his cock back out of me. I want to wrap my legs around him tightly, keep him inside me as much as possible. It's like an instinctive, almost animalistic need. To keep him. To hold him here. As though if I were to let him go, he might disappear into the fog rolling down across the beach. But I remember his words the other night at the bar: *I'm not going anywhere.*

Without warning, Luca suddenly slams into me, his cock hammering into my pussy. I let out a shriek of surprise and pleasure, and Luca claps a hand over my mouth as he begins to thrust harder and faster. A thrill runs through my body at the newness of this; I've never had anybody cover my mouth during sex before. After what I went through as a teenager, with anybody else I might be scared. But I trust Luca completely, without question. I know he would never, ever hurt me. And the joy of feeling so safe coupled with the hint of danger makes everything that much sexier.

"Shh," he whispers, passing his thumb delicately over my lips. "Someone might hear you."

"I'm sorry," I gasp, feeling my body tingle with ecstasy as he pumps into me again and again. "I'm trying to be quiet but— oh fuck— it feels so good."

I can barely get the words out, as wave after wave of pleasure rushes over me. Luca gives me a devilish grin and leans down to kiss me just as I open my mouth to let out another involuntary cry. He slips a hand down between my legs, his fingers finding my clit easily. I inhale sharply as he works my clit while his cock slams into me incessantly. His breath is hot on my neck, teasing me, until he finally kisses the ticklish skin there and starts to nip and suck. I'm overwhelmed with the competing sensations all over my body, my eyes rolling back and closing. I lift my hips again and again to meet his thrusts, moaning words without meaning.

"So good for me, baby," he purrs, the words dancing tantalizingly across my neck. I tremble with anticipation of looking in the mirror later to see the mark he's leaving there.

It might be juvenile, but I have always loved seeing those pink and purple love bites on my skin, a reminder of intense pleasure that lasts for days. It's a symbol, a trademark, telling the world that I belong to someone. And the thought of belonging to someone like Luca... well, it doesn't get any better than that.

"You're mine," he growls, almost as though he can read my thoughts. I groan, dragging my hands down his back and wrapping my legs around his waist, pulling him in close to me. I need to be closer, always closer to him. I can never get enough.

"I love it when you say that," I murmur. I can feel my pussy clenching around him, preparing for an inevitable climax. "I am yours. I belong to you. I always have."

"Gonna make sure everybody knows it. I'm going to claim you, mia passerotta. You're mine."

And with that, he lunges forward to suck a biting kiss into the flesh just above my collarbone and I yelp as my body trembles through an orgasm. I'm whimpering now, nearly incoherent with the over-whelming symphony of sensations.

"Good girl, very good," Luca whispers, stroking

the hair back from my face and planting a soft kiss on my lips. "I want you to ride me, sweetheart."

With one swift, fluid movement, he grabs hold of me and spins around so that his back is on the sand and I'm straddling him. I'm still swaying in the throes of pleasure, but I start working my hips, leaning forward to let my clit rub against him as I ride his cock. Luca reaches up to caress my breasts, rolling my nipples between his thumbs and forefingers, sending shockwaves of pleasure down to my core. I start to lose control, bouncing up and down on his cock with abandon, needing to feel him slam deep inside of me even though it almost hurts. I'm greedy for it now, all coyness and shyness completely faded away by my desire.

"Oh my god," I groan, leaning backward and arching my back as I ride him. Luca pulls up to a sitting position, tugging my legs around him so that we're straddling each other now, facing each other. He gently strokes my face before aggressively taking a fistful of my hair and holding me in place. I never thought I would love being manhandled like this, but everything Luca does is delicious. Perfect. With him, I can completely let go of my insecurities and anxieties and just *be*. At any moment, someone could come walking down the beach and find us here in the most vulnerable position. We could be discovered. A cop could show up. We could get in trouble for this.

But I don't care. It's worth the risk. Luca is worth every risk.

Even though I'm technically on top, Luca seizes control, thrusting into me while he holds me in place with both of his powerful hands firm on my hips. My second orgasm shatters over me and I start to scream, but Luca lets go of my hip to cover my mouth with his hand again.

"Such a good girl for me. I love feeling you come all over my cock, Serena. I want to make you feel so good," he snarls, never relenting in his fast, hard rhythm. I'm losing myself to the shivers of intense pleasure, the world melting away around me. All that matters is this: Luca and me. Together.

He picks up the pace while one of his hands slides around to cup my ass, giving it a hard slap as I bounce on his cock. "Oh, fuck," I moan. "Do that again. Please."

He spanks me harder, his other hand sliding down from my mouth to my throat, applying gentle, careful pressure. It's just enough to make me feel that edge of thrilling danger again, but never enough to scare or hurt me. He knows exactly what to do without even asking. He knows me.

"I knew you were a dirty girl underneath that sweet smile," he whispers, his breath warm against the shell of my ear. I shiver and lean into him as he gives my ass another hard slap. He's thrusting into me harder and harder, and I know I'm going to be aching later, but it doesn't matter. Nothing matters except for this. I couldn't stop even if I wanted to.

"You make me dirty," I respond breathlessly. "You make me feel like I've never felt before."

"And I'm going to keep you on your toes forever, *mia passerotta*. My sweet sparrow. I want to show you everything. Give you everything," he answers, giving my throat a momentary squeeze. The sensation fills me with adrenaline and spurs me to ride his cock faster, rolling my hips.

"I want you to come, Luca. Please," I beg, wrapping my arms around him.

"Anything for you, baby," he whispers.

And with that, he lets out a growl of pleasure, pumping his hot, sweet seed deep inside of me while I continue to bounce up and down on his cock, milking every last drop from him. He groans and leans in to kiss me hard, his tongue pushing into my mouth while my pussy fills with his cream. He thrusts a few more times and then stops, his hands roving down my back and up to my face, cupping my cheeks as we kiss. There's a passion, a desperation in his kisses, as though he's just as afraid of losing me as I am of losing him. We cling to each other this way for what has to be several minutes, just soaking up the glow of being together, the perfection of the moment.

Finally, we both start laughing softly, resting our foreheads against one another's while the ocean waves crash behind us in the fading light. "Now, time to take you home," Luca says.

My heart sinks for a moment until he adds, "I'm gonna cook you dinner. I think we've both earned that, don't you?"

I nod vigorously, overjoyed to spend more time with him. I never want to be out of his sight. I would follow him anywhere, and that thought doesn't scare me at all. Being vulnerable with Luca doesn't feel scary or forced—it feels *real*.

We gingerly get dressed, trying and probably failing to get all the sand off of our bodies and clothing as we make our way back to the car. On the drive home, we listen to a radio station playing old Sinatra and Elvis songs, the windows rolled down to let the evening air blow through our hair. Luca reaches across the console to take my hand, and I feel my heart swell. This is everything I've ever wanted. I never thought I could find this kind of bliss.

When we get to his apartment building and step out of the elevator onto his floor, there's a fluffy, fat cat meowing at us just as the doors open. Luca chuckles, shifting the groceries from the market to one arm and bending down to pick the cat up with his other arm, to my surprise. "*Ciao*, Grasso," he says, stroking the cat's head as it closes its yellow eyes and purrs.

"Whose cat is that?" I ask bemusedly.

"My neighbor, Mrs. Rodriguez— he's always sneaking out on her. Little bastard," he says, cooing fondly at the cat as he carries it toward the door next to his and knocks.

There's a pause, and then the tell-tale shuffle of slippered feet on carpet. The door rattles open to reveal a tiny, stooped older woman with snowy-white hair and big brown eyes. Her lipstick is slightly smudged, as though she'd wiped her mouth after forgetting she was wearing it. She's wearing a bathrobe over her floral-patterned pajamas, and when she realizes who's at the door, her wrinkled face splits into a genuine smile.

"Oh! Luca, you found Grasso!" she exclaims, reaching out to take the massive cat into her arms. It purrs happily, curling its tail around its body. "*Pobrecito*, he just gets so bored cooped up in here with me sometimes, he wants to go on an adventure. But when he gets out there, he's afraid. Thank you for bringing him back. I was just about to watch Jeopardy and go to bed without him!"

"No problem, Mrs. Rodriguez," Luca says, smiling. "I've brought you some groceries, too."

The woman's eyes light up. "Oh *gracias, mi querido*. You are too good to me."

"Just looking out for my favorite neighbor," Luca replies, handing her one of the bags. I can feel my heart swelling with pride and warmth. Luca puts an arm around me. "By the way, this is Serena. She's my—"

"*Tu novia! Que linda! Much gusto*," Mrs. Rodriguez gushes, pushing through the doorway to give me a hug, the cat still curled up in the crook of her arm.

"Oh, nice to meet you, too!" I reply, hugging her back. I give Luca a look over her shoulder and he grins, shrugging.

"I always tell Mister Luca, I say to him, 'Mister Luca! You need a woman to look after you! A handsome young man like you should not be spending so much time alone!'" she says, holding up one finger with mock sternness. "I am so happy for you, Mister Luca! You be sweet to Serena. I like her. And so does Grasso."

"I promise I'll be sweet," Luca says, nodding dutifully. He gives me a wink when she's not looking. Mrs. Rodriguez gives each of us a peck on the cheek, with Luca having to bend nearly perpendicular for her to reach, then she wishes us goodnight and retreats back into her apartment, still cooing to the cat.

Luca and I exchange expressions of amusement and then he takes me by the hand and leads me into his apartment. Once the door is shut, I burst out laughing.

"That was the cutest thing that's ever happened to me," I say genuinely. Luca chuckles and heads into the kitchen.

"She's a sweetheart. A little batty and forgetful sometimes, but she's a good neighbor. She bakes me a cake every April," Luca answers. I follow him into the kitchen, watching him take out ingredients for what looks to be a very impressive dinner.

"April? Why?" I ask, confused.

He shrugs and takes out a knife and cutting board to start chopping onions and tomatoes. "She thinks my birthday is in April. It's in September, but I don't have the heart to keep reminding her, so I just let it go."

"Aww," I reply, smiling. "You know, you've got to be one of the most surprising people I've ever met, Luca. Every time I think I have you all figured out, you go the other way entirely."

"Is that a bad thing?" he asks, glancing sidelong at me as I lean against the counter.

I grin and shake my head, walking over to kiss him on the cheek. "No. It's the best thing."

The rest of the evening I spend looking through his apartment, finally taking the time to look at the minimalist decor and little quirks that speak to his character and personality. He lives simply, without frills or opulence, but he lives well. Cleanly. I can see his appreciation for the nicer things, but he doesn't go over the top. There's a refurbished vintage record player in the corner of the living room, a set of dumbbells tucked into an alcove, a colorful blanket folded over the back of the couch.

I ask him about the blanket and he explains that it's a traditional pattern from the area of Italy he hails from. I run my fingers over it lovingly, as though I can get a glimpse of that version of Luca just from touching the vibrant threads. I want to know everything about him, but I know it's better to let him show me slowly, at his own pace. After all, I don't plan on ever losing him again, so we have all the time in the world to learn all those little things about each other. Sure enough, he explains that the blanket is one of the few things he was able to bring with him when he first came to the States to work as a carpenter under his uncle's tutelage. He's kept it all these years as a memento of home, reminding him where he comes from and who he is.

Dinner is, of course, another surprise. It's course after course of delicious, authentic Italian food. At first he tells me to just relax and let him do all the work, but I sidle up next to him in the kitchen and ask how I can help. As he goes along, he teaches me how to prepare everything, how to plate it.

"It's funny, my family is Italian but I never learned to cook," I tell him, slightly embarrassed. "When I was growing up, we always had a chef who came to the house to prepare most of our meals. Mom knew how to cook, but my dad didn't want her to have to lift a finger. She was spoiled, you know? And he wanted to keep spoiling her as much as he could. And then after my dad died...well, I just didn't get the chance to learn. We've had a lot of takeout over the years. Mom cooks sometimes, but I think it makes her kind of sad. A lot has had to change since Dad died, and I try to make it as easy on her as I can."

"You're a good daughter," Luca says, putting an arm around me and kissing the top of my head. "I know your father would be proud of you. Anybody would."

After an hour or so of working side-by-side in the kitchen, Luca shoos me away to the table so he can serve me. It's a parade of ridiculously rich, amazing food. Wine, prosciutto, fresh mozzarella, perfectly cooked pasta, massive shrimp cooked in a spicy red sauce, a tray of expertly cut and arranged fruit. By the second course I'm already stuffed, but I keep eating, unable to resist anything Luca brings to the table.

Over dinner, we talk about the old days, reminiscing about how young and stupid we used to be before the world knocked us off our feet.

We don't talk about that horrible thing that happened, and I'm more than okay with that. I don't want to think about it. Everything is so good right now, and I want it to stay this way as long as possible. I'm happy, truly happy, for the first time in a long, long while.

After dinner, we take our time cleaning up all the dishes together, just chatting and listening to the music playing from the record player. As I'm putting the wine bottle back into the rack, I notice a bottle of liquor in his cabinet that looks interesting. "Is that Campari?" I ask, pointing it out.

Luca walks over and takes it out, along with a bottle of Prosecco. "Ah, good eye. Here, let me make you our drink."

It's even better with the prosecco than the soda water, and immediately I feel lighter and happier than ever. "I feel like I should pinch myself," I laugh.

"I can assure you that the drink in your hand is real," Luca says coyly.

"I know that," I say, leaning into him and resting my cheek on his chest. "I just can't believe that you're real. That any of this is happening. It's too good to be true."

Luca tips my chin upward with his finger. He kisses me softly. "It's all real. I promise."

Finally, we both finish our drinks and sleepily make our way to his bed, where we curl up in each other's arms. I feel safe and wanted, like this is exactly where I'm supposed to be. Like I've been waiting my whole life for a moment this perfect. I've been dreaming about this, and now it's here.

And it's happening again—I'm falling for him. I've fallen for him.

For better or for worse, there's no denying it: I've fallen in love with a mafioso. Just like my mother.

I'm the disgraced mafia princess, following in my mother's footsteps.

Yet a pit in my stomach won't go away, it knows something has to go wrong. Something painfully soon.

"*B*uongiorno."

I open my eyes at the sound of Luca's velvety voice sending warm shivers down my body. His lips press against the back of my neck, making me twinge away from the ticklish sensation. His powerful arms are wrapped around me, with my head resting comfortably in the crook of his right elbow on the pillow. I have no idea what time it is, but I'm finding it really hard to care when there's a beautiful man pressed up against my back. I yawn and pull his left arm over me tighter, wiggling backward into him so that my ass is pushed against his crotch. He's so warm, radiating enough heat that I probably don't even need a blanket. He kisses my neck again and I giggle, shrugging my shoulders playfully.

"Good morning to you, too," I murmur, my

throat feeling scratchy as it always does when I first wake up. Despite the fact that I routinely get up early to go into Bathing Beauty, I am really, definitely not a morning person. Left to my own devices, I would gladly lie in bed until noon. I know today is a work day, and I'm dreading looking at the alarm clock on Luca's nightstand. I don't want to know. I want more time here in this warm, cozy heaven with the man I adore. The idea of getting out of this bed is completely repugnant to me right now.

"I should get up," I groan. "Gotta go to work."

"Mmm, that sounds terrible. Don't do that," Luca replies in a growly voice, pulling me closer and breathing hotly against the back of my neck. Goosebumps rise up along my arms and legs.

"You're making this very hard for me," I chide him, grinning. He rocks his hips forward and I can feel his massive shaft stiff against my ass.

"Oh, I think you're the one making it hard," he answers coyly.

"Who, me? I haven't done anything," I reply, with mock indignation. "I'm totally innocent."

Luca chuckles and sits up a little, leaning over to kiss the side of my neck and up to my cheek. He turns my face gently to kiss my lips, his cock still rock-hard against me.

"Oh no, I have morning breath," I protest weakly.

"You taste wonderful," he replies, kissing me again. "I don't care."

"You're going to make me late for work," I add, feeling myself start to give in. It's impossible to resist him, and every part of me wants desperately to stay in this bed.

"Well, we'd better get started then," he replies mischievously. Before I can even respond, he dives under the comforter, pushing it back out of the way as he exposes my body bit by bit. He sleeps naked, unsurprisingly, but I'm wearing one of his t-shirts, which is comically huge on me, and a pair of decidedly-unsexy black panties. Nothing special. I mean, they're not granny panties, but they're definitely not lingerie either. I feel my face flushing pink at the realization that Luca, the most blisteringly hot man I have ever been intimate with, is seeing this underwear on me.

"Sorry for the ugly undies," I mumble.

Luca, tugging them down my thighs to take them off, looks up at me with a wry smile. "First of all, you look fantastic in everything. Second of all, it doesn't matter anyway because they're about to come off. Lingerie is nice, but I think we both know I prefer you without anything on at all. You're the gift. I don't care about the wrapping paper."

I can't stop the grin that plasters itself on my face. I've never met anyone so good at putting my mind at ease. It's like magic. He just melts away all my anxiety, all those years of stress and fear. He cuts away all that bullshit to get to me— the real me. The version of myself I never thought I could find again. And it's liberating.

Luca drops the offending panties over the side of the bed and pushes my thighs wide open, kneeling down between my legs. I inhale sharply in anticipation as he leans in and gently begins to suck at my clit, his tongue flicking over it while one of his fingers slides inside of me. Fuck, I'm already wet. All it takes is Luca's presence to make me give in. I can't resist.

"Oh my God," I murmur, my eyes closing and my head falling backward onto the pillow. My hands instinctively reach down to comb through Luca's hair, and before long my hips are rolling, bucking up to meet him. He knows just how to work my clit, just how to angle the tip of his finger inside me to reach that little bundle of nerves that makes me weak. He's an expert, like he's been studying my body for years or something. I don't know how he knows, but he does. He just *knows*.

He groans, his finger sliding in and out up against that special spot faster and faster. I fling my arms outward to grasp at the bedsheets, gritting my teeth as my pleasure mounts to a climax.

Just before my orgasm hits, Luca backs off, grabs me by the hips, and flips me onto my stomach. Then he pulls me to my knees and rubs the head of his thick shaft against my slick opening, sliding over my sensitive clit. I back into him, desperate for that delicious friction, but he grabs my hips and holds me in place.

"Please, Luca," I whimper. "I want to come."

He lets out a growly kind of chuckle and says, "Oh, you're going to come, sweetheart. But only when I'm good and ready for it."

A shiver runs down my spine and I feel myself getting even wetter. I never expected to be the kind of woman who likes to be bossed around and dominated in bed, especially after what I went through years ago. But with Luca, it's different. I want him to tell me what to do. I want him to use me however he wants to, because I know he would never hurt me. I can trust him to push me right to the very edge and then bring me back over and over again, making it feel so good every time.

"So wet for me, Serena," he says softly, his voice gravelly and rough. I can tell this is taking all of his self-restraint, too. And the thought that he's struggling to keep it together, that he wants me just as badly as I want him, makes me feel powerful and desired.

"I want you inside me," I beg him, twisting to peer back at him. He's a formidable sight, all muscle and smooth skin, with that impossibly handsome face. Those flashing green eyes. And then, he smiles at me. A devilish grin. He knows just how badly I need this, and he's going to give it to me.

He slides the full length of his cock along my wet

slit, making me tremble. I'm so sensitive right now, all my nerves on fire, just hovering over the edge. Then he gives my ass a hard slap. I cry out, shuddering with the mingled pain and pleasure.

"Good girl," he says quietly, now circling the tip of his cock around my wet opening, teasing me.

"Please, I need you to fill me up, Luca," I plead. I'm aching for his cock.

"Oh, I'm going to, *mia passerotta*. I'm going to fill you up and fuck you hard. But I don't want you to come until I say so, *si?*" he explains, keeping his tone even-keeled even though I can hear that husky need in his voice.

"Whatever you say," I answer, grinding back against him. I'm a little scared that I won't be able to hold on— I'm already so close. He has me dangling over the edge, and I just know that the second his cock is inside of me, I'll be a goner.

And then, it happens. He grabs my hips and pushes his cock deep inside me, penetrating me to the hilt. I can feel my pussy clenching around him and I cry out, grabbing for the pillow to hold myself steady. I'm trying so hard to keep myself from coming. I want to do what he told me to do.

"Don't come yet, baby," he says, even as his hips start to move and his cock slides in and out of me while he reaches around my thigh to gently rub my clit with his finger. By now, I'm an incoherent mess.

Every last thread of my focus is centered on not giving in, not climaxing. But it's so hard.

"Oh God," I groan as he starts to fuck me deeper, but slower. "Luca, I-I'm gonna come, I can't take it. It feels so fucking good!"

"Yeah? You want to come for me, sweetheart? You want to come all over my cock?" he teases me, circling my clit with his finger and sending shock-waves of unbearable pleasure through me.

"Please, oh fuck," I whimper. He slaps my ass again, hard.

"You want me to fuck you harder, Serena?" he asks.

"I need it, I need you," I answer breathlessly. I'm hanging on by a mere thread. "Please!"

And with that, he starts to thrust harder, his cock hammering at my g-spot while his finger works my clit, fucking me hard and fast. "Are you ready? I know you want to come."

"Oh God! Please, I need it!" I cry out, my fingers twisting in the sheets.

"Come for me, baby. Come all over my cock. Now."

Instantly, my body seizes up in an overwhelming rush of pleasure. Wave after wave of electric bliss rolls over me and I let out an involuntary shriek, feeling my pussy pulsing intensely around his cock. Luca doesn't let up for even a second, fucking me harder and faster until I'm coming again and again, lost in a sea of extreme pleasure.

"Good girl, very good," he groans, and I can tell he's gritting his teeth, trying so hard to keep his own climax in check. I decide to take business into my own hands. He's not the only one who can play at this game. I begin to roll my hips back, impaling myself on his cock hard and fast, clenching as tightly as I can.

"It's. Your. Turn," I manage to mumble, and I can tell by his increasingly erratic thrusts that he's about to blow. He's almost there. The fact that I have this power to make this beautiful, amazing man feel so good is intoxicating.

"Fuck, Serena," Luca groans. "Just like that."

He thrusts a few more times quickly and sharply and then holds me still, his fingertips digging into my hips as he shoots his thick honey deep inside me. His deep voice thrums through my body as he cries out, and he shudders through his orgasm.

We're both still panting as I feel him lean forward to kiss a gentle line up the arch of my back before withdrawing. We fall on our backs side by side, and his hand finds mine underneath the tangle of sheets. I look over at him, beaming uncontrollably, to see an identical look of bliss on his face. Warmth. Every-thing about Luca is comfortable. Everything about him feels like home.

"Well, that was definitely worth being late to

work for," I laugh, turning over to get my phone from the nightstand. The battery is nearly dead, as I forgot to bring my charger last night, but it can still show me the time. Nine-thirty-eight, and then my phone dies.

"Shit," I mumble, wriggling out of bed and whipping Luca's huge t-shirt off. I hop into the bathroom, pulling on my socks which I'm pretty sure are inside out, but that's a problem for future me to sort out. "I don't have clean clothes!" I call out, staring around the bathroom in a mild panic.

Luca comes shuffling in behind me, totally naked and unreserved. He wraps his arms around me and presses a kiss to my cheek. "You can borrow one of my shirts again."

"Uh-huh, and it'll look like I'm a grifter who just wandered into the shop one day," I giggle, rolling my eyes. Then, I get an idea. "Actually, could you bring me your biggest, longest, most stretched-out shirt?"

Luca gives me a skeptical smirk but nods. "I feel like that's the opposite of what you'd want, but your wish is my command." He steps into the walk-in closet attached to the bathroom suite and starts poring through his surprisingly meticulous wardrobe.

"Any luck?" I ask, reluctantly slipping back into yesterday's bra, panties, and leggings. I can't just walk into the shop wearing the same dress as yesterday. Too obvious. Even if nobody else notices, I would still feel icky all day.

"Uhh, how do you feel about, um, vintage?" Luca says, making me laugh.

"How vintage?"

"Let's just say I had to dig back through my sort of nostalgic section of clothing for this one," he explains, giving me an apologetic shrug. "All my clothing from recent years has been tailored. I have a guy. So there's not a lot of wildly oversized stuff in here anymore."

I hold my hand out. "Alright. Just give it to me. Let's see."

He hesitantly hands over a faded, well-worn gray t-shirt with some kind of brand logo that has nearly been washed blank by the years. It's a little threadbare, but it will do. I tug it on, then knot the hem at one hip so that it falls almost like a stretched-out, slightly off-kilter shift dress.

Luca laughs. "Wow. That is real ingenuity."

"Shut up," I giggle, swatting at him playfully. "Well, no time to really do my makeup now."

"Can you do it in the car?"

I raise an eyebrow. "While driving? No, I value my life just a *little* more than that."

"As a passenger, of course. I'm driving you to work," he says, matter-of-factly.

"You sure? I could always get a cab."

"I'm going to work with you anyway, so we might as well carpool. Save the earth and all that," he adds, emerging from the walk-in closet again, this time fully dressed and looking like a million bucks. He's only wearing a white button-down, black pants, and gray blazer, but he looks like some kind of secret agent about to crack a case or steal a diamond or something.

"Wow, way to show me up," I comment, crossing my arms and eyeing him up and down.

"Well, I do have the advantage of my entire personal wardrobe here," he says, walking over to envelop me in his arms. He smells wonderful, like a mix of fancy cologne and his own particular, musky, delicious scent. "And besides, you make everyone in every room you walk into look terrible by comparison. Anyway, let's get you to work. Bath emergencies wait for no man."

We pile into his car and head out, with the mid-morning sun beaming joyfully overhead. Everything is so bright and crystal-clear today, with the kind of bright blue skies and puffy cotton-ball clouds that seem better suited for a painting than real life. It's hard to determine whether the beauty of the world is actually intensified today, or if I'm just seeing it this way because of the gorgeous man beside me in the driver's seat.

"This is gonna be a good day," I say softly. "I can feel it."

"Every day with you is a good day," Luca adds, squeezing my thigh gently.

As soon as the words leave his mouth, there is a sudden flash of gray across the windshield and Luca hits the brakes. I look out my window to see that there is a pillar of smoke blowing down from an alleyway next to us at the stop light. "What the hell?" I murmur, rolling down my window to look.

"Smoke," Luca says.

"From where?" I ask, squinting into the occasional clear spots. Then it hits me.

I know where we are.

Before the car can start rolling again, I unlock and hop out the door, taking off down the alleyway. Luca somehow manages to pull over and park, halfway on the sidewalk, and run after me. I burst through the alleyway and across the street to stand in front of the source of the fire.

Room With A View is in flames, a clamoring crowd gathering in a messy semicircle out into the road. There's a fire truck out front, its siren wailing while the firefighters run in and out of the burning building. I dart around, looking for Nico or Rafaela, my heart pounding in my chest. Luca catches up to me and takes my hand, pointing to an area closer to the front line. Police are blocking the crowd from getting much closer, and luckily Luca can see better over the crowd from his height than I can.

"Up there!" he says, pulling me along behind him as we push through the crowd.

I shove past lots of angry spectators, caring only about locating my friends. If they were inside when the place caught on fire…

"Rafaela!" I shout, catching sight of my best friend and wiggling past a couple of cops to reach her. There's ash on her skin and she's crying, but there's a hardened expression on her face. Rafaela is not the kind of girl to cry over just anything. She's incredibly tough, and even with the tears clearing a path down her sooty cheeks, she looks about ready to fight someone.

She turns to pull me into a hug, and I can tell she's been needing this. As strong as she is, I know that she can be vulnerable, too, with people she trusts. Like me.

"Oh, Serena, it's fucking horrible. Everything we have—had—it's all gone. This bar was our every-thing. I-I don't know how this happened. But I have an idea *who*," she says, her eyes flashing with anger.

"Are you okay? Where's Nico? Is there anybody inside?" I ask, panicked.

She shakes her head. "Not anymore. The fire-fighters got everyone out, but two of our boarders are already en route to the hospital. It—it doesn't look good," she adds, looking horrified. "But Nico is over there. The cops keep trying to talk to him but he doesn't want to say anything to them yet."

I glance around her to see Nico and Luca huddled together, several feet away from the line of policemen. Nico looks unscathed, and I silently thank the heavens that both of my friends are okay. I link arms with Rafaela and walk her away from the cops, trying to look unobtrusive.

"So, what do you think happened?" I ask quietly. She shakes her head, blinking back tears.

"I think it was one of those fucking gangs, *chica*. Probably the same shitheads who graffitied your shop and hurt those dogs," she says bitterly. "I just feel like this is my fault. I should've been here more. I've just been so distracted with school lately and leaving Nico to look after the Room by himself. I should've done something ages ago. *Mierda*. I fucked up."

I give her another tight hug. "No. No. You can't blame yourself for this, Raf. You're not a superhero. Nobody could've prevented this."

She sighs heavily and tucks her hair behind her ears like she does when she's nervous. She fixes me with a sorrowful look. "I just know there's something else going on here. *No sé*. I think—I think I'm a little out of my pay grade, you know? Like, maybe I should've just stayed in Harlem. Maybe I'm reaching too far trying to make it in this neighborhood."

I squeeze her hand supportively. "Hey, don't say that. You've achieved so much. Seriously, you know what I said a minute ago about you not being a superhero? I was wrong about that. You *are* a superhero, Raf. And you're gonna get through this just fine. Like you always do. Just don't blame yourself, okay? It's not like you set the fire."

"How do you know I didn't burn it down for insurance money or whatever?" she pipes up, a flicker of that old attitude flaring through.

I grin.

"There's my girl. Just, not so loud, the cops might hear. Now, let's go find Luca and Nico and regroup, okay?"

We weave through the crowd, gingerly avoiding eye contact with the cops. Rafaela is right. I may not know the details, but I'm pretty sure this fire is no accident. Somebody did this, and I have a feeling things are about to get worse before they get better. When we reach the guys, Nico puts his arms around Rafaela and points out a man in slightly nicer clothing than the rest of the crowd.

"Babe, that's a detective. We're gonna have to make a statement to him. No big deal. Just tell the truth, and nothing else. Everything is gonna be fine," he tells her. Then, looking at Luca and me, he gives a quick nod. "Thanks for being here."

"Of course," I say.

The two of them make their way down the street to the detective and Luca turns to me, giving me a quick kiss before staring into my eyes emphatically. "We need to get away from here. Now."

"What?"

"We're being watched. I'm sure of that. Let's go. Back to the car."

We quietly sneak back through the masses and down the alleyway to the car. Once we're inside and driving away, Luca continues. "The two men who were injured are mafiosi. They're in critical care. I do not expect that they will live through this."

"Oh my God," I murmur, my head starting to spin. "So, this is a *gang* thing."

"Essentially," he agrees. "The Cleaners are responsible for this, no doubt. I don't know if you were aware of this, but your friends have been running a kind of halfway house there. Mafia guys in hiding, a place for newcomers to blend into the city, a place to lay low when things get heated. Well, they just got too hot."

"How in the world… are you serious? Room With A View. A mafia den," I mutter, raking my fingers back through my hair. I never would have expected it. Rafaela can't possibly be involved with this stuff. But Nico—well, I don't know as much about him as I probably should.

"Nico is one of our guys. A casual. Low profile. But he does what he can," Luca explains. "This is a hit by the Cleaners. Everything up until now has just been a test run, trying out our limits, making plans. Now, the war is started. There's no telling how long the bar has been compromised. They could've had eyes on us for months, just waiting for the right time to strike."

I think about our night together in one of the boarding rooms and my stomach turns. All this time, they could've been watching us. Even that night, maybe.

"So, what the hell are we gonna do?" I ask, feeling like my entire world has been turned upside down. Luca glances over at me, those green eyes lighting up in the sunshine.

"We're going to bite back, of course."

"You're sure?" I say into my cellphone, a frown on my face. I'm standing in front of a counter in the back of Bathing Beauty, looking at a row of about four small TVs with camera feeds hooked up to them.

All is clear on the video feed, but as I listen to Diego over the phone, my frown only deepens. He's been helpful in giving me updates as they come in. The heat might be turning up with the Cleaners, but at least I can rely on my own allies to keep me informed. But the news isn't good.

"I see. I'll update the men. Keep your ass safe out there," I end the call while running a hand through my hair. The piece of news I just got is the worst yet. Just as I'm about to make a call to the men I have patrolling the block, I hear the door to the back room open, and Serena's face appears in the crack.

"Hey, you alive back here?" she asks, glancing at the flickering screens. I smile warmly at her. She's been incredibly strong through all this. Her store has practically become the front lines of a battleground she never wanted to set foot on, but she still manages to keep the doors of the shop open as if nothing's the matter.

"As far as I know," I say, and I stride over to her to pull her the rest of the way into the room and wrap my hands around her hips. "How's business?"

"It's going," she says, tilting her head to the side. "I'm not exactly advertising that there are mobsters patrolling the streets, so it's business as usual."

"Maybe you should try that," I say with a playful smile. "Think about it: 'Bathing Beauty, so fresh it's a crime.'"

She bites her lip and stares at me lovingly. "I...think we should leave the marketing to me."

"Probably," I say, and I plant a kiss on her forehead. She giggles and hugs me after a quick glance to make sure the front of the store is quiet, then looks back up at me with a slightly more serious look.

"Really though, you look kind of uneasy. Is everything alright? The streets have been quiet all day."

I pause, glancing down at my phone, and I decide it's best to be totally upfront with her. It's never done her any favors to leave her in the dark about what's happening in her own life.

"That was Diego on the phone," I say. "We knew

the Cleaners had cops in their pocket—that's not unusual for any organization." Serena nods slowly, and I go on. I squeeze her hips gently and give her the most reassuring look I can. "It goes deeper than I thought. They have someone on the take who's higher up than I thought—a detective."

Serena's eyes widen. "A detective?"

"Detective Will Price. He's a piece of shit," I say, and that's something I can say sincerely. "He's been crooked from the start, but he deals with drug runners and traffickers—the kind of man that helps scum like the Cleaners thrive."

"Is he going to be a problem for us?" Serena asks, but the look in her eyes tells me she already knows the answer. I run my hand through her hair, letting my strong fingers play gently with her golden locks.

"We don't know yet," I say. "Diego knows he's in the area, and he's making it easier for the Cleaners to do what they want, but none of our men have been in touch with him."

Serena nods, and I hug her close to me, kissing her on the top of the head. "I'd take on the whole NYPD before I let any danger come too close to you, Serena. We'll cross this bridge when we come to it. For now, we have enough on our plate."

Serena looks up at me, pink lips smiling, and the sight of her smiling softly at me is enough to give me all the strength in the world. "I'm glad you're here, whatever happens," she says, and then she steps away from me, heading back into the front. "It's about closing time, so I'm gonna start wrapping things up out front."

"I've got an eye on you," I say with a wink and a nod back to the CCTV feeds, and she blushes before heading back to the front.

Half an hour later, Serena is closing the blinds on the windows of the shop, and soon there's nothing but the lights keeping the shop bright inside. I step into the front of the shop as she closes up some of the displays and finishes cleaning a few surfaces off, and she turns to quirk an eyebrow at the two long objects in my hand.

"What are those?"

I hold up the two sheaths, then set them on the front counter. "Remember the tussle on the boardwalk the other night?"

"Sure."

"I wasn't kidding when I said you handled yourself well," I say, unbuttoning the sheaths and taking out the objects inside. I pull out two rubber knives, holding them up to show them to her. She cocks her head to the side.

"Are those…?"

"Not real," I say with a grin, "they're rubber. Training knives. Me and my boys are going to keep you safe, but if things get too hot," I say, stepping closer to her and looking down at her, "I won't let my *passerotta* be caught defenseless."

She looks up at me silently for a few moments, then down at the hilt of the rubber knife I'm offering her. She takes it and feels its weight, getting a firm grip on it. The way she holds it tells me she'll be a natural.

"I got lucky on the boardwalk," she says, brandishing the knife around a little experimentally. "I don't think I could go toe-to-toe with someone like that guy you took down."

"It shouldn't come to that," I say, stepping around behind her and adjusting her stance, bending her elbow just so and turning her hips. "But just in case, a little extra luck doesn't hurt," I say with a smile down at her.

"By 'luck' you mean a few inches of steel, right?" she says with a coy smile, and I grin.

"That helps, too."

"Okay," she says, taking a deep breath to relax as she tosses the knife up and down in her hand a few times and catching it. "I'm game. No problem. Soap shop owner and knife-fighter. I can make that work. Where do you want to practice?"

"This will do," I say, looking around the front of the shop. She raises her eyebrows at me, and I carefully slide some of the tables in the center out of the way to give us a little more room.

"Are you sure? Going out back might be a little more convenient."

"You don't get convenient space in a fight," I say,

"and besides, unless you changed your mind about branding this place as a mob front, I don't think a knife-fight out back will be the best public image."

"Fair enough," she says, and she sinks back into the stance that I showed her. As I finish moving the tables, I look at her and smile. Her body is good at remembering the posture.

"That's good," I say, "managing your own center of gravity is half the fight. You're light, you'll need to use that to your advantage a lot."

"How do I do that?"

I square up with her, holding my own knife at the ready. "I'll show you step by step. I'll move in, and I'll show you how to move yourself so you can use my weight against me. You might not be able to push me around, but I can't lift myself. Like this…"

I start showing her the basics of knife-fighting, the sounds of our feet scuffling around the shop the only noise besides my instruction.

Serena proves to be a good student. She seems naturally able to move where I tell her, and half the time, she anticipates what I'm going to tell her. I can see her athletic youth shining through, and her muscles serve her well.

I show her the basic amoves, how to keep an enemy from using his height to his advantage, how to move quickly and effortlessly to match an enemy's better reach. I have to be careful not to run into the displays in the shop, but it's good practice in using the limited space.

While I teach her how to use her body, it isn't long before she starts making use of the knife to fight back with the movements. "That's good," I tell her as I parry one of her quick jabs, "let the movement come first, and the attacks can follow. That's the trick—they'll see you coming from a mile away if you come in to attack. Let him come to you and make him regret it."

She nods and slips around me to make a stab at my kidney, and I roll around to pull her arm behind her back, gently. I tap her on the collar with the knife, and she huffs, getting back into position. "Again."

She gets into the swing of things fast, and soon, we're going back and forth at a steady rhythm, our pace only getting more regular. I move in, she moves around me, and I catch her.

After a few minutes of practicing a set of about five maneuvers, I finally feel a tap of the rubber on my kidney, and she gives a triumphant little laugh, skipping back and smiling brightly. "Ha!"

"Not bad," I admit, grinning proudly at her. "Now do it again."

Soon, the sound of our heavy breathing is in the air as we run through the routines until I feel that they're coming almost unconsciously to her. She moves in like a viper, and she's starting to learn my openings. I don't fight people as small as her, so she soon finds openings in my defenses even I didn't know were there. She's impressive.

And I know that the guys she'd potentially be fighting are no different than me. They don't fight women like her. They simply…

I shake my mind of the thought. I can't go back to that night. I can't let myself think of what would happen if I didn't show up.

I parry another stab, but Serena gets too bold soon, and when she tries to dart under my arms and bring the knife up to my throat, I catch her by the wrist and whirl her around, holding the knife to her own throat with her back pressed against my front.

We freeze there for a moment, our heavy breathing filling the air, and I let the rubber blade brush against her skin.

"Playing with fire, *carina*," I whisper into her ear. She smiles and twists away from my grip, twirling the blade in her hand a moment before darting in again. This time, she gets up under me, and I catch her before she can draw her knife across my thigh, but she shifts her weight the way I showed her, and I go down to one knee to keep her from getting out of my grasp.

I bring my knife down to her throat, but at the same moment that my rubber touches her neck, I feel a prod at my gut from her knife.

We look into each other's faces a moment, both of us 'dead' by the other's hand.

"You learn fast," I say in a low tone, between breaths.

She's panting as well, her skin glistening in the light of the shop. "Have to, with a big brute like you coming after me."

"It'll take more than that to keep me from coming after you," I say, my voice lowering into a husk, and before she can respond, I descend upon her and press my lips to hers.

Surprised, she moans into the kiss, her heart still beating fast from the exercise, and I soon drop my knife and use one hand to lower myself over her while the other slides up under her neck to lift it ever so slightly into my kiss. She squirms under me, and I hear her rubber hit the ground too as her hands slide up to my shirt, feeling the tight muscles under the thin fabric.

I let her explore me, her fingers going from my swollen pecs down to my abs. She feels my wounds, but the dull twinge of pain is nothing to me with Serena in my hands. The pleasure she gives me is worth a fresh gunshot wound. She wraps her arms around me, and I feel her ankles go around my waist as she clings to me tight, our lips still locked.

I stand up with her wrapped around me, and with no patience left in my body, I take her to the front counter and set her down on it. My hands run down her sides before they reach her leggings, and I roughly jerk them down as she wiggles to help them slide off.

"Spread your legs," I order her, and she puts her hands back to lean on as she obeys, color flushing into her cheeks. The fabric reveals her lips, looking as swollen as needy as ever, and I feel my hunger for them overwhelm me.

I kneel down and run my hands over her smooth thighs, gripping the sensitive skin. She seems so delicate, even though we've just spent nearly an hour teaching her how to be all the more deadly.

She's deadlier to others, at least. To me, Serena is already my fatal poison.

I lean forward and breathe in her scent, letting my breath wash over her pussy, and I hear her gasp as she grips the table, knuckles white already. I breathe along her slit, taunting her by coming so close, so very close to touching her, and when my stubble finally grazes her skin, she whimpers, trying to close her legs.

My strong, gentle grip holds them apart, though, and she pushes her hips in a little, begging for me, needing me.

"Do you think you've earned this?" I ask, teasing her with a smile curling on my lips.

"Fuck, Luca, don't do this to me!" she whines. Her face smiles, but as I let another quick breath roll over her lips, it fades into desperate need.

"Am I torturing you, *carina*?" I ask, using my thumbs to tease her inner thighs before I run my mouth along them, teeth grazing them, five o'clock shadow teasing them.

"I've been thinking about this all day," Serena whimpers, "fuck, I wanted you to bend me over the counter since you walked in this morning."

"That's not very professional," I growl, and I wait for her to open her mouth to reply before I let my tongue out over her cunt.

She tenses immediately, and I feel the beginnings of her honey on the tip of my tongue as it travels from the bottom of her slit, deep into her lips, then up to the tip of that sensitive nub that's so very desperate for attention. I've teased her, but she's done well tonight—she deserves a proper reward.

I let loose, my tongue attacking her clit relentlessly. Its tip rolls back and forth over it, up and down, rhythmically, slowly at first. But as I build up a little speed, her jaw hangs open, and I feel her hands go to my head to get a grip. My hair pokes through her tight fingers as she holds onto me, and I feel her honey start to flood my face freely. Her body is uninhibited—it knows what it wants, and what it wants is my mouth.

I let my teeth graze her as I lavish her clit with attention, and each time they touch, I feel her tighten her grip, hear another gasp escape her pretty mouth.

My tongue moves back and forth, darting in and out to kiss her swollen nub, and I feel her start to buck her hips ever so slightly, rhythmically, needfully. I hear her gasps start to get more regular, more like a steady pace of whining breaths, and her fingers start to tighten on my head.

"Oh, oh, oh Luca, Luca, fuck!" she gasps, breathing in sharply as my name dances across her tongue, and I feel her whole body convulse and tighten as she comes for me, hard. Exercise always makes your body more ready for release, more needy to get rid of all that tension. I feel my face getting so wet as she lets out a wonderfully satisfied sigh, head falling back as she struggles to keep herself up, the poor thing.

I don't give her a moment to breathe, though. I keep lavishing her clit, and soon, I let my tongue roll over the rest of her pussy, too. It runs deep, drawing out as much honey as she serves up to me. I'm devouring her, and it isn't long before she tenses up again, orgasm crashing through her frame.

Her beauty might be my weakness, but the things I can make her body do is my secret weapon against her.

I rise up to face her panting expression, and her hazy eyes meet mine, full of so much need that I haven't tapped yet. I smile and let out a rumbling groan from my chest as I wrap my hand around the back of her neck and pull her into a kiss. Her wetness gets all over her face as we messily embrace each other, and she brings her hips forward to push against my black pants.

"Baby, you're so wet," I groan between sloppy kisses. "You weren't kidding."

"We're making such a goddamn mess," she half-laughs as I bring my mouth down to her neck to tickle her with kisses, getting more aggressive and nipping her, nearly biting her as the scent of her drives me wild.

"You make me a mess, baby," I whisper, my accent coming out more thick as I get almost dizzy in the heady scent of her lust. "Now I'm going to give you what you want."

Without further warning, I seize her hips and slide her forward, smiling wickedly as I loom over her. I pick her up with ease and flip her around so that her ass is facing me, and I bend her over. She gasps as I press on her back, and I let my hands run down to her ass. I squeeze her, a low growl escaping me as I look on her body. We aren't naked, we're still in the clothes we've gone through the day in. It makes it feel so sudden, so wanton, and my cock grows at the sight of her with her pants pulled down, exposed and vulnerable before me.

While her ass taunts me, I unbutton my pants and let my thick shaft spring free. I stroke it, letting my fingers play across the veiny girth and up to the bulging crown. It's so stiff and ready for her that I could explode at any moment. But I want to savor her. I pick her hips up to help her get to just the right angle, and I slide my cock to caress her soaking-wet lips.

She whimpers and pushes her hips back, desperate for me to fill her. I bring my crown to her lips and just barely penetrate her, letting the stiff tip wander around her lips like my tongue did just moments ago.

"Oh, fuck you," she whimpers, "God, I need you in me so bad, Luca!"

"Every night I don't have you sheathed on my cock, Serena," I whisper in a husk, "I feel like something's missing."

"Glad it's not just me," she gasps, looking back at me with heavily lidded eyes, her mouth hanging open and her cheeks blushing.

"Better make up for lost time, then," I say, and seizing her hips, I enter her from behind.

The gasp that escapes her lips is a sound I could never get tired of. I feel her inner walls tight against my cock. My shaft pulses within her, as if roaring in triumph at being united with the depths it was meant to be in.

I thrust forward, and she arches her back for me, even as I hold her up. Her golden hair spills over her shoulders and hangs down as she grips the other end of the counter. This place is her livelihood, and I'm fucking her hard within it. I feel a ripple of pleasure run up my body as I thrust further up into her, rocking back and forth and caressing her ass with each thrust.

Serena never asked for any of this to fall into her lap. She never asked to get attacked by a mob, dragged back into a life she came so close to escaping. I still know in the back of my mind that this is wrong, that it's irresponsible to be with her like this…

But the one thing she did ask for is me. And I can't deny my girl anything.

I hear her gasp as I thrust hard against her upper walls, sliding against the slick, wonderfully hot sheath that is her pussy. My cock swells within her, and I grunt as I pound her fiercer, harder, faster.

Her gasping is getting louder, and she's letting whimpers and cries of pleasure flow more freely. I know if she's much louder, someone outside might hear, but I don't care. I'm taking her, *now*, and that's what she wants—that's all that matters right now.

She clenches her pussy, and I slap her on the ass with a sound that rings through the whole room. My heavy balls swing under her, and the sounds of our flesh slapping and grinding keeps me red-hot, harder than ever, and my whole body feels poised.

She gets a rhythm going, tightening each time I slide in, making it all the sweeter when I touch that sweet spot far within her, and she lets out an exasperated gasp. As the orgasm floods my cock, her strength gives out, and I have to hold her hips up entirely on my own as she loses her grip on the counter for a moment.

"I've got you, *dolcezza*," I growl, hoisting her up into me, and the way I bring her to sink onto my cock sends a shiver up her back that even I can feel. She stifles a yelp that sounds almost like a musical note, and the next moment, she's back on her hands, pushing her pert ass back onto me, and I do not hold back.

I feel tension building up within me, but I'm not ready to let it go just yet. There's a monster within me that wants me to give into my instincts, to let loose hard and fast with abandon. But I'm no beast— I'm a man who will please his woman well, and I'll finish when I'm good and done fucking her.

I start bucking into her like a piston, my rhythm unstoppable like a machine, and her shoulders freeze as her cunt clenches. She starts to look back at me, but her eyes are shut tight and her mouth hangs open. I can feel pressure in her body winding up like a spring. I don't let up, every muscle in my body driving forward with unstoppable heat.

And just before her spring uncoils, I withdraw from her.

The whimper she lets out his heartbreaking, and her eyes open wide, begging me for mercy. "Fuck, Luca, I'm so close!"

"And I'm going to take you there," I growl, slapping her on the ass before I pull her leggings the rest of the way down until they're off her legs, leaving her bare from the waist down in her own shop, but for the oversized shirt. I take a handful of her hair and gently tug her back until she's standing up in front of me. "Hold on tight."

Without warning, I sit up on the counter, my cock standing upright like a mast. Serena looks at it hungrily for a moment before I seize her by the waist and lift her up. She makes a surprised squeak as I lift her up high, but when she sees the waiting cock below her, a bead of precum glistening above the sheen of her honey she spreads her legs and starts to wrap them around me.

"I want to look into your eyes when we come," I say thickly, and I let her sink to the hilt onto my hot, throbbing cock. My precum mixes with her wetness. The sound of her loving sigh as our sexes are united again is like honey to my ears.

She rests her hands on my shoulders and looks down at me, but I'm supporting her hips with my hands. She's safe in my grasp, and I can see in her eyes just how much she trusts me.

When I start rocking my hips, it takes her no time to join right in with the rhythm again, as if we hadn't paused at all. Serena bites her lip and knits her brow, and her flushed face tells me she's using the last of her strength to work with me as I rock forward, my cock harder and stronger than ever.

My Serena feels like nothing I've ever felt in my lap, my cock perfectly sheathed deep inside her. Every time I help her rock forward and her hips dig deeper for more, we're both finding parts of her that we've never felt, feeling sensations only we can unlock in each other.

In a bold move, she reaches to the hem of her shirt, letting go of the support of my shoulders for a moment. She pulls it up over her head, but she manages to keep balance on my cock, even though I don't stop rocking and bucking up into her. It takes her a few moments, but she gets it off and shakes her gorgeous locks of golden hair out before tossing it to the side. Instinct kicks in, and I reach up to unhook her bra, which comes off next.

She exposes her breasts to me and rests her arms around my shoulders again. It brings her close enough that I reach behind her with one hand and put my teeth to her breast. She leans her chin against my head as I lick her nipple until it's soaked, then suck it between my teeth and toy with it more. I give both her breasts attention, never breaking pace for a moment, and her whole body begins to coil up in ecstatic tension once again.

"Luca...oh, Luca," she murmurs, almost chanting as I rock her into a trance-like pace, pumping up and rocking with her, my cock getting stiffer as pressure mounts in me, too. I feel her nails dig into my back, and I know it's time.

I pick up the pace, pounding up into her, any hope of finesse or precision getting thrown to the wind. My pounding gets savage, relentless, and I hold one hand in her hair in a fist while the other grips her hips, pulling her into me.

She breathes in sharply, and she starts losing control of her body as the pleasure wells up into an unstoppable flood. Just as she reaches the peak of the cliff, I let myself go. The incredible tension in my cock unlocks, floodgates opening as my seed bursts up into her at the same time as she lets out a scream of ecstasy, her whole pussy tightening and pulsing around me as I throb into her.

It isn't until the second pulse of hot seed that I realize a loud groan is escaping my lips too, and as we finish together, we melt into each other, soaking-wet sexes locked into each other, and the tide of bliss rocks us into a daze as I bring the rocking rhythm slower, slower, until we're just sitting there, sweating on the counter of her shop, seed spilling out her pussy onto my balls.

It's a mess, but god, I wouldn't trade that moment for the world.

Finally, she pushes herself up, shivering as my still-stiff cock twitches inside her, and her glowing face looks down at me like an angel. We're both at a loss for words. Smiles play across our faces, and we finally start laughing, bringing our foreheads together to rest on each other until we settle down and kiss playfully.

"So, do all knife-fights end like this?" she asks.

"Of course," I joke, grinning. "At least, the ones with us will."

"I might have to get more serious about this, then," she says, and I brush a lock of hair out of her eyes as I smile up at her before picking her up off my cock and setting her down gently. She wobbles a moment, but keeps her balance, putting her hands on her hips proudly.

I wet my lips as I button my pants back up. "You'd better get your clothes back on unless you want round two to be sooner than you think."

She raises her eyebrows and tilts her head to the side. "Oh yeah? Maybe we should take it back to my place."

I smile wickedly, but I put up a hand for her to wait as I move to the back room. "Hold that thought. I have something for you."

She blinks, confused, and calls after me, "Uh, seriously though, if gun practice is next then I might need a breather."

"Later," I say as I pull out my bag and dig through it to get two little black boxes. One is a long rectangle, the other is a square. I carry them back into the main room to find Serena pulling her leggings back on. She peers at the little boxes curiously.

"What are those?"

"A couple of things I want you to have," I say, setting them down on the counter. "You know, gifts. One of them I didn't want to give you until later, but I think you're ready."

Serena's eyes are wide with surprise, and she's even more surprised when I pick her up to set her on the edge of the counter and hold out the rectangular box first. In my massive palms, it looks a lot smaller than it actually is.

"Oh! Is there an occasion?" she asks. She looks at the box shyly, but I know my girl—she likes presents, and I like to spoil her.

"You want me to say something cheesy like 'every day is an occasion with you?' I mean, it is, but…"

"Stop!" she giggles, kicking playfully at my leg before she bites her lip. "Kinda." She takes the thing and sets it on her lap to open it carefully, sliding an inner compartment out, and her eyes shine at what she sees inside. "Oh my god, Luca, is this-"

"Yours," I say proudly. Inside the box in a foam casing is an ornate switchblade, its handle jet-black. "Be careful, it's brand-new and sharper than just about anything *I've* handled."

Her careful fingers reach in and take it out, holding it up to the light with round, wondrous eyes. "Woah, it's...a step up from the one I had. Luca, I don't know what to say!"

"Open it," I urge her, and she points the blade

away from us to push its switch. With a click, the blade pops out.

"It *looks* sharp," she says, experimentally holding the thing in her hand, and that's when she notices something on the base of the blade. She brings it closer to her eyes to squint at and read. When she reads it, I see tears start to well up in her eyes.

I start to say, "It says-"

"*Passerotta,*" she finishes, smiling and looking up at me.

"A *passerotta* for my *passerotta,*" I say, taking the blade from her hand and sheathing it again. "My sparrow. I had it made specially for you."

She throws her arms around me, and I chuckle as I hug her tightly. "That's the most dangerous and romantic gift I've ever gotten, Luca."

"I thought it was fitting," I say, kissing her on the forehead, "but that's not all."

"Oh, the square box!" she says, reaching over and taking it as I stow the switchblade. She opens the next box, and her face lights up—this one needs no explanation.

"Oh my *God*, Luca!"

She reaches in and draws out a necklace, silver glittering in the lights above us down to the set topaz pendant. "It's beautiful," she breathes.

"Serena, you deserve nothing but the best in life," I say, reaching out and sliding my hand around the back of her neck. She looks up at me, tears still welled up in her eyes, and when she blinks, they roll down her cheeks as she smiles, still glowing. "We're going through hell, but I wouldn't want to go through it with anyone but you. And if we're going through hell, I'll treat you like we're going to die tomorrow. And if we pull through this, I'll treat you like the princess you are, every day of our lives."

"Luca, I-I don't know what to say," she says softly. She sniffs, and I wipe away a tear, which makes her smile. "Thank you. For everything."

"Come on," I say, nodding to the door. "Let's get out of here."

"Let's? Are we going back to my place?" she asks, hopping down from the counter and finishing getting her shirt on.

"As much as I'd love to, not tonight," I say. "Rafaela agreed to let you stay at her place tonight. I messaged her earlier. Things are a little hot right now, and I don't want to make us easy to find until we can get a better grip on the situation."

"I'll text my mom and let her know. And… maybe suggest she stay in a hotel for the evening. Treat herself."

I'm about to say something when I hear my phone buzzing in the other room. I stride over to it and pick it up. Nico.

"What's up?" I answer the phone, my brow knit.

"Luca, where are you tonight?" he asks, sounding urgent.

"Why? What's the matter?" Serena is looking over at me with concern on her face.

"We got a tip, Luca."

"I'm not walking into another trap, Nico," I say.

"If we got any more bad informants on our radar, you can take my kidneys," Nico says. "This one's good, so good most of the Cleaners don't even know about it. Comes from someone we got among the Irish."

"The Irish? What the fuck do they want?" We've had a long history with the Irish—a lot of ups and downs, but things have been quiet from their end for a long time. The last thing we need is another front in this war.

"There's a meeting going down tonight, Luca," Nico says. "The Cleaners are reaching out to some of the higher-up Paddies. Probably want to sweet-talk them into an alliance if they can persuade them we're weak enough to take a shot at."

"Fucking hell," I hiss, pacing around the back room, and Serena comes to lean on the side of the door, biting her lip. "Tell me you've got something else."

"I do, and you're gonna owe me for this one," Nico says.

"Not if you keep me waiting, Nico."

"I got where the meeting's happening," Nico says in a low voice, and my eyes widen. "Some of the biggest names from both sides showing up to parley.

Probably a drug handoff, as a show of good faith. Something that shows the Irish that the Cleaners are worth their time."

"You're shitting me."

"There's more, Luca," Nico says. "The Cleaners aren't even telling a lot of their own men—Luca, Lorenzo's gonna be there to oversee the handoff personally."

From the expression darkening Luca's face, I can tell he's reading bad news on his phone screen. He heaves a sigh, slips the phone into his back pocket, and looks over at Giovanni, who is clearly waiting for some kind of order. He shakes his head and Giovanni's face settles into a stony look of resignation, his eyes narrowing. This wordless exchange is enough to throw my anxiety into high gear. I may not be in tune with how the mafia operates these days, but I am certainly in tune with Luca's body language, and I know this is not good.

He strides over to me and gently takes my face in his huge hands, staring into my eyes for a moment before kissing me. There's a sort of quiet desperation in his kiss, the way his fingers press against my cheeks as he leans close to me. I can tell something is wrong. Very wrong, from the way things feel right now. A knot of worry balls up in my stomach.

"I have to go," Luca tells me softly, those bright green eyes burning into mine. Somehow, I knew exactly what he was going to say before he even opened his mouth. But there's no use in fighting it. Luca is a mafioso and he does exactly what he has to do, whether I like it or not.

So I give him a quick nod. "You have to promise me that you'll come back safe, okay? I-I don't have a good feeling about any of this, Luca. I can't— I *won't* lose you again."

"*Mia passerotta,*" he says, tracing his thumb over my chin fondly, "I will never leave you for long. You can trust in that. I will be careful. I have something very important to live for."

It's almost as if there's a silent *now* missing at the end of his sentence, and it breaks my heart to think that before he found me again, he didn't think he had any real reason to keep going. I vow to myself to make his life beautiful again, to bring him the kind of joy that will make him happy to be alive. I want to give him everything.

But he has to survive this first. We both do.

Luca kisses me one more time and then slips out of the apartment, leaving me here with Rafaela and Giovanni, the two most unlikely companions for this situation. Rafaela comes up behind me and takes my arm, giving it an encouraging squeeze.

"Come on, *chica*. Let's have some of that cocoa and try to just relax," she suggests, holding up the box of fancy dark chocolate cocoa I brought as a sort of weak apology for getting Rafaela tangled up in this mess. Though, to be honest, her involvement with Nico probably would have made her a target at one point or another anyway. For such a big metropolitan city, New York is starting to feel like a claustrophobic little town. And we're all snagged in the same dangerous web.

"Giovanni, you want some?" Rafaela asks. He looks stoically amused for a moment, and then gives a shrug.

"Sure," he answers flatly.

"*Claro*," she replies, a smile tugging at the corner of her mouth as we go into the kitchen. She heats up some milk on the stove while I stare blankly at the tile floor, trying to remain as calm as possible despite the nervous energy bubbling in my veins.

"Ugh, I wish I could just turn my brain off for a while," I murmur, closing my eyes.

"I know what you mean," she says. "It's hard not to think of the worst-case scenario. But jumping to conclusions when you don't know anything for sure only adds unnecessary stress."

"Are you counseling me right now?" I ask, narrowing my eyes.

She smiles. "If that's what you need. But if I were your real therapist, I wouldn't do this."

She reaches up to take down a bottle of whiskey from a cabinet, pouring about half a shot into the cocoa mug before mixing in the hot milk and cocoa mix. Then she hands it to me.

"Wow, if I could get boozy cocoa at the therapist I might actually go," I tease, blowing gently on the mug to cool it down.

"Well, whatever it takes, I guess," Rafaela says. Then she calls out, "Giovanni, do you want some super special deluxe cocoa?"

Giovanni walks into the kitchen with a curious look on his face, having to tilt his head slightly walking through the doorway because he's so tall. When he sees the bottle of whiskey on the counter his face breaks into a surprisingly pleasant smile. He nods. "*Si*, a little bit."

"You got it," she answers, pouring his concoction and handing it over. She turns to me and says, "Okay. So, let's play therapist. Tell me what you're feeling right now."

I roll my eyes. "Oh, I don't know, Raf. I don't think I want to talk right now."

She shakes her head and puts a hand on her hip. "*Dale, ahora.* It'll help, I promise."

"Fine," I sigh, gently swirling the contents of my mug. "Well, first of all, I'm terrified that something bad is going to happen to Luca. I know this is some deep shit we're all in, and I'm afraid that it's at least partly my fault."

"Mhm, and why is that?"

"Well, because of the stuff with my dad. And the shop. And now Luca is back and we found each other but once again I'm in trouble and he has to save me and— ugh, I really hate this," I confess.

"And you're feeling worried about him, why?"

"Geez, you're relentless, you know that?" I groan. Rafaela shrugs, waiting patiently for me to keep going. "Okay. I'm upset because I care about him. A lot. In fact, I think I might be falling in love with him all over again. And you know me—that's totally not normal for me. I don't just fall head over heels and lose my mind like this. I'm ambitious. I have a lot of responsibilities to take care of and I don't usually let my feelings get in the way. But with Luca, it's impossible. I can't just ignore how I feel. It's too real and at the same time it feels like a dream, and now with everything going on, I'm just so afraid that I'll lose it all."

"I feel the same way about Nico," Rafaela agrees, taking a sip of her cocoa. "Here I was, fresh out of Harlem and ready to make something of myself. I'm gonna be a doctor. I'm gonna help people. I have to get perfect grades and work so hard and I can't lose focus but there he is: the man I can't help but fall in love with. And he's a distraction. He takes up all the space in my mind where I should be keeping information for my exams and my dissertation and stuff. Instead of just dreaming about having my own clinic and my own fancy office with a skyscraper view, I'm thinking about how cool it'll be to grow old with him. I'm thinking about marriage and babies and seeing the world together. I want all of it, my career and my love, and it looked like I was gonna make it happen. But now... I don't know anything. I'm scared, too, Serena."

"It is impossible to turn away from love when it burns so brightly and beautifully that it nearly hurts to look with your own eyes upon it. We are eternally trying to get as close to the fire as we can in the hopes of warming our hearts, but the closer we step, the more dangerous the flames become. Love will always be a dance between too close and not close enough, but it is a dance that makes life worth living. *'If good, why this effect: bitter, mortal? If bad, then why is every suffering sweet?'*" Giovanni says suddenly, his deep voice thick with emotion.

Rafaela and I stare at him wide-eyed, surprised at such a lyrical outburst from the most unsuspecting of speakers. "Whoa," she murmurs.

Giovanni shrugs and downs the rest of his spiked cocoa in one go. "I read a lot of Petrarch. These security jobs get very boring sometimes. The mind needs stimulation."

"You're going to make some girl very happy someday," I comment, shaking my head in awe.

Giovanni grins, almost looking bashful for a

moment. "Someday maybe, but for now my heart belongs to the most beautiful one of all: Italia."

"Speaking of Italy, I could really go for some pasta right now," Rafaela says, patting her stomach with a pitiful expression. "Serena, you want to help me get some dinner started? We may be on lockdown here but we still gotta eat."

"Sure," I answer, and the two of us start taking out ingredients for spaghetti while Giovanni pulls a small book from his jacket pocket and sits on a bar stool reading silently. "Raf, do you have a pasta strainer anywhere?" I ask.

"Oh yeah, we got a new one the other day. It's still in the foyer in a shopping bag if you want to go grab it," she says, chopping tomatoes at the counter.

I walk into the entranceway of the apartment to look for the bag, glancing at the door to make triple-sure it's locked and deadbolted while I'm at it. Just as I look over at the door, something dark passes by the peephole and my blood runs cold.

Surely it's just one of Raf's neighbors coming home from work or something. Or just a trick of the eye. Nothing to worry about. But just in case, I step closer and look through the peephole. There's another flash of black and then the door rattles with a loud thump from the other side. I fall backward with a cry, and Giovanni comes running.

"What is it?" Rafaela calls out from the kitchen.

"*Cazzo*," Giovanni says under his breath. He

reaches out and yanks me to my feet, pushing me behind him and gesturing for me to get out of the way. "Run! Hide!" he hisses.

I take off for the kitchen, grab Rafaela around the waist, and the two of us bolt for her bedroom. "I think they've found us," I whisper, hastily locking the bedroom door before we run into the en suite bathroom and lock ourselves in there.

"*Mierda*," she mumbles, her face going ashen gray. "What are we gonna do?"

"Be quiet and hide and hope Giovanni can keep them out, I guess," I reply, feeling totally helpless. Out of the corner of my eye I see my jacket lying on the bathroom counter and I reach for it to take the knife out of its pocket. Rafaela looks at it wide-eyed.

"What the fuck are you planning to do with that?" she mutters, clearly terrified.

"Whatever's necessary," I answer shortly. "Now hush."

We climb into the tub and pull the shower curtain closed, sitting in the dark, waiting for the inevitable battle to ensue. There's a short silence, and then several earsplitting bangs. Rafaela starts to scream and I clap a hand over her mouth, shielding her with my arms as we huddle in the bathtub. There's the unmistakable crack of the front door being kicked in, and the shouts of angry male voices out in the apartment. Next we hear the sound of breaking glass, the grunts and thumps of men fighting, and my heart aches for Giovanni, worrying that he might already be dead by now. From the sound of it, he's definitely outnumbered, and it's only a matter of time.

Suddenly, more silence.

All I can hear is Rafaela's shallow, panicked breathing beside me in the darkness. And then a horrible voice cracking across the apartment, a familiar one I hoped to never hear again.

"Miss De Laurentis!" Lorenzo calls out, his heavy footsteps thumping the floor as he approaches the bedroom. I can hear him clearly, even through the two locked entrances. "I did tell you I'd be back to see you again, didn't I? I have to admit, it hurts to see that you're shacking up with other men, having a real party here tonight. Maybe my invitation got lost in the mail. I'll give you the benefit of the doubt one more time, *bella*. But my patience is wearing very, very thin. Come out and see me."

Tears pulse down Rafaela's cheeks as she struggles to keep quiet. My heart sinks. This can't be how this goes down. It can't happen like this. Where is Luca? What happened to Giovanni?

"Knock, knock!" Lorenzo shouts, banging on the bedroom door. "Come out and play!"

He tries the lock for a moment and then I hear him bark an order in Italian. A moment later, there's a resounding crash and I just know they've kicked the bedroom door down.

Lorenzo laughs, a terrible, nasally sound. "Oh, these cheap apartments in the city are so shoddily made. Just fall apart all over the place. Now, those houses out in Riverdale are much better quality, aren't they, Serena? Your daddy kept you up there in that damn mansion of his, guarding you just like all the good fortune that didn't rightly belong to him."

There's a sharp rap at the bathroom door and Rafaela squeals in fear, burrowing into my side and sobbing. Lorenzo laughs again. "I wonder what your daddy would think now, hmm? His precious virginal little daughter caught up in the same shit that killed him. I doubt he'd be very proud."

I grit my teeth, closing my eyes and tightening my grip on the knife. He's wrong. Maybe I have made some big mistakes, but I'll be damned if I go down without a battle. My father would've wanted me to fight for my life. I've always had to fight, ever since the day he died, and I won't stop now.

"Last chance," Lorenzo continues, his voice sharp and low. "Open the door and we won't kill your Costa side piece here. We're not after him or your little friend in there. I want you. I think we both know it's in everybody's best interest if you just come quietly."

I sit there for a moment, soaking in his words. On the one hand, I don't want to give up. It goes against my nature entirely to just surrender now. It's what Lorenzo wants, and I would hate to ever give him the satisfaction of beating me down. And I don't trust him to just completely let Rafaela and Giovanni go free. Lorenzo is a lying, scamming, treacherous piece of shit. I can't take his word.

On the other hand, maybe if I give myself up without a fight he'll take pity on me. I don't want to risk pissing him off further and putting Rafaela and Giovanni in any more danger than they're already in. My heart thumps away in my chest as my mind races in every direction. What the hell can I do? I'm caged here, cornered like a wild animal.

"I'm giving you a chance here, Miss De Laurentis. Give yourself up and save your friends. Or my associate here can kick the door down and kill both of them. It's up to you. Will you sell out your friends to benefit yourself? Like your good-for-nothing daddy did?" Lorenzo snarls.

Sneering, I sit up and pull the shower curtain to one side.

"No," Rafaela breathes. "Don't."

"I have to. If it gives you any chance of survival, I have to," I reply simply, climbing out of the tub to unlock the door and deliver myself to the devil. I turn the lock and open the door, letting the light stream into the darkened bathroom. Lorenzo takes me by my knife arm and pulls me close, looking me up and down with rakish glee. One of his henchmen runs into the bathroom and grabs hold of Rafaela.

Giovanni is slumped over the combined shoulders of two henchmen, looking void of life.

"You said you wouldn't hurt them!" I shout, slapping Lorenzo across the face. He grabs my hand and wrenches it behind my back, his eyes flashing with fury.

"No, I said I would not kill them. Your guard dog here will catch a nice ransom from the Costa family. And as for you and your pretty friend, I have my own plans," he says, smirking cruelly. Remembering my training, I manage to quickly wiggle free of Lorenzo's grasp, using his own weight against him to pin him in the doorway with my knife pressed against his throat. I can tell the only reason I'm able to get the upper hand is by the element of surprise, but regardless I'm grateful. Two henchmen come barreling toward us to presumably free Lorenzo from me, but he shakes his head ever so slightly.

He raises an eyebrow and says, "No, no, boys. Leave us be. Miss Serena, if you kill me it will be your friend's blood on your hands."

I glance over to see a man holding the barrel of a gun to Rafaela's head and my stomach turns.

Shit.

There's nothing I can do.

"Now, let's all just calm down and walk out of here like nothing is wrong," Lorenzo orders.

Reluctantly, I lower my knife and allow one of the henchmen to wrest my arms behind my back, confiscating my blade in the process. Lorenzo rubs at his neck gingerly and gestures for everyone to leave, leading the way through Rafaela's ravaged apartment. Then he falls back to walk beside me, the henchman handing me over. Lorenzo holds my wrists tightly at the small of my back, leaning in to perversely sniff at my neck.

"Smells like a glorious addition to my collection," he says quietly as we file out of the apartment and down the hallway. "Don't worry, there's room enough for you and your Spanish friend in my bedroom. I think you'll be very happy there."

"How many do you see?" I ask into the burner phone, my other wrist resting on the wheel of the car as I sit back and let my shoulders relax. I wonder if I'll ever be immune to that tension I feel in my back that wells up when I know I'm about to take a life.

Tonight, it will be many lives.

"At least eight," says Nico through the phone, his voice so hushed I wouldn't be able to hear him if I weren't in the privacy of the car. "The intel was good. Irish are here. I've seen a couple of them before. Nobody too important. They must be cautious."

"Smart," I say, putting my phone between my shoulder and jaw to free up my hands and let me check over the weapons I have strapped to me.

Nico is about a block away, perched up on a

rooftop and watching the meeting site through the scope of a sniper rifle. I'm sitting in my car around the block, out of sight until I'm ready to move.

He's being my eyes for now, but he's a damn good shot, too. A weapon like the one he has isn't one you use lightly, so this needs to count. He offered it to me, but I'm more of a hands-on man.

I want to look Lorenzo in the eyes when I kill him.

"Five Cleaners, three Irish," Nico confirms.

"And Lorenzo?" I ask.

"No sight of him…" Nico says, trailing off. "Wait. There's a car pulling up. Tinted windows, but the Irish are watching it."

"There he is," I say, smiling.

"Window's coming down," Nico whispers. "Someone inside is saying something. I think it's Lorenzo in there, but it's hard to tell. Shit, I can't line up a good shot, the people outside keep moving too much. One miss and that car will tear out of here."

"I'll take care of that," I say casually, rolling my shoulders back and putting my car into gear.

"What?"

"Be ready."

"Luca, what are y-" but I end the call before Nico can finish. Headlights off, I pull out, my jaw set.

I'm not giving Lorenzo half a chance to slip away again.

My engine tears down the narrow road as I near

the meeting site. They've heard me by now, and in a few moments, they'll realize I'm coming their way. No time for hesitation now, I have to strike fast.

I come up on the corner fast, and I use the handbrake to pull a hard, screeching turn to point the front of my car right down the alley. As soon as I do, I flip my brights on, and I'm treated to the sight of exactly what Nico described: one black sedan and eight men looking at me, wide-eyed and stunned.

I throw the car back into gear and barrel down the alley.

A couple of the men are sharp and quick enough to dive for cover, but the car doesn't have the blessing of being able to get moving so fast.

I can hear curses and shouts from the group and I tear forward, and I brace myself for impact.

Metal groans with a loud crash and glass shatters as my car rams the black sedan, my whole body lurching forward with the momentum. I had time to see the driver's door crumple and the driver throw his arms up in defense before I covered my eyes with my arm, and I feel the sting of glass in my own skin.

In the next moment, a stunned silence like the calm before the storm, I roll out of the car and draw my weapons.

"*Lorenzo!*" I shout, and the word has hardly left my mouth before I hear bullets start flying.

A pistol in each hand, I open fire on the car while I run for cover. The driver is slumped over his wheel and a man in the back isn't moving, but the rest are scrambling to spill out the other side.

In front of the car, two Cleaners are already firing at me, and with a quiet *thud* I see one of them jolt, a bullet wound in his head, and he slumps to the ground.

Nico is giving me cover with his rifle.

"A fucking sniper!" the other man calls, a moment before another bullet silences him too.

Three Cleaners are still standing, not counting the three more from the car who I can now see clearly. I feel rage boil up within me as I see each of their faces.

Lorenzo isn't among them.

As the three remaining Cleaners open fire, I dive behind a battered dumpster. I hear the sound of hurried footsteps, and I turn to see the three Irish making a run for it. I let them go—someone will need to spread the word tonight.

Bullets spray my cover, and as I blindfire back at them, I hear another dull *thud*, and the firing stops as the men shout at each other to take cover from the sniper. It's a chance I have to seize.

I leap out from cover and charge after the three from the car who are trying to dig their heels in behind its ruins. I leap over my own car and rain bullets down on them, catching one in the heart and putting him to the ground while the others scramble to react.

They weren't expecting such a flagrant attack, and if I'm honest, neither was I—but I'm seeing red, and these men will pay for their deception.

At close range, one man tries to swing at me. I dodge his blow and catch his wrist, pulling him around my front with the sickening sound of his elbow getting broken. I use his shoulder as a rest to fire at the third man, who takes a bullet to the shoulder and staggers back, diving around the front of their car.

I curse and put my gun to my captive's head, executing him swiftly. I have just half a second to take cover before the injured man starts blind-firing at me.

He's got me pinned down, and I know Nico can't get a good shot at him while he's crouching behind the front of the car. I'm crouching by the driver's door—we're so close I can hear him breathing, but neither of us can pop out of cover without getting shot, and with the other three Cleaners still alive and trying to get a shot at me, my time is running out.

Then a steady rumbling sound catches my attention—the Cleaners' car is still running. Without a second thought, I pull the car door open, pull the dead man out, climb in, and keep my head down before flooring the acceleration.

I hear a surprised scream from the man as the car plows over him, and I roll back out the moment he's down to finish him off with a quick shot. A loud clang tells me the force of the impact knocked the already-loose car door off its hinges, and it now lies flat on the ground nearby.

I feel the sting of a bullet hit my arm, and I draw in a sharp breath through my teeth—the three remaining Cleaners are getting bolder, and I turn to see they've found cover behind the dumpster.

My adrenaline is pumping, I'm exposed, and I don't have time to think. In a fluid motion, I seize the car door and lift it up like a shield to cover my body. I hardly feel its weight with the rush of the fight coursing through my veins. It's by no means good protection, but it's better than nothing.

Nothing else to lose, I charge them.

I see one of them peek around the corner, and his face goes white at the sight of me, battered, half-covered in blood, furiously rushing them with a car door for a shield. I must look like some lunatic barbarian warrior, out of time and place in reality.

Bullets start raining in on my barrier, and some ricochet off to the brick walls around us, while some make it through, and I feel the hot sting pierce my other arm and my shoulders as bullets graze them.

But by the time I make it to them, two of them stagger back when I hurl the thing at them. One man gets the full force of it, and the others stagger back for fear that I'm going to charge through the lot of them.

I put a bullet in one of the two while Nico picks off the other.

Before he can struggle for his gun, I put my foot on top of the car door, pinning the man under it with a pained grunt as I point my pistol at him. I don't know when I dropped my other one, but at this point, I don't care.

"Lorenzo," I bark, bloodthirsty eyes boring into his pained face. "Where is he?"

"*Vaffanculo*," he spits, and I have no patience to twist him for information.

I pull the trigger, leaving his brains on the asphalt.

I hold my weapon pointed at the body for a few moments before I realize I can hear the ringing in my ears, feel my chest rising and falling, the tension in my gritted teeth. I lower my gun, looking around at the scene.

Eight bodies, two wrecked cars, walls and ground riddled with bullet holes, and more blood than I've seen in a long time. The Cleaners' car is devastated, but somehow, mine looks...well, it's serviceable. I hear the engine still running, at least, and there are only a few bullet holes in it.

For a moment, everything around me feels like it's dulled by the ringing in my ears, but that soon fades as I realize I can hear the buzz of my phone from my car. I stride toward it, broken glass crunching underfoot. I calmly pull the car door open and reach to the floorboard to pick up the phone.

It's Nico.

I put the phone to my ear and look up to his location. "Still with me up there?"

"Luca, what in the everloving fuck was that?!" he snaps, but I just grin up at him and wink.

"Come on, dinner with Rafaela's parents can't be much worse than this," I say. There's a solid five seconds of silence from the other end of the call. "What, did I cross the line?"

"Hold still, I'm deciding whether to shoot you now or later," Nico says. "Christ, Luca, warn me before you pull that cowboy bullshit next time. You alright? You're covered in blood."

I look down at myself. I can't feel much of the pain yet, thanks to the rush of adrenaline still surging through me. "Most of it's not mine. Glass cuts, a few grazing shots, and I'd say they got two good shots in," I say, checking out the bloody mess of my shoulder.

"There's a saint watching over you somewhere, I swear," Nico says.

"Lorenzo wasn't here, Nico," I say. I'm oddly calm. "Was this another trap?"

"I don't know," Nico admits, "I'll go take care of my informant. Luca, do you-"

"You do that," I say, striding back to my car and stowing my weapons, picking up the one I'd dropped. I'm going to need every bullet I've got left. "Save yourself some time and put a bullet in him for me."

"Luca, what are you doing?"

I get into my car, putting it into reverse and moving my battered car back out of the wreckage, a grim look on my face.

"I have a bad feeling. I need to get to Serena. *Now.*"

"Where are you taking us?" I ask, sitting blindfolded in the back seat of what feels like a rickety old van. Every time we go over a speed bump the whole vehicle rattles ominously, like it's just seconds away from falling apart completely. It feels like quite a departure from the usual sleek, shiny black company cars the mafia uses.

"Somewhere very nice," Lorenzo answers smugly from somewhere ahead of me. I assume he's in the front passenger seat, with one of his henchmen driving. I'm seated next to Rafaela, whose hand is clutched in mine. Her fingers are clammy and cold and every now and then I give her a squeeze of reassurance, even though I'm desperately in need of reassurance myself. The guilt I feel for getting her involved in this mess is overwhelming. After my mother and Luca, Rafaela is the most important person in my life, and I can't believe I've allowed my own mess to infect her life, too.

I just wish I knew where we were going. Again and again the urge to rip off my blindfold and take a look comes over me, but I know that would only put us in danger. I've dealt with the mafia and seen enough crime television to know that it's best to just go along with their plans. They're like wild animals —you can't make any sudden movements or they'll be on you with their claws.

"What's going to happen to Giovanni?" I press on. I'm not being disobedient by asking questions, at least. They can kidnap me and blind me but they haven't made me shut up yet, so I'm going to keep talking until they do, just in case Lorenzo lets some important tidbit of information slip.

"Why are you so concerned about him? Here I thought the Lomaglio boy was your beau. Or is that too old-fashioned of me? Maybe you're fucking both of them. After all, your mother was a Gaspari slut, and the apple doesn't fall far from the tree," Lorenzo sneers. There's a thick layer of bitterness in his voice, jealousy even.

The dig at my mother is almost laughable. I know her reputation— long before she met my father, when she was just a teenager, she was notoriously known to be an ice queen. My father once joked that he had managed to melt her icy heart and charm the *untouchable Luisa Gaspari* even though all his friends said it was impossible. It was a story my father liked to tell when he'd had a little too much to drink, and even though my mother would roll her eyes in typical ice-queen fashion, there was always just a hint of a smile on her face. Even though they seemed like total opposites, and despite all the trickiness of dealing with their combined mafia ties, my parents were truly in love. That much I know for certain. Nothing can tarnish the memories I have of them dancing together to old Sinatra vinyls in the living room, holding hands at the dinner table, my father doing the most outlandish things to make Mom laugh even though she fought so hard to maintain that cool composure.

In spite of everything, I smile.

Of course, I quickly remember the direness of my current situation and the smile melts away. But thinking about my parents and their love for each other and for me has warmed me up a little bit, and I feel a little less afraid.

Their love was truly one for the books, and now that I have Luca, I know what that feels like.

True love within the mafia was always a little bit dangerous. And maybe that makes it just a little bit sweeter. With the threat of death never far from you, you learn to appreciate those you love and trust so much more.

I just hope he's okay.

"Are--are you going to hurt us?" Rafaela pipes up,

her voice thin and quaking. It's obvious without even having to see her face that she's crying. I give her hand another light squeeze.

"Only if that's what you're into," Lorenzo replies flippantly. My heart sinks. What the hell does he have planned for us? He mentioned having enough space in his bed for both of us…

Suddenly, those horrible memories come flashing back. The ones I so desperately forgot. The ones that even Luca's reappearance in my life couldn't bring back.

A dark room. Goosebumps prickling across my skin. Feeling exposed. Violated. Terrified. Cold.

No!

"You'll have to pass inspection first, of course," Lorenzo adds, breaking me out of my thoughts. "The Don will want to look you over, make sure you're in mint condition. I know he'll be pleased that I've brought him two different flavors of slut: Italian *and* Spanish," Lorenzo laughs.

"*Soy venezolana, pajizo,*" Rafaela quips indignantly, a surprising note of strength in her tone. There's the fiery woman I call my best friend.

"Mexican, Cuban, Venezuelan, doesn't matter. You're all the same to me. Either way, you'll be a treat for the boys. Maybe I'll let them taste my sloppy seconds when I'm done with you," he replies.

Rafaela lets out a tiny whimper and I lean into her, nudging her shoulder with mine. I wish I could hug her or tell her it will all be okay, but I don't want to do anything that might provoke the henchmen to tie my hands.

We ride along in silence for a while longer. I have no idea how much time passes. It could be five minutes, it could be five hours. I just try to focus on keeping cool. At the moment, our lives don't seem to be in immediate danger, and Lorenzo's threats seem to be lewd rather than murderous, not that it's much better this way.

Especially with the trauma of what happened to me years ago still hovering in the back of my mind like a storm cloud. I can't let him get into my head, though. For my sake and Rafaela's, I have to keep calm as much as possible. There's nothing else I can do right now.

I push down the memories, back into the dark corner of my psyche where they've lived for so long. I don't have the luxury of having Rafaela play psychologist for me right now. No, I have to stay strong for the both of us.

I've survived the mafia's wrath before. I'll survive it again.

There's the rattle of wheels on gravel, perhaps even on dirt, for what seems to be a few minutes. This frightens me because it signals to me that we're not in the city anymore. When the car stops, my stomach starts to twist, fear settling into my bones. I don't know where we are, but we've evidently reached our destination.

"Take off the blindfolds. They'll have no fucking clue where we are anyway. Grab them and don't let them go," Lorenzo says. "We're going to march into the building."

The henchmen take off our blindfolds and we both blink uncomfortably in the onslaught of light. We've apparently been driving all through the night, because the sun is peeking out over the horizon in a splash of gorgeous pink and orange. It's a strange sight, seeing something so lovely when we're in such an awful situation. We're hauled out of the van with our arms twisted behind our backs.

Up ahead of us is a massive, classical-style villa surrounded by countryside. There are thick white pillars and balconies, wide windows with shining glass panes, and immaculately-maintained hedges leading up to the pearly front door. It looks like some sort of ancient pleasure palace. The henchmen drag us away, up the front steps and through the entrance, which opens into an impressive foyer with a vaulted ceiling and a grand staircase.

"*Coño*, what the hell is this?" Rafaela murmurs quietly.

Lorenzo steps up to us and bids the henchmen to move away. Lorenzo looks us up and down and then barks at one of the henchmen, "Get the Don. They're ready. No time like the present."

One of the men goes upstairs and we wait

nervously for a few minutes while Lorenzo stands back and gazes at us, his arms crossed and a sly grin on his stupid face. There's the click-clack of dress shoes on marble and we all turn to see an older man, with steel-gray hair and a stern expression. He's wearing an exquisitely-tailored suit with a tie nearly the same color as his hair. Even though he's considerably shorter than the massive henchman walking behind him, there's a disquieting, commanding presence about the man. Lorenzo steps out of his way with an ingratiating gesture of deference, and the man walks up to stand in front of Rafaela and me.

His expression stays exactly the same as he looks us up and down, his eyes critical and his mouth set in a hard line. He reaches out to take Raf's chin in his fingers, turning her face side to side. He grabs a handful of her thick, curly hair and tugs it gently. Rafaela is frozen in place, her brown eyes wide and fearful.

The man says, "Turn around slowly." His voice is deep and flat.

Rafaela hesitates for a moment before giving in and doing a slow spin. The man pauses, then snaps his fingers, and another man comes up to take Rafaela by the arm and drag her away down the hall. She starts to cry again, wordlessly pleading with her eyes for me to help her.

"No! No! Don't take her," I burst out, making a move forward. But the Don reaches out and stops me with one hand, giving me a stern look. He holds me by my shoulders, keeping me still while he surveys my body, like I'm some prize cow about to be sold for slaughter. He turns my head side to side, running his thumb over my bottom lip and opening my mouth to check my teeth. Then he cups my breasts with both hands, and I gasp sharply.

Like a reflex, I knock his hands away and stumble backward. Two men hurriedly grab hold of me and to my horror the Don is now grinning, as though this is the reaction he was hoping for. I want to spit at him, slap him across the face, kick him in the balls. Anything. Something. But there is nothing I can do. I'm helpless again, just like I was all those years before.

"So this is the bitch my nephew has been so worked up about," says the Don coolly. "The other girl is a fine toy for my men, but this one… well, she will make a fantastic trophy. Might even bear a few of his children before we're finished with the takeover. Good work, boys."

"Thank you, sir," Lorenzo says. The fucking brown-noser.

"Well, I have business to attend to upstate," the Don continues, dusting off his immaculate suit. "Enjoy yourselves while I'm away, but try not to get killed in my absence. You're all expendable, but I hardly have the time for new recruits."

The Don snaps his fingers and I, too, get dragged

away down the hall, with Lorenzo's eyes following me hungrily. The men push me into a darkened room and lock the door. A moment later, someone is wrapping their arms around me and I let out a shriek of fear.

"Serena! *Chica*, it's me," Raf says tearfully. I relax and turn around to hug her. "What the hell is going on? What are they gonna do to us? Who the fuck was that guy?"

"I think that was the Don," I answer, sighing. "The head honcho."

"*El jefe*," she breathes, her shoulders sagging. "I'm so scared, Serena. I don't know what to do. I-I'm really worried about Nico. And I know it's stupid but I'm supposed to be in class right now, you know? I have a life out there that isn't gonna wait for me and now I don't even know if I'm ever gonna make it out of this place alive."

"Hey. Hey. It's gonna be alright. I promise. We're gonna get through this. We just have to stick together as much as we can, okay?" I tell her, petting her hair. She nods, and as my eyes readjust to the low light, I can see tears shining on her face.

"Breathe in. Breathe out. You're a powerful goddess woman who can handle whatever life throws her way," I say to her, repeating the daily affirmations she's so fond of repeating to me. She gives me an incredulous look that makes me smile despite myself. Now she knows how I feel when she says it to me.

There's a knock at the door and we both jump in fear, clinging to each other as the door opens just a fraction. A few skimpy items of what looks like lacy lingerie are thrown into the room. Lorenzo's awful voice hisses, "Fix yourselves up nice for me. I'll be waiting in the bedroom. While the Don is away, Lorenzo will play. My men will come to get you soon. I'm going to blow your fucking minds, you little sluts. Don Abruzzi won't mind if I break you in, get that filthy Costa scent off of you before we hand you over to his nephew."

The door closes and we're both left staring down at the little pile of lingerie. A sense of heavy despair has fallen over the room. We know what we have to do. Feeling utterly helpless, we silently strip out of our clothes and dress ourselves in our new digs. There doesn't seem to be any point in fighting this. I'm going into survival mode now. Dignity isn't important anymore. We just have to keep living, keep fighting to stay alive despite whatever these disgusting pieces of shit do to us.

"I-I'm scared of what Nico will think," Rafaela whispers sadly.

I hug her.

"He'll understand. You and I have to do whatever it takes to survive, okay? You and me— we're going to live through this to see the other side. I don't know how long we'll be here, but don't give up. Just… try not to think too hard about it. I know that sounds impossible, but you have to just pretend none of this is happening. I'm here with you. You are not alone."

I hesitate for a moment, letting those long-buried memories start to wash back over me. I swallow hard and continue, "Look, Rafaela. I've been through something like this before. I—"

Before I can go on, the door swings open. One of the henchmen gives us a wry smile, looking at our exposed bodies, and then says, "Lorenzo is ready for you."

My car tears down the road as if it's on fire like my heart. I weave in and out of traffic, handling the battered remains of this sedan with more finesse than it should be able to pull off. This is going to be the car's last ride, and for all I know, it could be mine as well.

I don't care anymore. There's only one life on my mind, and that's Serena.

I arrived at Rafaela's house barely five minutes earlier. There was a single black sedan parked out front, and I knew that she wasn't alone in the house. When I made my way inside through a window, silent as a shadow, the first man I found never heard me when I caught him from behind and broke his neck.

Moving silently through the house, I found the second man in Rafaela's bedroom, picking through some of her things in a drawer. He looked like he was going to shit himself when he looked up and saw me aiming a gun at him.

The gun should have been the least of his fears. I got the information I wanted from him. He and his comrade were Abruzzi soldiers, looting the house after they'd been taken.

Once I had the information I needed from him, and I put him down with a single shot to the head. I'd deal with cleanup later.

Serena was in the dragon's lair.

He told me that Lorenzo had her and Rafaela taken into the Abruzzi compound, and he told me where it was. He was a tough man, but a little pressure went a long way. Men who put on a tough face are always the weakest, just under the surface.

I take a corner hard, and I hear the sounds of car horns around me as I speed by. I give the clutch a squeeze. *Come on, just a little further now...!*

In the back of my mind, I hear a voice reminding me that what I'm doing is insane. A family compound is just that—a fortress housing the most important members of a crime family. As I see the estate come into view in the distance, I glance down at my arsenal. After that fight in the alley, I haven't even stopped to take stock of everything I have. Time is too pressing.

I'm armed with two guns, a few spare cases of bullets, and two knives. My clothes are torn and bloody, and the best I can say about my injuries is that they've stopped bleeding. Taking a moment to wrap some duct tape around them did the trick.

But love makes you push your limits.

I grip the steering wheel as I fly down the road toward the entrance of the compound. It's a beautiful place, with dark red ivy spilling down its walls, and the driveway leading up to the place is nicely taken care of.

Almost a shame to spill so much blood in a place that shows off this city's beauty so well.

The man posted at the entrance steps out of his guardhouse at the sight of me, his face growing alarmed, and he has time to raise what looks like a cellphone to his ear before I blow past him, pulling my handbrake as I screech into the courtyard of the estate.

I keep my head down since I'm coming in hot. The screams and couple of *thumps* I feel against the car as it screeches over the cobblestone tells me there were a few guards on their way to investigate when I peeled in.

Immediately, I throw the car door open and dive out, keeping low and whipping my guns out.

The courtyard is a small square decorated with simple hedges, a fountain, and the bodies of the three men I ran over on my way in, sprawled on the ground. Up by the door, there are two stunned men watching me get out, and they waste no time in raising their own guns.

Bullets start flying.

I dive behind the fountain as a bullet chips the concrete to the right of my head, and I hear them cursing and calling for backup in Italian. Getting on my stomach, I use the fountain for cover and crawl along the side until they come into view, firing on where I'd been a moment ago. Two quick shots, and one of the men drops.

The other swears and fires at me to cover himself as he throws the door open and heads inside, on his way to raise the alarm, I assume.

If I wanted secrecy, I wouldn't have hurdled into the place at 50mph.

A bullet grazes my leg from behind, and I curse and whip around to fire on the gate guard, who takes the shot to the gut and drops his weapon, doubling over on the ground. Stowing my weapons, I race over to him and tackle him to his back, resting my knee on his neck.

"Keys, *stronzo*," I growl as he groans in pain. "Get me into this place."

"You're a dead man, Lomaglio," he gurgles with a pained grin on his face. With a grunt, I slam his head back into the ground and put him out.

I have to move fast. In a matter of seconds, this courtyard will become a killzone with as many Cleaners as there are windows in the manor popping out to gun me down. No time to strategize, I have to make an entrance. If I have any chance at surviving this, it'll be in a lightning fast rampage that's all bravado and luck. It's way too late for stopping and planning.

I race around to the side of the building, and I can hear scuffling and shouting inside from behind the walls. The walls aren't exactly made for climbing, but there's enough stonework between the windows that it will have to do. A tall cypress tree grows by the wall as part of a row, and I leap up onto it and start climbing.

By the time I near the second story of the building, I can hear the sounds of footsteps in the courtyard. Someone must have figured out I'm not in sight, and they're sending men to look for me. I can't be exposed any longer than I have to be.

I look to the nearest window. It has a balconette, just what I need to get a grip. But the window is shut, of course. Wrapping my legs around the tree, I slip my jacket off and toss it to the balconette. It hangs there, and clad in nothing more on my torso than a white shirt stained with blood, I leap after it.

I catch the railing and haul myself up, getting a sturdy foothold. I take my jacket and ball it up over my fist like a glove, and without hesitating, I throw my fist into the window by the handle inside.

The panel smashes to pieces, and I let my glass-ridden jacket fall to the ground as I unlock the window and push it open, climbing inside. I've made a lot of noise, and I need to get to cover fast.

"East wing guest room, move!" I hear from down the hall, and the sound of feet approaching tells me I have only a few seconds. It's a lavish room, decorated in true Sicilian style with lavish rugs and exposed stonework. I don't bother gathering my jacket. I make my way to the door and press myself against the wall to the side and wait, drawing my knife.

I let the first man rush in unharmed, but when the second follows, I turn my knife downward and drive it into the base of his skull. Before his comrade can so much as turn around, I shove the dying man's body into him, throwing him off-balance.

The two of them topple to the ground, and I dive onto the living man and put the knife to his throat, a finger to my lips as he glares up at me with pure hatred in his eyes.

"Will you be as stubborn as the corpses outside?" I ask in a hushed tone.

"I don't talk to dead men," he hisses back. "That's what you and your whole family are."

"To hell with the Costa," I say, "this is personal business. Tell me where Serena is and I'll let you get out of here."

"Probably moaning through Lorenzo's co-" he tries to say, but I silence him with my blade, and I cover his mouth as he convulses under me.

I stand to my feet over the two dead men. The soldiers in this compound aren't going to fess up— these must be the men who made the Cleaners a force to be feared. Still, there aren't as many as I would have expected.

That's a shame. If they had more men, the odds might be more even. That's cockiness speaking, but it's all I have left at this point. That, my knives and some bullets.

I stow my knife and draw a gun out, holding it at the ready as I move out into the hallway.

The manor is lavish, but I can tell it's new. There's no soul to this place yet, and everything looks too clean to be authentic. Whether the Abruzzis are new or old money doesn't matter to me, but the place reeks of lavish spending and bad taste.

I make my way down a long hallway toward what I can see to be a set of marble stairs. I'm about halfway down when I hear the sounds of footsteps coming up fast. Cursing, I kick open the door to a room on the side and take cover.

As soon as I do, a terrified woman inside screams and covers her mouth as she staggers back. I don't bother trying to hush her—my kicking down the door already let them know I'm here. Judging by how she's dressed, I'd guess she's a cleaning lady. I gesture for her to get down, and she nods, moving further back into the room and crouching down.

I use the doorframe to stabilize my arm as I wait for the men to come into sight. Three of them come up the stairway, and I wait for all three to show themselves before I start firing. My first shot catches one in the heart, and as he falls back down the stairs with a cry of pain, the others move for cover in side-rooms of their own. I get a shot into one of their shoulders before they dig themselves in safely, but when they start shooting from cover, I know this is a useless battle. I'll just waste bullets while reinforcements have time to get here.

My jaw set, I'm thinking of my options when I hear a voice from behind me.

"Sir!" the domestic whispers loudly. I fire off a couple shots down the hall before I glance back at her. She's standing beside a panel in the wall that I would have missed, but she finds a subtle handle on it and pulls it aside, revealing a small staircase leading up and down. My eyes widen.

"This is a laundry room," she hisses, "stairs go up and down to other servants' quarters. Take it up, these men won't find you."

Hardly able to believe my eyes, I fire off another shot down the hall before I move over and look down on her. "Why are you helping me?"

"These men are monsters," she says, "whatever you're here for, it can't be worse than them. I'll take the stairs down, they won't catch me."

I give a curt nod. "Lorenzo's room, where is it?"

"Three floors up from here," she says, "it won't take you to his room, but close."

I glance at the door, then nod. "Thank you," I grunt before squeezing my body into the narrow opening. True to her word, while shots ring out in the hallway, she heads down the stairs and closes the panel behind us. I draw my knife and start my climb.

The stairs are surprisingly quiet. They have to be, if service workers are supposed to be seen and not heard, I would guess.

I climb past several panels that look like doorways, counting them as I go. When I reach the third, I put my ear to it before carefully sliding it open. Sure enough, I find myself in what looks like a utility room, and the door at the far end of the little space is closed, but I can hear the sounds of walking footsteps and voices outside it.

I move carefully up to it, swapping my knife for my gun, and I put my ear close to the door.

"I don't care if the second floor looks clear, sweep it again, he didn't vanish into thin goddamn air," a scruffy voice says. I don't hear a response, so I gather that he's on a cellphone. "No, you'll get him to the doctor after we have this God damned ordeal dealt with. I want this fucker's head on a plate before Don Abruzzi gets wind of anything that goes on here, understand? Because if word gets out, he'll have *my* head after I get *yours*." I hear the beep of the call ending.

I take that as my cue, and I simply push the door open, gun raised at the man now about three feet from me.

He's a middle-aged man with a tired face and graying hair. Despite his age, the muscles under the rolled-up sleeves of his shirt tell me this guy can pull his weight. A capo, no doubt. These Cleaners were just shaping up to be a real crime family.

"Son of a bitch," he mutters, letting his phone fall to the ground as he raises his hands.

"Let's make this easy," I say in a low tone in Italian.

"You went past 'easy' when you drove a fuckin' sedan into our front yard, you cock-sucker," he says in a grizzled voice, speaking in the same language. He has a tired look in his eyes, but they're still the eyes of a killer. "I knew Lorenzo was in over his head going after the De Laurentis girl, but shit, kid, I gotta hand it to you, you know how to make waves."

I frown at him and set my jaw. "And what do you think you know about Serena?"

He gives a scoffing laugh. "Look at me, you think I'm one of these bloodthirsty young fucks? I know who she is. *She's mafia royalty*. I know who her dad was—he was the guy who used to run the Costas you work for. I know there was a power struggle, and her daddy got taken out by the guys who are your bosses now. And I heard she was next on the chopping block, until *someone* intervened."

My eyes narrow. The old guy is looking at me meaningfully. As much as I've tried to bury the past, it can't stay hidden forever. But it's strange to hear it spoke out loud again after so long.

"And I'm willing to bet that someone was you," he says. "You think you can bring down the whole Abruzzi family over some spoiled mafia princess? You're sticking your neck out under a big sword, kid."

"Enough," I growl, raising my gun.

"Not so fast," he says quickly, holding his hands up higher. "Lorenzo's room is right down this hall. One gunshot, and they'll know something's up too close for comfort. That door's locked and I've got the key. You really think you got time to make it down there and unlock the door before Lorenzo puts a bullet in your girl's pretty head?"

"You look like an old-school kind of guy. Is it a duel you want?"

"Fuck that," he half-laughs, "look at you, you look like Rambo just crawled fresh out of 'Nam." He stretches his arms out to the side. "Look, you got lucky, kid. Disarm me, and I'll unlock that door and disappear. Even if Lorenzo kills your ass, I'm a dead man to Don Abruzzi."

I don't like it, but I don't have time to bargain. I give a sharp nod and approach him with my gun trained on his head. He turns around and lets me remove the guns from his person, and he walks forward toward the door.

My eyes follow his hand to his coat pocket as he pulls out a cardkey and hands it to me. I take it, and he whirls around to face me as he steps backward. He gives Lorenzo's door a final glance, then nods to me before walking backward to the stairs and moving down them, out of sight.

As I hold the key near the door, knife in my other hand, I take a breath and say a quick prayer in my head to whoever might be listening. The door lock clicks, and a little green light flashes. I drop the key and throw the door open.

"The fuck do you think you're-" comes Lorenzo's voice as he turns around, and the scene I walk in on freezes in place for half a second in time. At the far end of the room, Lorenzo stands with his shirt off, half-kneeling on the bed where I see Serena and Rafaela laying, eyes widening at the sight of me, Serena's mouth falling open and tears coming to her eyes. On either side of the door I just burst through are two guards, each holding guns.

But I've burst in on enough meetings to be ready for that, and I move before they can gather themselves.

I go to the right first, one hand grabbing the wrist of the hand that holds his gun and pointing it down. The gun goes off just before I slash his throat with one quick motion and roll around his body, just in time for the man on the left to shoot. The guard's body takes the shot for me, and I have enough time to flip the blade around and throw it at him. The blade sinks into his eye, and his hand squeezes as his body convulses, another shot ringing through the room before he falls to the ground.

I draw my spare knife and point it at Lorenzo, standing there covered in blood, chest breathing heavily, and all the fury I've ever known burning in my eyes at the sight of what he was about to do to my girl and to Rafaela.

"Get away from them, Lorenzo," I snarl, "I've got the blood of half this compound on my hands, and I'm not leaving without yours."

Lorenzo moves fast, diving for the dresser and seizing a long hunting knife mounted on it, and he turns to face me. His eyes are wild, and there's a smile on his face.

"I was wondering if you'd make it," he says, readying himself in a stance. "I love a good fight before I take a woman."

I have no more patience for words, and I lunge forward at him. He moves faster than I thought he could, and he dodges me and thrusts up toward my gut. I roll with the attack, and it only grazes my side. I bring my fist around and feel it connect with his jaw in payback, and he staggers back.

Lorenzo spits blood, and he charges me again. This time, I'm ready for him. I feign like I'm going to move in to tackle him, and when he brings his knife in to catch me from above, I move to the side and bring my knee up into his gut.

He groans, but he keeps his momentum and wraps his arms around my waist to bring me to the ground. We hit the wooden floor together, and I immediately try to get on top of him, wary of the thrusting knife. We're evenly matched as we struggle. One moment, I'm about to get on top of him and bring my knife to his throat, and the next, he's got his elbow in my gut and is worming his way away before I get my hands on him again, trading blows and grappling with each other.

Out of the corner of my eye, I notice something —Serena. She's crawling out of bed and is moving toward what I recognize as Lorenzo's coat on the ground, and she starts digging through it hastily.

But I can't focus on it too long—whatever Serena's doing, I don't want Lorenzo to put his attention on it. I pull him up to his knees with me and bring my head down on his, hard, dazing both of us before I stagger back and he tries to jump up, shaky on his feet.

"Is that how you learned to fight in the Bronx?" he laughs, spitting blood to the side as he tries to refocus his eyes. "If that's the best you've got then-*AAAAGHHHH!*"

Lorenzo shrieks in pain and falls to his knee as Serena scrambles away from his legs, blood pouring from the Achilles tendon she just cut. In her right hand, her knife *Passerotta* glistens with its first ruby-red blood. I see the telltale look of an adrenaline rush in her eyes, and when he opens his eyes in a rage to slash behind him at her, she skillfully dodges out of the way, just like I taught her.

He struggles to his good leg to come at her again, but in the millisecond he turns his back on me, I fly at him, and I catch him from behind, putting my knife to his throat.

"Tell the devil there's more where you came from," I growl before my knife rips through his throat, opening his neck to let hot blood run over my arms as Serena watches the life fade from Lorenzo Abruzzi.

I release him, and his body crumples to the ground, blood pooling around him.

For a moment, we just stand there. My eyes move from Lorenzo, then up to Serena standing before me and Rafaela looking stunned on the bed. The next moment I step forward and Serena is already halfway to meeting me, our arms locking as I hug her tight to me.

"You're alive!" Serena says through a sob, "Luca, I thought you were dead!"

"Hell wouldn't keep me away from you, *passerotta mia*," I say, my heart soaring as we're reunited, breathing the same air and feeling each other's warmth once again. Just as it should be.

But we don't have time for a proper reunion. I look between Rafaela and Serena. "Are either of you hurt?"

"No," Rafaela says, her smile of relief fading as she stands up from the bed, looking at the door as if making sure nobody was coming. "Our egos are a little bruised, but seeing these bastards on the ground makes up for it, I think."

"Luca, he was going to-" Serena starts, but she's unable to finish as I hug her to me. I know just what kinds of memories this dragged back up for her.

"It's over now," I say reassuringly, holding her close. "It's all over. I told you, Serena, as long as I'm alive, nobody will hold you against your will."

Serena smiles warmly up at me, but I can tell she's shaken badly. These aren't the kinds of scars that heal overnight.

"We need to get out of here," I say, nodding to the door. "There's still a compound full of soldiers who don't know their boss is dead."

"I got Lorenzo's keys," Rafaela says, holding up Lorenzo's jacket. "Any ideas how to get out of here?"

"A worker showed me a way up here," I say, remembering the cleaning lady heading downstairs. "And I have a feeling we can take it down to somewhere that won't be crawling with gunmen. Stay close to me and move as quietly as you can."

~

*I*t's nearly twenty minutes later that we've peeled out of the compound in Lorenzo's own car, out the back road and to civilization where it's too crowded to chase us. Besides, with Lorenzo dead and his capo gone, the organization in the compound is shot to hell.

We make it out without trouble, and before we know it, it's like we're in a totally different world.

I'm driving, my bloodstained shirt drying in the sunlight as the luxury sports car rolls down the roads just outside New York City proper. Serena sits in the passenger's seat, her legs close together as she holds her arms, looking out the window with a dreamy look in her eyes. Rafaela is in the back seat, looking up at the ceiling with a look of disbelief on her face.

Back in the city, the abrupt change in scenery feels jarring. It's like moving from a warzone to civilization in the blink of an eye, like waking up from a nightmare.

"I just can't believe it," Serena finally says softly, turning her head to look at the road in front of us."

"What?" I'm starting to feel twinges of pain as my adrenaline starts to fade, letting my wounds take their toll, but I'm not about to show pain right now.

"That we made it out of there," says Serena. "I know this is like, a regular Saturday for you, Luca, but it just doesn't feel real."

"Maybe a slightly more exciting Saturday than usual," I say with a smile.

That earns a smile from her, but she shakes her head. "I don't know why, but I just had this sense of things coming to an end when we got taken. Rafaela, if you hadn't been there with me…"

"You'd have been alright, give yourself some credit," Rafaela says with the kind of smile only a good friend can give. "You're the one who cut that fucker's legs out from under him."

"You two handled yourselves well," I say, and I mean it. "Not many people could keep it together under so much pressure."

Serena is quiet for a moment, but there's a soft smile on her face. After about a minute, she speaks again. "So, what happens now?"

"Now," I say, getting off the highway, "I'm taking you to a safehouse. Both of you. You're going to need to vanish for a few weeks while we figure out where things stand with the Abruzzi. Best case scenario, they're willing to call a truce while the Don buries Lorenzo and mourns. I never bet on the best case, but this is a blow the Cleaners won't recover from anytime soon."

"No," Rafaela says, raising her eyebrows. "It's a hell of a blow to their spirits, too. You might have stopped a much longer, bloodier war here, Luca."

"No offense, Rafaela," I say honestly, "but the only family I'm interested in protecting is my own, not the mobsters we work for." I smile at Serena, who returns it, and Rafaela grins.

"You won't hear me arguing. Maybe it's time I convince Nico to move upstate and get out of all this noise."

"So, where is this safehouse?" Serena asks.

"Just around this corner," I say, pointing to the turn I'm about to make. "It's a cozy little place we don't use much, and…"

The thought trails off as I turn the corner. The apartment complex the safehouse is in has no less than four police cars parked out front, and nearly a dozen officers standing outside.

"Luca, what-" Serena starts to say, and without a moment to lose, I try to take a turn down a side-road and slip out of sight before we're noticed.

But the moment I do, a fifth car pulls up to block my path, coming to a screeching halt while the beat cops start running up to the car, guns coming out.

"What the fuck is this?!" Rafaela hisses.

"*No,*" I whisper through gritted teeth, and from the fifth car, I watch a tall man with a thin face and short dark hair step out of the car, pulling a shining badge out of his trench coat in one hand while he moves to the car and uses his other hand to pull the door open.

"Luca Lomaglio," the man says in a tone that tells me exactly what's coming next. I put my hands up as another cop pulls me out of the car, and

Serena and Rafaela are take out from the other side.

"What the fuck are you doing?" I say in a gravelly, warning tone, glaring at the man as he takes out a pair of handcuffs.

"Detective William Price," he barks, gesturing for me to turn around. "You're under arrest for racketeering, assault with a deadly weapon, possession of unlicensed firearms..." His voice trails off to me as my ears start ringing, and I feel another cop pulling my hands down and trying to shove me against the front of my car.

"Serena!" I shout, watching the girls getting pulled away by the cops. Her terrified face looks to me desperately.

"Luca! Luca, what-"

"Stay calm!" I shout as I try to pull away from the officers to stay in sight of her. Immediately, I feel two officers wrestling me back, shoving me into the back of a police car, "I love you, baby!"

"I love you, Luca!" she calls, tears streaking down her face.

And that's the last sight I see before the police car door slams shut.

~

hank you so much for reading! I hope you enjoyed <3 If you have a moment, please leave a review. Other readers are dying to know what you thought.

Make sure to buy Killer Desire & Killer on Fire now so you can find out what happens next!

~Alexis Abbott

ALSO BY ALEXIS ABBOTT

<u>Romantic Suspense:</u>

HITMEN SERIES:

Owned by the Hitman

Sold to the Hitman

Saved by the Hitman

Captive of the Hitman

Stolen from the Hitman

Hostage of the Hitman

Taken by the Hitman

The Hitman's Masquerade (Short Story)

THE KILLER TRILOGY:

Book 1: Killer for Hire

Book 2: Killer Desire

Book 3: Killer on Fire

SEXY SEALs

Sweetheart for the SEAL

Sights on the SEAL

HOSTAGES:

Stealing Her

The Assassin's Heart

Killing For Her

Abducted

Stepbrothers:

Ruthless

Criminal

Standalones:

Betting on Love

Hunter's Baby

I Hired A Hitman

Vegas Boss

Rock Hard Bodyguard

Innocence For Sale: Jane

Redeeming Viktor

<u>Romance:</u>

Falling for her Boss (Novella)

Most Wanted: Lilly (Novella)

Bound as the World Burns (SFF)

<u>Erotic Thriller:</u>

The Dangerous Men Series:

The Narrow Path

Strayed from the Path

Path to Ruin

Alexis Abbott is a Wall Street Journal & USA Today bestselling author who writes about bad boys protecting their girls! Pick up her books today if you can't resist a bad boy who is a good man, and find yourself transported with super steamy sex, gritty suspense, and lots of romance.

She lives in beautiful St. John's, NL, Canada with her amazing husband.

facebook.com/abbottauthor

twitter.com/abbottauthor

instagram.com/alexisabbottauthor

bookbub.com/authors/alexis-abbott

pinterest.com/badboyromance

youtube.com/AlexisAbbott

CONNECT WITH ALEXIS

Get an EXCLUSIVE book, **FREE** just as a thank you for signing up for my newsletter! Plus you'll never miss a new release, cover reveal, or promotion!

http://alexisabbott.com/newsletter

facebook.com/abbottauthor

twitter.com/abbottauthor

instagram.com/alexisabbottauthor

bookbub.com/authors/alexis-abbott

pinterest.com/badboyromance

ACKNOWLEDGMENTS

Thank you to my amazing Patrons. I'm constantly humbled and grateful for your support.

Ramona Cabrera
Melissa Hedrick
Virginia Swanson
Dawn Daughenbaugh
Don Doss
Stacie Currie

If you'd like to join them — and get my ebooks or paperbacks — you can find me here on Patreon.
https://www.patreon.com/alexisabbott

www.ingramcontent.com/pod-product-compliance
Lightning Source LLC
Chambersburg PA
CBHW051209190726
48288CB00006B/1880